"You want me to look at those figures *now?*

"I was in bed!" Meridee said irritably.

"You were?" Zeb's eyes raked over her green trench coat.

Then she did something totally out of character. She flashed open her coat.

Zeb cleared his throat. "I just need fifteen minutes of your time," he said hoarsely.

Meridee bent down to pick up her yapping bichon frise, but Vanna headed straight for Zeb's legs, jumping excitedly.

Zeb crouched to pet the hyperactive animal. "I think she has something in her mouth— something metal."

"Oh ... those are her braces."

"You've got to be kidding!"

Meridee yanked Vanna from his arms. Once again he'd managed to make her feel like a complete fool.

ABOUT THE AUTHOR

Swinging on a Star is the third book in Pam Bauer's trilogy of stories about the Osborne family. But not all of the relationships she explores are familial.

"After watching my niece pamper her bichon frise, I knew that one of my heroines would have to be a dog lover," says Pam. "Little did I know that I'd become a dog lover myself and get my own bichon. Like Meridee's dog, Vanna, Max is a white ball of fluff, but he's just an ordinary canine—no braces and no doggie day care."

Pam and her husband, Gerr, make their home in Minnesota with their children, Amy, fifteen, and Aaron, twelve, and, of course, Max.

Books by Pamela Bauer

HARLEQUIN SUPERROMANCE

378–THE HONEY TRAP
406–MEMORIES
481–SEVENTH HEAVEN
484–ON CLOUD NINE

Don't miss any of our special offers. Write to us at the following address for information on our newest releases.

Harlequin Reader Service
P.O. Box 1397, Buffalo, NY 14240
Canadian address: P.O. Box 603,
Fort Erie, Ont. L2A 5X3

Swinging on a Star

PAMELA BAUER

Harlequin Books

TORONTO • NEW YORK • LONDON
AMSTERDAM • PARIS • SYDNEY • HAMBURG
STOCKHOLM • ATHENS • TOKYO • MILAN
MADRID • WARSAW • BUDAPEST • AUCKLAND

For my sisters, Carol, Kathy and Sharon.

Published February 1992

ISBN 0-373-70487-9

SWINGING ON A STAR

PROLOGUE

"I HOPE I'M DOING the right thing," Juliet Osborne Harper said as she stood in front of the mirror, her fingers nervously tugging at the shirred bodice of her wedding dress.

"You're not having second thoughts about getting married, are you?" Meridee asked cautiously, running a critical eye up and down her sister's slim silk-and-taffeta dress. "If you are, you have about ten minutes to call it off."

"I don't want to call it off!" Juliet said, alarmed. "I'm a little uneasy about the way we're doing it, that's all. It's become such a big production. Look at me." She spread her hands expressively. "I look like I'm off to a New Year's Eve party."

"You look the way the bride of a jazz saxophonist should look," Meridee told her. "Trust me, your dress is perfect." Her fingers poufed out the hip-hugging ruffle circling her sister's trim figure. "It's glamorous, it's sophisticated...."

"It's not me," Juliet interrupted with a tiny moan. "I should have gone with the ivory chiffon."

"Chiffon is for mothers-of-the-bride, and if you had chosen that dreary ivory dress, no one would have noticed your legs," Meridee answered, observing the shapely legs protruding from the knee-length skirt.

"It's not my legs I'm worried about. It's all of *this*." She gestured to the exposed skin on her shoulders and once more tugged at the shirred taffeta. She sighed impatiently and dropped her hands. "Besides, I feel funny in white."

Meridee exhaled a sigh of frustration. "Will you stop it? You're worrying about nothing. You heard what that woman in the bridal shop said. Just because this isn't your first marriage doesn't mean you can't wear white, and you, my dear sister, look drop-dead gorgeous in white."

Juliet smiled gratefully. "Is my hair all right?"

Meridee examined the cascade of red curls spilling out from under the satin headpiece. "Every inch of you looks perfect," she declared firmly.

The door to the dressing room opened, and their younger sister, Brenda, entered, an astonished look on her face. "Hey, Jules, you look like you could have stepped out of the pages of *Bride* magazine. That dress is perfect!"

"See." Meridee gave Juliet an "I told you so" glance as their eyes met once more in the full-length mirror.

"You are a lovely sight," her grandmother agreed, entering the room on Brenda's heels. "All of you look picture perfect." Her gaze swept across her three granddaughters affectionately. "This is such a happy day for me." She dabbed at her eyes with her handkerchief.

"You were right about Ross, Gran. He really is a prince of a guy." Juliet put her arm around the fragile old lady and gave her a gentle hug.

"He's going to be a good father to Sara and Annie and a good husband to you," Gran continued. "You're a lucky girl, Juliet."

"I know, Gran," Juliet said. "I'm happy, too."

"At least now I can stop worrying about *one* of my granddaughters," Gran said with a sigh.

Meridee muffled an automatic protest. "You don't need to worry about me, either, Gran."

The old lady's eyes brightened. "Does this mean you and Richard are going to be making an announcement?"

"No!" The word came quickly and emphatically. "Gran, I'm never going to marry Richard."

"Oh? I thought maybe he was the right man for you."

"He wasn't even close, Gran." Meridee tried to keep the bitterness from her voice. Seeing the concern in her grandmother's eyes, she said in a lighter tone, "I think the fairy godmother's already set a limit of one Prince Charming per family."

"I hope not," Brenda piped up. "I'm counting on Gran finding one for me."

"You be patient," Gran replied, patting her hand. "Your time will come soon enough. But first, we have to get Meridee settled."

This time Meridee couldn't stifle a groan of protest. "I *am* settled, Gran. I have a successful career and a nice place to live. I don't need to find a prince."

Gran dismissed her comment with a wave of her hand. "You just haven't met the right man yet, that's all."

"I just don't want to get married, Gran," Meridee answered in an exasperated tone.

"But Juliet does," Brenda interjected, "and if we don't get moving, everyone's going to wonder where she is. If I know Mom, she is probably pacing outside the door right now." She reached for one of the floral bouquets resting on the table. "Is everyone ready?"

Juliet took a deep breath. "I'm ready. Where's my bouquet?"

Meridee reached for the garland of pink roses and baby's breath and handed it to her. "Just make sure you don't toss this thing anywhere near me," she said in an aside her grandmother couldn't hear.

Juliet ignored her sister's remark and looked in the mirror one last time.

"Okay?" Brenda asked.

"Okay," Juliet replied.

"Then let the wedding begin," Brenda proclaimed, holding the door open for her sister.

As Brenda had predicted, Kate was waiting for her daughters on the other side. When Juliet stepped out of the dressing room, Kate held out her arms to her. She smiled her approval, then enfolded her daughter in a warm embrace. "You look perfect," she said through her tears.

Meridee was the last one out of the dressing room. As she passed, Brenda said in a low voice, "What's with you, Meridee? Can't you at least look at little bit happy for Juliet?"

"I am happy for her," Meridee insisted. "How's this?"

She pasted on an artificial smile.

"Real cute," Brenda said sarcastically. "It would serve you right if you did catch the bouquet."

Meridee laughed. "I'm going to have my hands behind my back."

Brenda could only shake her head. "Someday you're going to be the one saying the wedding vows and I'm going to be the one laughing."

"In your dreams, little sister," Meridee answered smugly.

CHAPTER ONE

AS SOON AS SHE THOUGHT no one would notice her absence from the wedding reception in the elegant St. Paul hotel, Meridee made her way to the ladies' room furthest from the ballroom. She sank down onto one of the velvet padded stools at the vanity and sighed. For the first time all evening, she didn't need to pretend she was having a good time, and she took great pleasure in making a face in the mirror.

"Weddings," she murmured disdainfully. "Who needs them?"

The sound of the door opening made her sit up straight, and she quickly chased her frown away as her mother came into view.

"When Brenda said she thought you had gone to powder your nose, I didn't think I'd have to hike clear across the hotel to find you," Kate said as she sat down next to her.

"The other rest rooms were crowded," Meridee told her, hoping her mother would accept that explanation.

Kate's glance was skeptical. "Are you sure that's all it is?"

"Of course. What else would it be?"

"That's what I'd like to know," Kate said gently. "Despite the smile you've had plastered on your face all day, your behavior is not that of someone who's happy to be at her sister's wedding."

"Have you been checking up on me, Mother?" Meridee asked, trying to keep her voice light.

"No, but I can't help but notice that the sparkle in your smile doesn't reach your eyes and that there's an edge to your laughter. You've also been at the champagne punch table quite a few times—and you seldom drink anything at all."

"I'm celebrating," Meridee said with false gaiety, dabbing at her nose with a powder puff.

"I think you're upset," Kate said perceptively.

Meridee didn't reply, but snapped her compact shut and returned it to her purse.

"Are you going to tell me about it?" Kate asked, her eyes riveted to Meridee's face. "Are you unhappy because Richard came down with the flu at the last minute and you don't have an escort?"

Meridee looked at her mother's concerned face and knew she couldn't pretend with her. "He didn't get sick."

Puzzled, Kate said, "He didn't?"

Meridee shook her head. "When I stopped by his apartment last night, he had company."

"What kind of company?" Kate asked suspiciously.

"Female company," Meridee replied sourly. "Some wench with purple-painted nails to match her purple negligee."

"Negligee?" Kate's eyes widened in disbelief.

Meridee nodded. "It even had purple maribou trim. You know, the kind movie stars parade around in but no one actually sleeps in. Not that she and Richard had been sleeping," she said sardonically.

"I can't believe this," Kate said, her face registering her shock.

"It's true, Mother. Richard's been seeing her ever since he moved back to Minnesota, and I didn't even know about it until last night. I've been dumped for a purple passionflower and her Persian cat," she said dryly, holding back the tears that had suddenly gathered in her eyes. "And that's another thing. She has a cat! A great big gray thing that looks as though it could eat my dog for breakfast."

"But I thought Richard hated animals."

"He does! He wouldn't even let Vanna in the door." Meridee clicked her tongue in dismay. "Can you believe it? I couldn't even bring a tiny little bichon who doesn't shed into his apartment, yet there was this monstrous cat leaving gobs of hair all over the place." She bit down on her lower lip to keep it from quivering.

"Oh, Meridee, I'm sorry," Kate said, slipping her arm around her daughter's shoulders in a comforting gesture. "No wonder you're having to pretend you're happy for Juliet."

"Mom, I *am* happy for Juliet," Meridee insisted. "That's why I didn't say anything about this to anyone. I didn't want to spoil her special day."

Kate gave her a gentle, understanding hug. "You should have told me this morning. I wouldn't have made all those comments about you getting married."

"It doesn't matter," she said, struggling to maintain her composure. Although she felt like crying, pride kept her from letting her mother see how deeply she was hurt. "I know I always said that Richard and I would never get married, but I honestly never thought it would end this way."

"Then it's definitely over between the two of you?"

"It's over," she said quietly. "They're getting married. Mom, I don't know what he sees in her. She's nothing special to look at, and she doesn't even have a decent job."

Kate stilled Meridee's flaying hands. "Maybe she wants the same things in life that he does . . . marriage, a home, children."

"And you think I don't want those things?" Meridee asked defensively.

"Do you?"

Meridee paused before answering. "Not yet, maybe. But someday I might."

"That's my point, darling. For eight years Richard has been asking you to make a commitment to those things, but you didn't want them. He once told me he felt he was in competition with your career and that he was losing by six touchdowns."

"Then why is it that I feel like I'm the one who lost the ball game?" Meridee asked sadly.

"Oh, Meridee." Kate could only shake her head in sympathy.

"I know you and Juliet think I'm cool and dispassionate, but I have feelings, too," Meridee insisted, dashing away a solitary tear that dared to trickle down her cheek.

"Of course you do," Kate said soothingly, giving her another squeeze. "And I'm truly sorry about Richard, dear. I wish there were something I could do to ease your pain."

Meridee squared her shoulders and sat up straight. "I'm all right, Mom."

Kate's eyes were skeptical. "Just try not to let it keep you from enjoying the reception," she urged.

"I won't," Meridee answered, forcing a weak smile to her face. "I'll be just fine."

"Go easy on the champagne punch, okay? It goes down so smoothly you don't realize that it has a little kick until it's too late," Kate warned as she turned to freshen her makeup.

"I'm not going to get drunk, Mom," Meridee reassured her. "I'm meeting with someone a little later," she said, glancing at the slim gold watch on her wrist.

"What do you mean you're meeting someone?" Kate demanded, her lipstick poised at her lips.

"I need to talk to Ingrid."

Kate quickly blotted her freshly applied lipstick with a tissue, then said, "Meridee, you didn't schedule a business meeting on your sister's wedding day, did you?"

Meridee didn't need to look at her mother to know she was glowering at her. "It's not what you think. There's this guy coming from New York, and as it turns out, he's staying here at this hotel. Since I knew there'd be a short break between the dinner and the dance, I arranged to meet with him and Ingrid for a few minutes." Her fingers fussed with the short waves of blond hair stiff with mousse. "I'll be back before the dancing starts, I promise."

Kate stared at her daughter in the mirror. "I don't believe this! What could be so important that you have to leave your sister's wedding reception to meet with some stranger from New York?"

Meridee sighed impatiently. "Mom, I'm not exactly leaving the reception. We're meeting across the hall in the hotel bar. No one will even notice I'm gone."

"Of course they'll notice. You're the maid of honor, and it's one of your duties to greet our guests."

"I've already pumped more hands in a couple of hours than I did all of last year at the office," Meridee said dryly, then pivoted on the stool to face her mother. "Fifteen minutes is all I'm asking for, Mom."

"The point is, you shouldn't be asking," Kate said sternly.

"I wouldn't if it weren't so important, Mom." Her eyes held an appeal for understanding. "You know that Krystalene's in the middle of a takeover. For months rumors have been flying as to what would happen to all of us. Well, tonight I'm finally going to find out."

"I don't see why you can't wait until Monday morning to do this." Kate dropped her lipstick back into her beaded bag and closed it with a decisive click.

"Because by Monday morning this guy will have already gone through the company's records. I'm going to make sure that he doesn't create more problems than he solves," she said with a sparkle of determination in her eyes. "I've worked too hard to let some hotshot with a sharp nose for opportunity ride roughshod over our people."

"Darling, I admire your dedication to your employees, but I really think that you can delegate this responsibility to Ingrid." She reached over and covered Meridee's hand with her own. "Just this once, will you please leave your work at the office?"

Meridee rolled her eyes toward the ceiling. The last thing she wanted was to argue with her mother tonight, especially over a fifteen-minute consultation with a man she didn't even like.

"I can't leave Ingrid to face this guy alone," she said, wishing the look of disappointment on her mother's face didn't make her feel so guilty. If only there were some way she could make her mother understand her commitment to her job. Time and time again they had argued over her missing family gatherings because of business appointments, and every time Kate said the same things. Leave your problems at the office. Use your authority and delegate work to responsible employees. Only tonight, Meridee knew she couldn't do either.

Kate sighed as she stood and adjusted the lace tunic of her two-piece dress. "Fifteen minutes?" she asked in a resigned tone of voice.

"I'll try to make it fifteen, thirty minutes max," Meridee promised, getting to her feet.

"If you're not back by the time the band's onstage, I'm sending the police in after you," Kate warned, turning Meridee around by the shoulders so that she could straighten the bow on the back of her dress.

"And won't that look cute?" Meridee drawled sarcastically. "The purpose of this meeting is to give this guy from New York the impression that I'm a capable executive. What do you suppose he's going to think if my stepfather, the police commissioner, leads me away by my hand?''

Kate gave her a contrite smile. "All right. I won't send Donovan. I'll send Grandpa George instead."

"Gee, thanks, Mom. I feel much better knowing that. Maybe you want to send Gran with him. I mean, two little old people dragging me off by my ears should convince this guy I'm management material, shouldn't it?"

Kate held the door open and gestured for her daughter to exit. "All you have to do is be back on time and you won't need to worry about anyone dragging you anywhere."

"I'll be back," she promised.

EVER SINCE the announcement that Krystalene Products had been bought by one of the largest investment firms in New York, Meridee had been uneasy about the security of her job. In the six years she had been employed at the personal-care-products company, she had worked her way up from accounting clerk to junior vice-president of finance.

It hadn't been an easy climb. Despite having the encouragement of upper management, there had been obstacles along the way, including the egos of men who hadn't wanted to see a woman get ahead of them on the corporate ladder. But Meridee had always hated gender games, and she had found the aggressive tactics of her male coworkers challenging. Instead of backing down, she had worked twice as hard and convinced everyone that she was in it for the long haul.

Only now she wasn't sure what the long haul would be. Krystalene was about to be swallowed up by a large corporation, and her fate rested in the hands of a man named Zeb Farrell.

As she walked into the hotel bar, the first person she spotted was Ingrid Peterson, one of Krystalene's accountants, who was waving to her from a padded leather booth.

"Am I ever glad you came!" Ingrid exclaimed with relief. "I was worried you wouldn't be able to get away. How was the wedding?"

Meridee slid in across from her. "It was as close to perfect as you can get. Any sign of our Mr. Farrell?"

The slightly overweight blonde shook her head. "I left word at the front desk that we'd be in here." She took one last drag on her cigarette and ground the tip into the ashtray.

Meridee knew the other woman was nervous, for she seldom smoked except in times of stress. "I hope Zeb Farrell isn't responsible for that," she said, pointing to the butts in the ashtray.

Ingrid shook her kinky blond curls. "My willpower's on the low side, that's all." She shoved the ashtray into the corner. "I really am glad you were able to get away for a few minutes. By the way, you make a lovely bridesmaid. It's quite a transformation from the Meridee I know."

"It's this dress," she answered dryly, giving the bouffant skirt a cursory glance.

"The color's gorgeous," Ingrid crooned.

"It's called raspberry. See . . . my nails match." She held up her hands, palms inward, and wiggled her fingers. "I bet this is the first time you've seen me with ten perfect fingernails."

"It's the first time I've seen you with your nails polished."

"They're acrylic... it was Brenda's idea," she said, clicking the tips against the tabletop in amusement.

"Your hair's different, too, and you're not wearing your glasses," Ingrid observed, eyeing her more closely.

"Juliet wanted me to look like a maid of honor instead of an executive, so I put in my contacts and gelled up my hair. I don't know how I'm going to convince Zeb Farrell to take me seriously when I'm dressed like this."

"You look terrific. You should have seen the way the men in this bar looked at you when you walked in," Ingrid said, her fingers playing with the lime in her mineral water.

Meridee laughed sardonically. "Isn't that typical? Put a woman in a prom dress and men's hormones start jumping. Put her in a business suit and their hackles are raised."

"Yes, well, right now I'd rather be sitting here in your party dress than my plain gray suit."

Meridee sighed. "It's too bad we can't trade places."

"I'll say," Ingrid agreed, a hint of envy in her voice that didn't go unnoticed by Meridee.

"Believe me, Ingrid, you wouldn't want to be in my shoes tonight."

"Aren't you having a good time at your sister's wedding?"

Meridee took a sip of the ice water on the table, then said, "I'd rather be having a root canal."

"Meridee!" Ingrid's jaw dropped open.

"I can't help it. Weddings depress me," she said dismally.

"But you're the one who told me Juliet and Ross are perfect for each other."

"Oh, they are. And I'm happy that their wedding celebration is turning out exactly as they planned it. I just don't want to be there, that's all."

"Because of Richard?" Ingrid probed carefully.

Meridee made a derisive sound. "You want to know what I think about Richard? Good riddance to bad rubbish," she declared, lifting her glass in the air before downing the contents.

"Do you want a refill—something more appropriate for a wedding?" Ingrid asked, signaling for the waitress.

"Maybe I'd better have something nonalcoholic. I try not to drink at business meetings," she answered.

"I know, but one glass of white wine won't hurt," Ingrid insisted, ordering a sparkling wine for Meridee and a gin and tonic for herself when the waitress arrived.

Meridee watched the waitress walk away and sighed. "I suppose it doesn't matter. As long as I'm sitting here in a poufy prom dress with my hair all fluffed out, I might as well break all the rules," she replied dryly.

"Personally, I think you have a much better chance of winning Zeb Farrell over to our side the way you're dressed tonight than you would if you were sitting there in one of your suits," Ingrid told her. Before Meridee could protest she added, "I know you're a firm believer in this dress-for-success stuff, but the man would have to have ice water in his veins not to react favorably to the way you look."

"Ingrid, I've never had to resort to feminine wiles to get my point across," Meridee said indignantly. "I'm certainly not going to start now."

"Then maybe you want to go back to the ball and leave me in my plain old gray suit to handle our Mr. Farrell?"

The waitress returned with their drinks and Meridee glanced at her watch. "It's eight-forty. Where do you suppose he is?" She made a quick survey of the lounge.

"Should I check at the front desk to see if he's registered?" Ingrid offered.

"We'll give him a few more minutes." Again Meridee looked around the bar. "At least in here, everyone isn't in couples," she remarked. "Have you ever noticed how at weddings everyone seems to be in pairs? I mean, people you've never even seen with a date before suddenly seem joined at the hip to someone else."

Ingrid took a sip of her gin and tonic and nodded in agreement. "I know exactly what you mean. I hate going to weddings by myself. Talk about feeling out of place."

"That's my point. Why should we feel out of place?" Meridee demanded. "Normally I'm perfectly happy to go to any party or restaurant alone. But gather a bunch of people together to celebrate a wedding and I feel like a failure because I don't have a man's arm linked in mine."

"You're hardly a failure, Meridee. There aren't many men, let alone women, who have accomplished what you have in the short time you've been with Krystalene," Ingrid said, admiration in her voice. "I bet all those people in that ballroom are impressed by your success."

Meridee made a tiny sound of disbelief. "They might be impressed, but they still see marriage as the ultimate measure of success for a woman." She looked again at the narrow strip of gold on her wrist. "You did tell Zeb Farrell eight-thirty, didn't you?"

"Yes, and I told him we'd be sitting close to the door. Two blondes—one dressed for success, the other dressed to make men's hormones jump," she said with a teasing grin.

"Real funny, Ingrid," Meridee drawled as she looked around the bar. "What do you suppose a troubleshooter looks like?"

"He said he's six-one and dark haired."

Meridee chuckled. "He's probably five-eleven. Haven't you noticed how men always add an inch or two to their height?"

"He also said he'd be wearing a tie with fish on it."

"A what?" Meridee wrinkled her nose. "You mean to tell me I'm sitting here worrying about wearing a dress that swooshes and this guy's wearing a tie with fish on it?"

Ingrid lifted her shoulders and grinned. "He has an awfully nice-sounding voice, and he wasn't abrupt the way so many people are when they're on the phone."

"Well, don't expect him to be nice when he's auditing our books. Keep in mind that this is the man who's going to decide whether we're in the unemployment lines next month.''

Ingrid's pencil-darkened eyebrows drew together. ''I thought Mr. Griggs said that one of the conditions of the takeover was that everyone's job would be secure.''

''Sure, if you're one of the union workers. Management is a different story,'' she stated with a skeptical frown.

''Your performance should speak for itself,'' Ingrid stated loyally.

Meridee smiled weakly. ''I appreciate your vote of confidence, but we both know Krystalene's been struggling to stay out of the red for quite some time now.''

''And we both know that's not your fault,'' Ingrid added.

Meridee made a sound of derision, then took another sip of her wine, trying not to think about the arguments she had had with several members of the board of directors in recent months. ''We'll have to do our best to convince Mr. Farrell of that,'' she said soberly.

A shadow darkened Ingrid's face. ''Meridee, I don't know what I'd do if I lost my job. I'm barely making both ends meet now, and next month Tommy's scheduled for surgery on his knee.''

Meridee looked at the anxious face of the woman sitting across from her and felt a rush of sympathy. Ever since the first day Ingrid had come to work at Krystalene, she had felt an affinity with the thirty-nine-year-old divorced mother of three. Normally Meridee was able to keep her emotions from entering into professional decisions, but when the opportunity had arisen for her to promote someone to a senior accounting position, she hadn't chosen the person with the most experience. Upon learning that Ingrid was struggling to put her life back together after breaking up with her alcoholic husband, Meridee had given her the job, hoping the increase in wages would be the help she needed.

Not once since that day had Meridee regretted her decision. Ingrid was a dedicated and loyal employee who worked just as long and hard as she did. In many ways Ingrid was a lot like herself. She held people at a safe distance, which meant others often regarded her as cold and dispassionate. She could also be very single-minded at times, refusing to give up on an idea if she thought it was of merit, and Meridee had learned to trust her intuition, which was more often right than wrong.

Together the two of them had become known as the "Refrigerator Twins." It was a nickname most women would have resented, but Meridee chose to regard it as a compliment. She had climbed to her spot in the corporate structure because of clear reasoning, not emotional decisions.

With her promotion, Ingrid was able to make a new life for herself and her boys. Although she seldom talked about her relationship with her ex-husband, or the hardships she had suffered because of his drinking, Meridee knew the wounds hadn't completely healed. She also knew that her ex-husband occasionally phoned, and Meridee suspected that despite everything that had happened in the past, Ingrid still had feelings for him. The thought that she might return to a codependent relationship disturbed Meridee, and she did everything she could to support Ingrid in her efforts to be independent.

"Your insurance will cover the operation," Meridee assured her, aware of Ingrid's still-precarious financial situation.

"Yes, but if I lose my job, I lose my insurance coverage," Ingrid said uneasily.

"Well, we won't let that happen," Meridee said with more confidence than she was feeling. "You and I are going to convince Mr. Zeb Farrell that we are Krystalene's greatest assets."

This time it was Ingrid who looked at her watch. "It's after nine. His plane must have been delayed."

Meridee groaned. "If I don't get back soon, my mother will send in the troops to find me. I told her I'd be there in time for the dancing. Do you think you can handle this on your own?"

Ingrid looked apprehensive. "I can stay until nine-thirty, but then I have to go pick up the boys. I left two of them at the movies on my way over here."

Meridee pondered their predicament for several moments, then said, "Why don't you leave. I'll stop by the front desk and leave a message for our Mr. Farrell. If he wants to see me, he can come find me in the ballroom." She stood, smoothing her hands down the taffeta dress.

"I'm sorry, Meridee. If the boys had another way of getting home..."

Meridee waved her apology away with a flick of her hand. "Don't worry about it. I'm probably going to be looking for an excuse to leave the dance, anyway. My grandmother's arranged for several of George's nephews to ask me to dance. Can you believe it? At my age I have a matchmaking grandmother."

"She's still trying to find you a prince, huh?"

"Unfortunately. The last time she tried to fix me up with the grandson of one of her friends, it was a total disaster. He looked like a frog. I swear it's the truth." She held up her hand.

Ingrid laughed. "She just wants you to be happy."

"I *am* happy," Meridee insisted. "There must be a way I can convince her of that without having a man dangling from my arm."

"I'm afraid your grandmother sounds like the type who's not going to believe you until you put a ring on your finger," Ingrid warned as she slid out of the booth.

"You're probably right," Meridee agreed as the two of them headed for the exit. Before they were through the door, one of the men leaning up against the bar made a pass at Meridee, which she chose to ignore.

"Didn't I tell you you look terrific?" Ingrid said in a low voice when they were out in the lobby.

Meridee chuckled mirthlessly. "I'd better get back into the ballroom where the only men I have to worry about are the frogs my grandmother's going to send over to ask me to dance."

The door to the ballroom opened and the sound of music drifted into the lobby. "Oh, oh. The band's already playing. You'd better go have some fun. It'll be good for you," Ingrid told her in an almost maternal tone.

"Some fun," Meridee said dryly, then waved as she slipped inside the large ornate doors.

AN HOUR LATER, Meridee was no closer to having fun than she had been at the start of the evening. Ignoring her mother's warning and forgetting that Zeb Farrell could still put in an appearance, she continued to sip the champagne punch, appreciating the warm, easy feeling it gave her. After posing for more pictures and doing all the dances required of the wedding party, she wanted nothing better than to sit down with her aching feet propped up on a chair.

Her grandmother, however, refused to allow that. Meridee was convinced she knew every single man in the ballroom and was going to see that she was personally introduced to all of them. It was with that thought in mind that Meridee grabbed another glass of punch and took a seat at a table in the corner of the ballroom where several of her cigar-smoking uncles were discussing the prospects of the Minnesota Twins winning the World Series.

She was in the middle of discussing RBIs and ERAs when Brenda tapped her on the shoulder.

"Meridee, Gran's looking for you. She says there's a man here for you."

Meridee groaned. "Not another one! I've already danced with six of them. Can't you tell her I'm in the bathroom?"

"I think you ought to come meet this one. He's definitely different from the others."

Meridee made a sound of disbelief and craned her neck toward the area where her grandmother was sitting. "Where is he?" she asked, squinting as she looked across the dimly lit ballroom. She had been at the reception long enough to have seen every face in the crowd, and there hadn't been a single one that could make her want to get back on her sore feet.

Brenda gently tugged on her arm. "Come on. You can't stare at the guy then ignore him."

Meridee turned her back to the dance floor. "Oh, yes I can," she said, the champagne punch giving her cocky courage. "I'm not dancing anymore."

"Meridee! You're going to make a scene," Brenda said beneath her breath. "Gran thinks she's doing you a favor."

"Well, I don't need any more favors." She finished the liquid in her glass.

"What is Gran supposed to tell this guy?" Brenda asked as Meridee reached for another glass from a passing waiter.

Meridee ignored the question. "You're lucky you came with Steven, otherwise Gran would be doing this to you."

"I really think you should dance with this one," Brenda advised her. "He's cute."

"I don't want to dance. I'd rather talk baseball with the boys," Meridee said stubbornly, then turned back to the conversation.

"You're going to be sorry," Brenda said in a singsong voice as she walked away.

Several minutes later, Meridee felt another tap on her shoulder as a tentative male voice said, "Meridee Osborne?"

She briefly closed her eyes and braced herself for yet another of her grandmother's matchmaking attempts. She was starting to feel giddy from the champagne and a bit reckless, too. She spun around in her chair and confronted her grandmother's latest protégé.

She wasn't ready for the man who stood before her. Here at last was a man who could change her mind about wanting to dance. He was tall, dark and very handsome—the most handsome man she had seen in a long, long time. The kind of man every woman hopes will tap her on the shoulder and sweep her out onto the dance floor to some romantic love song.

Meridee slowly rose to her feet.

"I'm Meridee," she said with a flirtatious grin.

"I'm sorry to have to disturb you like this," he said with the kind of smile movie stars beamed at their leading ladies, "but your grandmother insisted I come right over."

Suddenly Meridee felt light-headed and carefree. For the first time all evening her smile wasn't forced. "I'm glad you came."

"Good, because we really should get down to business," he said with an equally charming grin.

"Business?" She stared at the broadly patterned tie around his neck. It was a mass of swirling colors. A closer inspection revealed that the swirls of color were actually giant fish. "You're the troubleshooter from New York?"

He smiled as he offered her his hand. "I'm Zeb Farrell."

CHAPTER TWO

MERIDEE SHOOK the proffered big, strong hand, and her smile slipped from her face. This attractive man hadn't come to ask her to dance. He was here on business. Business that she needed to be clearheaded to discuss.

Mergers, budgets, audits . . . she tried to concentrate on what she wanted to say to the troubleshooter, but drew a blank. The only thought on her mind was what it would be like to dance with the man standing before her. She felt a tug on her skirt and looked down to see her seven-year-old niece, Sara, alongside her.

"My mom's looking for you," Sara told her. "She says you're supposed to find someone to dance with."

"I can't right now, Sara," Meridee answered. "Tell your mom I need to talk to Mr. Farrell." She nodded in Zeb's direction.

"But my mom said they can't have the dance without you. It's for everyone in the family," Sara insisted, staring up at Zeb and Meridee with big blue eyes.

"It's all right," Zeb spoke up. "You go ahead. I can wait until you're finished."

Meridee glanced across the dance floor and saw Juliet waving at her. Brenda and Steven, her mother and

Donovan, her grandparents and the groomsmen and
their dates were all gathered in front of the band.

"I don't think they're going to start without me."
She gave Zeb Farrell an apologetic smile, flushing with
embarrassment.

"It's all right," he assured her.

Right was exactly what it wasn't, Meridee thought
miserably. Everyone had a dance partner but her, and
as she looked around for someone she could ask to
dance, she felt her humiliation growing. Everyone she
felt comfortable asking was already out on the dance
floor. Helplessly, she looked around the ballroom and
finally ended up asking one of her uncles seated at the
table.

Unfortunately, she asked the wrong one. "I'm too
old for a pretty little thing like you," he told her. Then
he looked up at Zeb and said, "You're the one who
should be dancing with her."

Meridee could have cheerfully cut out her uncle's
tongue.

"Mr. Farrell's here on business, Uncle Leo," Meridee explained, offering Zeb another apologetic smile.

The band gave a short introduction to the music,
announcing that the family of the bride would be
dancing to the next song.

"I think they're getting restless," Zeb commented,
nodding in Juliet and Ross's direction.

Meridee's anxiety grew as she looked toward her
family and saw her mother motioning for her to hurry.

"Who are you going to dance with?" Sara wanted
to know, her glance moving from her aunt to the tall
man at her side. "Him?" She pointed a finger at Zeb.

"I wouldn't pass up the opportunity to dance with Meridee if I were you," Uncle Leo advised Zeb, and Meridee nearly stuffed a napkin in his mouth.

"Look, why don't I meet you outside after I'm finished?" Meridee suggested with as much dignity as she could muster.

"I do know how to dance," Zeb told her.

Meridee stared at him, her head still whirling. "It's not necessary."

"Do you want to dance?" he asked, looking at her expressionlessly.

Meridee wanted to refuse, but by now all of the guests were looking in her direction, wondering why she wasn't with the rest of the family on the dance floor. Several voices called out in unison, "Come on, Meridee."

"I guess we might as well," she said, boldly taking him by the hand and leading him onto the dance floor. As soon as they had joined the others, the band began to play a lively contemporary number that eased Meridee's mind somewhat, for it allowed them to dance without touching.

She was soon caught up in the rhythm of the music, her body moving in time to the drummer's contagious beat.

Zeb, too, soon lost his air of detachment, for the woman across from him was wriggling her body in a most tantalizing manner. Dancing was the last thing he had expected to do this evening, yet here he was in the middle of a ballroom filled with strangers, bobbing up and down like a jack-in-the-box—with a very surprising woman.

The report on Meridee Osborne had indicated she was aggressive, competitive and about as warm as the polar ice cap. He had expected her to be tough, able to trade locker-room vulgarities and belt back stingers with the boys—not to be some fragile-looking blonde shimmying and shaking her luscious curves in gleeful abandon. She was hardly the sturdy, no-nonsense woman he had thought he would find. Kittenish was the word that came to his mind, although there was nothing coy in her demeanor.

Finally, the song came to an end, and immediately the band introduced a slow love song, inviting everyone to dance to the special request of the bride and groom.

Meridee looked at him, almost shyly, and in that moment, when her big blue eyes met his, things began to happen inside him—things he didn't want to happen. He felt like a basketball that someone was slowly letting the air out of. She wanted to dance to the popular love song—he could see it in her eyes.

When she said on an airy, uneven note, "I love this song," Zeb did what any man would have done in such a situation. He pulled her into his arms, one hand holding hers, the other finding the smooth taffeta at the middle of her back. As the hauntingly beautiful melody filled the ballroom, he momentarily forgot the reason he was at the St. Paul hotel.

All his thoughts were on the woman in his arms. She was smaller than he had expected her to be, and he smiled to himself as he recalled the drill-sergeant image he had mentally slapped on her bio. The scent of her perfume reached his nose, a fresh, sweet fragrance that tempted him to tuck his head closer to hers.

As they slowly swayed to the music, he tried to ignore the sensations of pleasure he was feeling. This was supposed to be a business meeting. However, it was hard to think of data systems and balance sheets while a beautiful woman nestled against him and hummed softly in his ear.

He knew he should distance himself from her and put things on a professional level, but she was clinging to him in a way that played on all his masculine instincts. And then there was her dress. It was swishing against him in a teasing rhythm, and through the slippery fabric he could feel her thighs connecting with his, her breasts pressing up against his chest. The hand in the middle of her back inched its way upward until it found bare skin. Hot bare skin that made him want to touch more of her.

Her head had been cradled against his shoulder, but as his fingers grazed her bare flesh, she lifted her eyes to his. She had the bluest eyes he had ever seen, and they looked into his with a refreshing openness he didn't often see these days—especially not in the business world.

"This isn't so bad, after all, is it?" she said with an enchanting smile. He noticed that her unforgettable eyes were almost unnaturally bright, and he began to suspect the freely flowing champagne punch was partly to blame for her uninhibited behavior.

"Not bad at all," he agreed, his eyes fastened to hers while his hand caressed her back. "Did you think it would be?"

Meridee studied the face of the man in her arms. It was a strong face. A face that had character. Yet there was humor lurking behind those deep-set eyes. She'd bet on it. Never before had she felt such an instant rapport with a man. "Let's just say this is a surprise... a very pleasant surprise."

"It's funny you should say that. I was thinking the same thing."

"You were?"

He grinned. "Let's hope we do this well working together."

At the mention of work, Meridee stiffened. For a few moments she had forgotten that the man who held her in his arms was the troubleshooter who had come to St. Paul to make decisions that could affect her future at Krystalene. As the music came to an end, she deliberately put a safe distance between them and said, "Thank you for filling in for my uncle."

"You're welcome," he replied, eyeing her curiously.

"We'd better get down to business. Why don't we find someplace quiet." She spoke as clearly and authoritatively as she could, angry with herself for not keeping closer tabs on how much she had been drinking. If she was going to discuss anything with a man like Zeb Farrell, she definitely needed a clear head.

Zeb followed her as she started for the exit. With his free hand, he pushed open the ballroom door, and they stepped out into the foyer.

She couldn't help but smile at several of her cousins, enjoying the curiosity on their faces as she floated past them with the best-looking guy at the party at her side. If only they knew the truth, she thought. Out of the corner of her eye she saw Brenda, who gave her a furtive thumbs-up gesture.

Everywhere they turned there seemed to be small groups of people, and after several unsuccessful attempts to speak privately, Zeb finally said, "Maybe we should step outside for a few minutes. I don't think we're going to find anyplace quiet around here."

"All right," she told him, hoping the fresh air would clear the fuzziness from her brain.

As they walked toward the lobby, he apologized for missing the meeting with Ingrid, explaining that his plane had been delayed leaving New York. When they reached the main entry, a thunderstorm was pelting the city streets with sheets of rain.

"It's raining," Meridee said inanely.

"Why don't we go to my suite, then?" Zeb suggested.

"Your suite?" A faint warning sounded in Meridee's head, but she immediately chastised herself for even thinking that he had anything but business on his mind.

"One of the company perks," he said with a grin, steering her toward the elevators. Noting her apprehension, he paused to say, "If you'd rather we went into the lounge, that's fine, but we're less likely to be interrupted if we use my rooms."

"Your suite is fine," she told him, unable to quash a tingly sensation at the thought. "Just let me tell someone I'm going to be gone for a while."

He nodded, and she hurried through the foyer outside the ballroom, searching for the other raspberry taffeta dress in the crowd, but Brenda was nowhere in sight. Nor was Juliet or her mother or her grandmother. Peeking inside the ballroom, she saw her stepfather and one of her uncles sitting alone at the table reserved for the wedding party.

"Donovan, where is everybody?" she asked, sitting down on the vacant chair beside him.

"Powdering their noses, I guess," he said with a grin. "Are you having a good time?"

"My feet hurt, I'm tired and I've had too much punch," she admitted candidly. "Will you tell Mom that I'm going to take a break from the party?"

"A break?" Donovan glanced at the watch poking out from beneath his stiff white cuff. "There's not much party left."

"That's why I need a break," she said with a weary smile. "If Mom asks about me, tell her not to worry. I'm with the businessman I was supposed to meet earlier this evening." She reached for her purse as she stood.

"Oh, oh. She's not going to like you doing business on a night like tonight," he warned.

"Maybe you should tell her I met some wonderful guy who wanted to take me out for coffee," she suggested, wishing that that had truly been the case with Zeb.

"Are you coming back, or won't you be needing a ride home?"

"Don't worry about me. I can get myself home," she said with more confidence than she felt.

"I know you can," he said, patting her hand affectionately. "Don't worry about your mother. I'll cover for you."

"Thanks." She bent down to kiss him on the cheek, then retraced her steps to the elevators. Zeb was right where she had left him, standing with his hands in his pants pockets and looking even more attractive than she remembered.

"All set?" he asked, pressing the call button.

A pair of chrome elevator doors slid open and he motioned for her to precede him inside. As the elevator soared to the twentieth floor, Meridee reeled ever so slightly. She grabbed on to the metal railing and hoped the dizziness would disappear when she stepped out onto terra firma. It didn't. As she walked beside Zeb, she found it increasingly difficult to prevent herself from swaying, and she wondered how she could possibly conduct business in this condition.

"You know, you're not at all what I expected you to be," Zeb told her, inserting a key into a lock on a door at the end of the hall.

Meridee tried to keep her voice professional, but even to her own ears it sounded less than authoritative. She felt a horrible urge to giggle. "You're not at all what I expected, either."

His room was a corner suite with two walls of glass, giving a panoramic view of downtown St. Paul, including the state capitol. Meridee couldn't help but gasp. "Oh! What a great view! I love the city at night," she said wistfully as she wandered over to gaze out the rain-streaked windows.

Zeb turned on a table lamp resting on a cherrywood desk and watched her press her nose to the glass like a child. "St. Paul is a great city," he remarked, loosening his tie.

"I'm glad you brought me up here. This is much nicer than being in a bar, isn't it?" She flashed him an innocent yet conspiratorial smile.

"Much nicer," he agreed, unsure as to whether he should trust that innocence. He wondered if the reports on Meridee Osborne had been wrong. Maybe her climb to the top hadn't been a result of hard work, but of feminine wiles. The idea bothered him, and he deliberately looked away from the blue eyes trained on his. He was here to straighten out Krystalene. He would be more successful if he kept that in mind and forgot about finding pleasure with Meridee Osborne, although at the moment, a growing desire to touch her was almost overwhelming.

She moved away from the window, looking around the room curiously.

"Can I get you something to drink?" he asked, turning on an overhead light and stepping behind the wet bar.

"I'll have whatever you're having," Meridee said absently, thinking he'd probably get her some soda or mineral water. She dropped down onto the soft leather sofa with a sigh.

"I'm really sorry about dragging you away from your sister's wedding," he said as he filled two glasses with a bubbly clear liquid.

"I'm the one who should be apologizing," she said, stifling a yawn. "I'm sure getting roped into dancing at a family wedding isn't exactly in your job description."

He handed her one of the glasses and sat down beside her. "I enjoyed meeting your grandmother."

"Did she give you a hard time? She thinks I spend too much time at my job."

"She did say I should either ask you to dance or leave you alone."

Mortified, Meridee said, "Gran said that?"

He nodded. "She gave me a postage-stamp lecture. Something about this being the one night you shouldn't be discussing business."

She tilted her head to one side in an unconsciously seductive movement, then removed her shoes, one at a time. Normally she would never have done that while conducting business, but tonight it no longer seemed to matter.

"I was glad to leave the party. My feet are killing me," she told him, unaware of the charming picture she made. Zeb wondered what it would be like to watch her remove more than her shoes—slowly and deliberately, as though she were tempting him.

Meridee took a sip of her drink, eyeing him over the rim of her glass. "This is champagne," she said, surprised.

"Would you like something else?" he asked, again wondering if her innocence was an act.

"No, this is fine," she answered, thinking she would only take a sip and then set it down. She briefly closed her eyes and tried to concentrate, but her mind kept going off in different directions and she wasn't sure which path to follow.

Zeb reached for the briefcase sitting on the coffee table and opened it. "Well, I guess we should get down to business," he stated smoothly, hoping that putting things on a professional level would squelch his desire to reach out and touch the creamy smooth skin exposed on her shoulders.

"I've never known anyone named Zeb before," she said thoughtfully.

"It's short for Zebulon. One of the twelve tribes of Israel," he explained. "At least that's my mother's explanation. My father says I was named for the American explorer, Zebulon Pike."

"You mean as in Pike's Peak?" she asked with a crooked smile.

"That's the one." He leaned closer to her. "Meridee is quite unusual, too."

She had never liked her name, yet the way he said it made her feel rather special. "It was supposed to have been Meredith—that's what my father wanted, but my mother said that none of her daughters would end with a 'dith.' They compromised, and here I am... Meridee." She spread her arms and shrugged, still holding her glass of champagne.

She pressed her other hand to her head. "I'd better not drink any more of this." She set the glass down on the table. "Ah, let's see. We're supposed to be talking merger, right? And you're the man who's coming to Krystalene's rescue."

Although she smiled, Zeb didn't think she was happy about his being in St. Paul. "Coming to the rescue is my business," he said, lifting his glass in the air.

Meridee thought about how he had already rescued her once this evening. If it hadn't been for Zeb, everyone in the ballroom would have known she didn't have anyone to dance with. If she hadn't consumed so much champagne, she would have been horrified. As it was, she found the situation funny and had to smother a laugh.

As Zeb shuffled papers in his briefcase, she studied his face. He had to be the sexiest-looking man she had ever seen, and she could only believe that she was thinking that way because of all she'd had to drink. When he caught her staring at him, she slid toward the opposite end of the sofa, her dress making a swishing sound against the leather.

"Maybe it would be better if we waited until tomorrow to go over the plans," she suggested, not wanting to be at a disadvantage. "It is getting late."

He smiled at her and said, "No problem." Then he pulled an appointment book from his briefcase and opened it to a page marked with a silver clip. "Let's see. Tomorrow at nine o'clock will work. We can have breakfast here at the hotel." He jotted something in pencil, then snapped the book shut.

He was talking as though it were a done deal, and Meridee felt control slipping out of her hands. This was not going as she had planned—not at all. The reason she had arranged to meet Zeb this evening was to take charge of the situation. It was critical that she set the tempo for their meeting. Now he was the one calling the shots, and she had to find a way to turn the tables.

"I should get you back downstairs to your sister's wedding," he said before she could decide on a course of action. He lifted his glass and swallowed the remaining champagne, then rose to his feet, indicating that their discussion was finished. He walked over to the cherrywood desk and picked up the room key he had deposited there only a short time ago.

"Wait a minute!" She shakily got to her feet and confronted him. Without her heels, she felt at an even greater disadvantage. She lifted her chin and said, "What if I don't want to meet you for breakfast tomorrow?"

There. She had asserted herself. She wasn't going to let some troubleshooter from New York walk in and tell her what to do. Not after everything she had gone through to arrange a meeting on the night of her sister's wedding.

"You have a more convenient time in mind?" he asked, a hint of amusement in his eyes.

She thought for a moment. "I prefer ten o'clock," she told him, unaware that she was holding on to his sleeves as she struggled to fight off the effects of the champagne.

"Then ten o'clock it will be," he stated amiably, his eyes on the raspberry-painted fingernails clinging to his suitcoat.

She could see that he didn't take her seriously, and it annoyed her. But weariness was causing her body to sag against his. Everything in the room seemed to take on a warm, rosy glow, including Zeb Farrell. When she looked up into his face, all thoughts of Krystalene and the takeover by Denton Diversified, disappeared. All she could think about was how close they were standing to each other.

"It's too bad we have to work together, Zeb Farrell," she murmured to herself, but he heard her as well.

"You don't want to work with me?" he asked, wrapping his arms around her in order to help her stay on her feet. His eyes roamed across her flushed face, then drifted lower to the soft curves revealed by the strapless dress.

"I guess I was just imagining what it would be like if we had met under different circumstances . . . if you had been one of the men my grandmother was trying to match me up with."

Suddenly she didn't care that he was the troubleshooter from New York. She wanted him to kiss her. She wanted to know what it would be like to have his lips on hers.

She sagged slightly, and the light cast a shadow across the gentle swell of her breasts. Zeb wanted to pull his eyes away, but found he couldn't. Seducing Meridee Osborne was definitely not in his game plan for Krystalene Products, yet ever since he had first set eyes on her, he had found himself wanting to do just that.

Unable to resist, he lowered his head and touched her lips with his, brushing them lightly, almost teasingly. Each time he pressed his mouth to hers, it lingered a little longer, until her lips parted beneath his. She moved her hands from the sleeves of his suit, coiling them around his neck as she pressed closer to him.

At age twenty-nine, Meridee thought she had experienced her share of passionate kisses, but nothing in her past had prepared her for the wild and reckless feelings his lips evoked. His arms were strong, his mouth demanding, his body firm. Never had she felt so wonderfully out of control, either physically or emotionally.

Incredible sensations of pleasure were swirling inside her. Champagne punch and Zeb Farrell were a heady combination. When he lifted his mouth from hers, she felt lost and gave a little moan, staring up at him with wide eyes and moist lips.

"We're supposed to be discussing business," she reminded him, fighting for composure but looking extremely vulnerable as she clung to him.

"I think I'm going to like doing business with you, Meridee Osborne." His voice was low and tinged with amusement.

Her smile was a bit impudent, and for Zeb, very appealing. He was finding it difficult to resist kissing her again, especially when she was standing on her tiptoes with her arms locked around his neck.

"Business." She chuckled, letting her arms fall to her sides. She made an effort to stand up straight, but Zeb could see that the champagne had taken its toll.

"I think I'd better go." She looked around for her purse, swaying ever so slightly. "The champagne punch has definitely kicked."

"Why don't you come with me?" Zeb suggested, reaching out to grasp her waist. "I'll take you back downstairs."

"Sure, only I need to use the bathroom first," she said in a near whisper.

"It's right through here," he said, escorting her to the door leading into the bedroom. He flicked on another light for her, and watched as she walked un-steadily out of sight.

While he waited for her to return, he stood with his hands in his pockets, looking out at the St. Paul sky-line. The city was beautiful at night, he thought, a smile playing at the corners of his mouth as he re-called Meridee's childish delight upon seeing the view.

The summer thunderstorm had moved off to the east, leaving the streets and sidewalks gleaming with puddles. As Zeb looked out at the myriad lights of the city, he wondered where among the rooftops Meri-dee's home was located.

What an evening it had turned out to be, he mused, rubbing his hand across the tense muscles at the back of his neck. He had come prepared to do battle with the young female executive, expecting resistance every step of the way. Now that he had met Meridee, he was be-ginning to think it might not be such a difficult task straightening out Krystalene, after all.

If he had any misgivings about the task ahead of him, it was that Meridee wasn't at all the sort of woman he had been expecting. She might not be a hin-drance to his job, but she definitely would be a dis-traction. It was that blond hair and those blue eyes. She had a Scandinavian look about her, as did half the population of Minnesota, he thought with a smile.

He waited for her to return. And he waited. Five minutes became ten, then fifteen. Hearing no sounds coming from any part of the hotel suite, he decided he'd better check on her. He was about to knock on the bathroom door when his attention was drawn to the king-size bed in the middle of the bedroom. Curled up in one corner was Meridee Osborne.

The raspberry silk dress had ridden up her thigh, exposing a generous portion of leg, including the light pink garter holding up a stocking. Zeb moved closer to the bed, calling out to her, "Meridee, are you all right?"

He leaned over and gently shook her shoulder. She stirred, sleepily mumbling something that sounded like, "I need to rest for a few minutes."

"Meridee, what are you doing?" he asked as she rolled over, her body as limp as a rag doll. "Meridee?" he repeated her name several times, but she paid no attention. From where he stood it looked as though Meridee Osborne was going to need more than a few minutes before she was up on her feet again. Unless he was mistaken, she was out for the night.

CHAPTER THREE

THE WORLD WORE A BLANKET of fuzz when Meridee opened her eyes the following morning. She felt a sharp, stabbing pain and quickly squeezed her eyes shut again. She grimaced, wondering how she could have gone to bed wearing her contacts.

Warily she reached up and touched her head with her fingertips. There was nothing there but hair, although it felt as though somebody had clamped a steel helmet on her head. The throbbing was relentless, but what was worse was the agonizing discomfort she had felt when she had forced her eyes open.

With a tiny moan she lifted her head, only to let it fall back down to the pillow. Movement of any sort was difficult, and she could have easily stayed right where she was if it weren't for her eyes. They felt as though she had spent the night in the Sahara Desert instead of an air-conditioned room. She needed to get to the bathroom and get her contacts out. The problem was, how was she going to get up when every inch of her body was screaming, "Don't make me move!"

She wiggled her toes, then cautiously moved one foot, expecting that any minute, Vanna, her bichon frise, would be all over her. She moved the other foot and then a leg, but there was no sign of Vanna.

Something was wrong here, her brain slowly registered. She shifted uneasily. The cotton sheets felt almost coarse beneath her fingertips, the pillow beneath her head polyester-hard, not downy-soft. Had she spent the night at her mother's?

It was a major effort to open her eyes, and the pain made her wince as she surveyed the unfamiliar setting. The guest bedroom at her mother's house did not have blue drapes or a television. Suddenly the memory of last night came back with a vengeance, and she realized she was not at her mother's, but in a hotel room— Zeb Farrell's hotel room!

With a sinking feeling in her stomach, she slowly rotated her head to see if there was anyone else in bed with her. There was. A startled gasp escaped from her throat and she quickly clamped a hand across her mouth.

He was big and handsome and naked, except for a pair of briefs that were stark white next to the dark skin of his thighs. Zeb Farrell was one good-looking man. He was also above the covers and at least two feet away, a small comfort, but still a comfort.

Raising herself up on one elbow, she felt a sickening sensation in her stomach. What was she doing in the troubleshooter's bed? Or maybe the question should be, what had she done in this bed? she thought miserably. The last thing she could recall was kissing him....

She couldn't have...

Or could she?

She swallowed with great difficulty. Her mouth was as dry as her eyeballs. She rubbed her knees together. Nylon slid across nylon. She was still wearing the garter belt and stockings. Her fingers crept beneath the covers and felt the satiny-smooth fabric of her bra and briefs. She sighed in relief, ignoring the tiny voice from the past—the one that sounded like her best friend in high school saying, "You don't have to be naked to do it."

Meridee refused to believe that she could have done "it." Not since she had been fifteen had she believed that anyone could do "it" and not remember. But then, not since she had been a teenager had she been foolish enough not to keep tabs on her alcohol consumption.

Self-pity made her want to bury her face in the pillow. Instead, she sneaked another peek in Zeb's direction and grimaced. There was a contented look on his face that did absolutely nothing to ease her anxiety.

She put both of her hands to her throbbing temples to steady herself and swung her legs over the edge of the bed. She needed to get out of his hotel room, and get out fast! Now. Before he woke up. She'd deal with the matter of facing him when she was better equipped to handle it.

Zeb stirred and she nearly catapulted from the bed. Clutching her head, she staggered into the bathroom, where she immediately bent over the sink to splash water in her eyes. She reached for one of the water glasses on the vanity and popped her contact lenses into it.

Catching her blurred reflection in the mirror, she groaned. With her hair resembling a haystack, and dressed in a push-up strapless bra and a lacy garter belt, she looked like something out of a bad B movie.

She splashed more cold water on her face, then rubbed a towel over what remained of her makeup, wondering how she could have spent the night in bed with a man she had met less than twelve hours ago. Not just any man, she reminded herself, but the man who had come to evaluate her performance at Krystalene!

She clutched the edge of the vanity until her knuckles grew white. She wanted to cry, but she had disciplined herself never to cry over business. And this most definitely was business. She tried not to remember the physical attraction she had felt for Zeb Farrell. It was something she dared not remember.

"Damn!" she swore at her reflection. "How could you be so stupid?" she asked herself in a frantic whisper. She grabbed the glass containing her contacts and went in search of her dress and shoes.

The raspberry dress was draped across a large leather chair in the bedroom. Picking it up carefully so as not to make any noise, Meridee kept one eye on the sleeping Zeb, praying he wouldn't awaken.

He didn't. She was able to slip the dress on and tiptoe out to the sitting area, where she found her shoes next to the sofa. She sank down onto the soft leather, fighting the urge to lie down. Instead, she leaned her head back and closed her eyes, willing the throbbing to cease.

After several minutes she realized the hammering wasn't going to let up until she was back in the comfort of her own home. She leaned forward and reached for her shoes. When Zeb appeared, she was quietly cursing under her breath, trying to squeeze her sore feet into satin pumps that felt several sizes too small.

"If you wait a couple of minutes, I'll give you a ride home," Zeb said in a sleepy voice.

He stood in the doorway to the bedroom, clad only in the snug white briefs. If Meridee had thought he was attractive in a Brooks Brothers suit, it was nothing compared to the way he looked this morning. He could have easily been an athlete posing for an underwear commercial. His lean, well-developed muscles held her eyes captive.

"No. That's not necessary," she assured him, dragging her eyes away from his chest. "I'll take a cab." She looked around for her purse.

As if he could read her mind, he walked across the thick carpet and retrieved the beaded bag from the cherrywood desk. "Is this what you're looking for?" He handed it to her, looking completely at ease.

She rose to her feet, conscious of his eyes on her. "I can see myself out," she mumbled, thinking Ingrid had been right. He was every bit six foot one.

"Meridee, wait," he ordered as she made a rather shaky beeline for the door, the beaded bag in one hand, the glass with her contacts in the other.

"I'll call you later," she said before hurrying out of the room. She wasn't sure how she made it out or where she was going to find the strength to make it down to the lobby and out the front door into a cab. She leaned back against the closed door of his suite and sighed, shutting her eyes briefly as she summoned up the strength to go on. Unable to resist the temptation, she removed the satin pumps and padded barefoot across the corridor to the elevator.

She sagged against the wall while she waited for a car to arrive. Expecting to hear a ping announcing the elevator, she was startled when she heard a male voice say, "It's here."

She opened her eyes and saw Zeb standing in front of her—dressed. As the elevator doors slid open, he ushered her inside with a hand at her back.

"I told you I'm taking a cab," she said stiffly, hating the way her pulse raced at the sight of him.

"And I told you I'm taking you home," he said in an authoritative manner, punching the button that read Lobby as they stepped inside the elevator. "It'll give us a chance to discuss a few things we didn't get to last night."

The doors slid closed and Meridee shuddered. She tried to concentrate on the business she would be discussing with Zeb Farrell, but all she could think of was how she must look in her day-old bridesmaid dress with her uncombed hair and her smudged makeup.

Humiliating. There was no other word to describe the entire experience. She still couldn't believe any of it. How could she have drunk so much punch that she couldn't remember parts of last night? Worse yet, how could she have spent the night in Zeb's hotel room?

Remorse washed over her, and she sagged against the elevator's mirrored wall, catching her reflection in the process. Just what she needed, she thought miserably, staring into the mirror. Another reminder of how awful she looked. She squeezed her eyes shut, which was a mistake, for as the car began its descent, she became queasy.

She must have turned a little green, for Zeb reached out to grab her by the arm, asking, "Are you all right?"

She gave him an almost hostile look and shrugged away from his hand. "I'm fine," she assured him in a voice that was anything but reassuring. "I'm just wondering what we *did* get to last night." She hated saying the words, but until she found out exactly what had happened between them, she wouldn't be able to talk to this man about business.

"Professionally or socially?" he asked lifting an eyebrow.

He appeared to be amused by her embarrassment, which only added to Meridee's irritation. She would not allow him to have the upper hand. "You're not a cat and I'm not a mouse, Mr. Farrell."

"Meaning?" His tone was steely.

"I would appreciate some straightforward answers about last night."

"If we're going to work together successfully, I expect us both to be up-front with each other," he said coolly.

Before she could respond, the elevator doors slid open, and she stepped out into the hotel lobby. As Zeb steered her toward the main entrance, he asked, "Why are you carrying that glass?"

"My contacts are in here," she answered, aware of several curious glances in their direction.

He ushered her past the front desk, stopping briefly to speak to the concierge. While they waited for his car to be brought up from the underground garage, Zeb

commented on the unusually warm, muggy weather the
Twin Cities were experiencing.

Within minutes, a large dark Lincoln Town Car
pulled up, and he motioned for her to get inside. He
slid in behind the steering wheel, allowing the bellman
to hold the passenger door open for her.

"Where to?" he asked as soon as she was settled in
the front seat.

"I live over by Lake Como," she told him, wishing
he didn't look so forbidding this morning. "You want
to go west on I-94. If you take a left at the corner,
you'll run right into it."

He nodded and pulled out into the flow of traffic. As
soon as they were heading west on the freeway, he said,
"I have the air conditioning on, but if you need some
fresh air, you can open the window."

"I'm all right," she told him, wondering exactly how
bad she looked.

They drove in silence until Meridee thought she'd go
crazy if she didn't resolve what had or hadn't happened last night.

Meridee swallowed with difficulty. "Mr. Farrell . . ."

"Don't you think you'd better call me Zeb after last
night?" he cut in.

She swallowed again, wondering what had happened to her salivary glands. "Very well, Zeb. About
last night . . ." She searched for the right words to ask
him the question foremost in her mind. She had always been a very direct person, and despite feeling at a
tremendous disadvantage, decided to be frank.

"I'm not in the habit of waking up in strange hotel rooms, and the fact that it happened to be the hotel room of someone I was supposed to meet on a professional basis..." she trailed off uneasily. "Well, it's very disturbing. The only explanation I have is that the punch had more champagne in it than I thought it did."

"I realize that," he said, giving her no indication of what he was thinking.

"Before we get down to business, I need to ask you something." She licked her lips and stared down at her hands. "I have to know if we did anything besides well...some kissing," she said, wishing she could throw herself out of the car.

"Actually, we did rather a lot of kissing," he said, a smile playing at the corners of his mouth, but Meridee didn't see it. She was too busy watching her fingers grind against one another as she folded and unfolded them in her lap.

"A lot?" she repeated uneasily.

"Yes, and then you went to the bathroom," he said evenly.

"And then?" She glanced at him expectantly.

He saw the apprehension in her eyes and said more reassuringly, "You didn't come out, so I went to check on you. I found you on the bed." He paused, then added, "You had fallen asleep."

Her sigh was audible. "So you took off my dress?"

"It seemed like a good idea. You looked rather uncomfortable. It was all twisted around you."

"I see," she said quietly, returning her gaze to her hands. "I don't know what to say."

He could think of plenty to say, but he didn't expect Meridee Osborne was in any mood to listen to what he had on his mind. He liked the fact that she hadn't asked him why he hadn't slept on the couch. If it weren't for her resolute attempts to act as though she wasn't suffering from a hangover, he would have been tempted to reach out and comfort her. But she was sitting ramrod-straight, acting as though she were on her way to the office instead of going home at seven o'clock in the morning wearing last night's clothes and carrying her shoes.

"If you're worrying that anything happened that might jeopardize our business relationship, you don't need to be," he told her gently.

"What happened last night does not fall under the heading of proper business etiquette," she said stiffly.

"But it did happen, Meridee." He wanted to add that he was glad that it had happened, but he could see by the expression on her face that that was not what she wanted to hear.

"Well, it won't happen again," she declared, wincing as the car beside them honked its horn. "Just for the record, I want you to know I keep my professional life separate from my personal life. I don't mix business and pleasure."

He found her rigid attitude rather annoying. She had enjoyed being with him just as much as he had enjoyed being with her, yet this morning she was all business and he didn't like it. He preferred to talk to her as man to woman. "Maybe you'll have to make an exception in this case," he suggested.

"If you don't mind, I'd like to forget last night ever happened," she said in a voice that told Zeb exactly how she had acquired her nickname. "Unfortunately, all I can do at this point is apologize for my unprofessional behavior and assure you that in the future you will have no reason to question my professional ethics."

"There's no need for any apology," he said, his annoyance growing. "If I had known it was your sister's wedding, I would have waited to see you until this morning."

"You were the one who wanted to get started as soon as you arrived," she reminded him, sounding offended.

He laughed shortly. "I'm sure I could have found something to do with my time until you were available."

Meridee didn't know whether to take his remark as a criticism or not. Her head felt as if it were about to pop right off, and if he didn't get her home soon, she was afraid she would humiliate herself even worse by getting sick in his car.

"Take the next exit," she told him, grateful to see the Dale Street sign. The next few minutes were spent giving him directions that would take them to the Lake Como neighborhood. When they passed a bank that had the time and temperature flashing over the door, she asked, "Do you still want to meet for breakfast this morning?"

"I think we'd better change it to lunch," he answered dryly.

Meridee was too relieved to be annoyed by his comment. The way she felt right now, she'd be lucky if she could face food by noon.

"There's a restaurant right across the street from the company headquarters," she suggested, trying not to feel repulsed by the thought.

"That'll be fine," he acknowledged. "How about if I pick you up at noon?"

"Why don't I pick you up at the hotel?" she countered, still wanting to feel in control of the situation.

"That won't be necessary. I'm going to stop in and look over the offices this morning."

Again she felt the beginning of a power struggle. "But there's no one there on Sunday."

"That's why I'm going. I get most of my work done on weekends. That way there's less chance for interference."

"I don't think you'll find the employees at Krystalene difficult," she said, struggling to keep her temper.

She must have failed, for he said, "I'm not here to take over anything, Meridee. My job is to incorporate your company into mine in the smoothest way possible." They were stopped at a red light, and he looked at her and said, "Understand?"

She had all sorts of snappy rejoinders she could have made, but she felt too ill to do anything but nod. She'd have her say as to what she thought about his coming to Krystalene, but it would be when she was of sound mind *and* body. "The light's green," she said dully, wishing for the hundredth time that they hadn't met the way they had.

She spent the rest of the trip directing him through the city streets that wound around the lake. When he pulled up in front of her house, she couldn't get out of the car fast enough.

"Thank you for bringing me home," she called over her shoulder as she climbed out.

He, too, got out of the car, and she hadn't gone more than two feet before he was at her side. "You're looking awfully pale. Why don't we wait until tomorrow to talk?" he suggested, eyeing her critically. "You shouldn't have to give up your Sunday just because I want to get a jump on things."

Meridee should have been angry with the suggestion, but the truth was, she was feeling too miserable to be anything but relieved. Of greater concern to her at the moment was how wretched she must look for him to make such a suggestion.

"That's fine with me," she agreed quickly. "I'll see you tomorrow."

Again, she started toward the house, but Zeb placed a hand on her arm.

"Aren't you forgetting something?"

She gave him a puzzled look.

"I need the keys to the office."

"Here. Hold this," she told him, handing him the glass with her contacts inside. She quickly pulled the office keys from her bag and exchanged them for the glass.

At the house next door the garage door opened and a station wagon rolled down the drive. Meridee was suddenly conscious of the fact that she was coming home wearing the dress she had worn for her sister's wedding yesterday. As her neighbor waved through his car window, she managed to lift a couple of fingers in return.

"I'd better go in," she told Zeb.

He nodded and said, "Have a good day, Meridee."

She stared at him in disbelief. "You've got to be kidding," she said to herself as he jiggled the office keys in his hand. *A good day?* She'd be lucky if she still had a job by the end of it. Summoning up every bit of strength she could find, she offered him her hand and said, "It was nice meeting you," then practically crawled into the house.

THE FIRST THING MERIDEE did when she went inside was head for the medicine cabinet in the main bathroom upstairs, ignoring Vanna, who had been dancing at her feet the minute she opened the door. She filled a glass with water, then ripped open two foil packages.

Plop. Plop. Fizz. She watched the tablets quickly dissolve in the water, then lifted the glass to her lips and drained the liquid all at once.

"Oh, please work," she muttered to herself, pressing her forehead against the cool ceramic wall tile. Vanna continued to whine, and Meridee reluctantly pushed herself away from the wall and plodded back downstairs to let the dog out.

"Make it quick, Vanna. Mommy's sick," she murmured to the tiny ball of white fur, who obediently scampered out and back in as though aware of her mistress's plight.

Instead of dragging her aching body back up the stairs to her bedroom, Meridee sauntered into the living room and was about to drop down onto the rattan sofa when she realized there was already a body stretched out on the blue floral cushions. A rather large, male body wearing a wrinkled suit. Even though his face was turned away from her, Meridee could tell that it was Brenda's boyfriend, Steven Krane.

Her head throbbing, eyes burning and limbs trembling, Meridee plodded back up the stairs and straight into her sister's room. "Brenda, wake up." She mercilessly shook the younger girl's shoulder.

After a couple of groans and a futile attempt to pull the covers up over her head, Brenda opened her eyes. "What do you want?" she asked in a groggy voice, squinting up at Meridee.

"There's a man sleeping on the sofa."

"I know. It's all right," she said sleepily. "It's only Steven." She turned over, punching her pillow.

Meridee was not about to allow her to go back to sleep. "It's not all right. We both agreed when you moved in with me there'd be no overnight male guests," Meridee reminded her, grabbing her by the shoulder.

Brenda groaned. "Aw, come on, Meridee. I'm up here and he's down there. What's the big deal?"

"The big deal is I don't want any men sleeping in my house. It's an invasion of my privacy," she said, her patience nearly depleted.

Another groan escaped from Brenda's throat. "Good grief. Steven drank too much at the wedding, so I offered to let him stay here rather than have him driving around drunk. Do you have to harp at me for acting in a responsible way?''

"You could have driven him home.''

"I was too tired.'' As though finally aware that Meridee was still in her bridesmaid dress and that the sun was peeking through the slats in the window blinds, she asked, ''Are you just getting home now?''

Meridee realized it was a little late to deny anything. ''Yes, and I feel awful, so I'm going to bed.'' She got up and started for the door.

''Meridee, you didn't spend the night with Zeb Farrell, did you?'' Brenda raked her eyes up and down her sister's bedraggled figure.

''It's not what you're thinking,'' Meridee said defensively.

''Oh, I suppose you're going to tell me you were discussing the merger.''

''I'm not going to tell you anything because it's none of your business,'' Meridee retorted and slipped out the door.

As she walked down the hall to her room she heard Brenda call out, ''I work for Krystalene, too, you know.''

Meridee closed her bedroom door and quickly peeled off her nylon stockings. She replaced the crumpled taffeta dress with a pair of cotton pajamas and slid between the covers of her bed. When the bichon jumped up beside her, she scratched the dog's head affectionately.

''Oh, Vanna, I'm afraid your mommy's made a mess of things,'' she told the fluffy white ball nestled in the crook of her arm.

Vanna moaned sympathetically, and Meridee said, "It's all Richard's fault. If he had come with me to the wedding, I wouldn't have drunk all that punch—and I wouldn't have been stuck without a dance partner." She sighed loudly. "Men. Who needs any of them?"

A small pink tongue licked her hand. "From now on it's going to be just you and me," Meridee declared as Vanna snuggled up closer to her. "I don't need a prince. I have my work," she said softly, not wanting to even consider the possibility that that might not be true.

"MERIDEE, WAKE UP."

Meridee felt a hand tugging on her shoulder and opened her eyes to see Brenda dressed in a lime-green cotton crop top and white leggings, looking disgustingly perky.

"It's almost one," Brenda informed her, running a suspicious eye over her prone figure. "You'd better change if you're going over to Mom's."

Meridee shifted uneasily, carefully lifting her head. The throbbing was gone, and except for a cramp in her left leg, she felt surprisingly good—at least physically.

"I don't think I'm going," she announced, mumbling into the pillow.

"You have to go," Brenda insisted. "Juliet and Ross are opening their wedding gifts, and Mom wants the whole family there. She's made all sorts of hors d'oeuvres and stuff."

"Just what I need after last night," Meridee said, pulling a face.

"Come on. It'll be fun."

Meridee made a sound of disbelief. "Is your boy-friend gone?"

"Yup. The coast is clear," Brenda said cheerfully, perching on the edge of the bed.

Slowly, Meridee swung her legs over the side of the bed and sat up. "Never again will I drink champagne punch," she declared resolutely.

"You're not the only one suffering today. Mom said the catering staff called her to apologize. It seems someone goofed and put in too much champagne," Brenda told her.

"I ought to sue for damages," Meridee said, wincing.

"Aren't you really going to tell me what happened last night?" Brenda asked, her big blue eyes guilelessly appealing.

"You don't want to know," Meridee said miserably.

"Why? What went wrong?"

Meridee almost laughed out loud. "Let's just say not much went right."

"But you looked as though you were having a great time."

Meridee heaved a long sigh. "I wasn't supposed to be having a great time, Brenda. I was supposed to be discussing business. Look, if you don't mind, I'd rather not talk about this just now." She trudged over to the closet to get her robe.

"Can't you at least tell me if he said anything about layoffs?" Brenda asked anxiously, following her sister across the room.

"We didn't get that far in our discussion."

"Are you going into the office this afternoon? Is that why you're not going over to Mom's?"

Meridee sighed. "I don't know what I'm doing this afternoon. All I know is that if I don't get into the shower right now I'm going to go crazy."

"Okay. I'll wait for you downstairs. But I think you ought to know—Mom's already called once this morning, and I don't think she's going to understand if you decide to go to work instead of getting together with the family."

MERIDEE FIGURED that if there was anything good that had come out of her unorthodox meeting with Zeb Farrell, it was that it made her want to spend Sunday afternoon with her family instead of at the office. For the first time in a long time she found herself eating Sunday dinner at her mother's, although her thoughts were not on the wedding stories everyone shared, but on the man who was working at Krystalene.

As it turned out, Meridee found the afternoon at the Cade home almost comforting. It was hard not to feel good when the bride and groom were radiating such joy. Between the pictures Kate had already had developed at a one-hour photo shop and the home video Grandpa George had taken at the wedding, they were able to relive many of the special moments of the happy occasion.

Much to Meridee's surprise, her grandmother didn't launch into her usual interrogation when Zeb's face appeared on the video. "Isn't he a handsome boy?" she commented.

Meridee took a deep breath and braced herself for the questions she knew would follow, but when Brenda said, "Grandma, that's the man Meridee's going to be working with on the merger," her grandmother simply nodded and said, "Oh, I see."

Looking at Zeb's undeniably attractive face on the video, Meridee thought she would be wise to remember just that. Zeb Farrell was here on business. But as she caught a glimpse of him on the video tape, she couldn't stop the pitter-pat of her heartbeat or the tiny thrill of pleasure tickling her stomach.

CHAPTER FOUR

HAD IT BEEN ANY OTHER Monday, Meridee would have begun her day with her usual morning swim, either at the local health club or at the house directly behind hers where her mother and stepfather lived. This morning, however, she decided to forgo her swim in order to be sitting at her desk when Zeb Farrell came looking for her. She was determined to be prepared for their next meeting. When she arrived at her office, however, Zeb was the one who was sitting at her desk, poring over a computer printout.

When he saw her, he frowned and said, "Is it that time already?"

"I'm afraid it is, and I'm going to need my desk," she said coolly, noticing the monitor to her computer had graphics on the screen. She shifted her briefcase to her left hand, and extended her right hand to him. "Good morning, Mr. Farrell."

He stood to shake her hand, his eyes raking over her curiously as he said, "Good morning, Meridee, and I thought we agreed it'd be Zeb." He didn't wait for a response but sank back down onto her executive chair and rolled over to the terminal, where he punched several keys, saying, "I just need to print one more file and I'll be out of your way."

She wanted to ask him what he was working on and why he was sitting at her desk, but seeing him again made her insides feel as though they were scrolling as fast as the graphics on the computer monitor. Despite the fact that he was dressed in a white shirt and navy trousers, the forbidden memory of how he had looked in his underwear flashed through her mind.

"Mr. Griggs was supposed to have an office ready for you to use," she told him, annoyed that her first reaction to him was physical.

He kept his attention on the printer that was spewing forth a stream of paper. "He does, but it's minus a terminal. I hope you don't mind that I used yours. Griggs said it would be all right." He gave her a look that said he wasn't expecting her to object.

Not that she had a chance to voice any objections, for Mr. Griggs entered her office as if on cue. "Oh, good. You two have already met. Everything going smoothly?" he asked Zeb.

Zeb nodded. "It helped to get into the computer files."

"I'm glad to see you took my suggestion and used Meridee's system. Meridee will be the best person to show you the ropes around here, so I'll leave you in her hands. She already understands that you have complete authority." He turned to Meridee. "You'll see that he gets everything he needs, won't you?" With a cursory nod, he left them on their own.

Meridee looked at Zeb coolly.

"Who am I to argue with Mr. Griggs?" she asked rhetorically. She would have set her briefcase on the credenza beside her desk, but Zeb's was already there, so she dropped it to the floor. The action didn't go unnoticed by him.

He quickly gathered together the data sheets that had been spread across the top of her mahogany desk. When he opened his briefcase to slip the papers inside, Meridee noticed that besides papers and folders, there was a small electronic game tucked inside. She glanced up at his face, thinking he wasn't as intense as the image he presented.

"There. That should do it," he said, snapping his briefcase shut. "By the way, I've called a staff meeting of all the department heads for nine o'clock this morning."

Meridee nodded. "Ingrid and I will be there."

"Ingrid?"

"Our senior accountant. She always attends staff meetings," she explained.

"Not this one," he said, pulling on the suit coat that had been draped across the back of Meridee's chair. "It's strictly upper management. No senior accountants."

"Ingrid is an integral part of this department," she told him, resenting his high-handed attitude.

"That may be, but she's still not coming to the meeting," he said firmly.

Normally Meridee would have protested, but after Saturday night, she decided it was better not to press the issue. She hadn't scored any points with her performance thus far, and from experience she knew it was better to tread slowly with a man like Zeb.

"Very well," she acquiesced. "Do you need me to provide any information?"

"I believe I have it all here." He patted the leather briefcase, then glanced at his watch. "It's still early. Can I buy you a cup of coffee?"

"No, thank you," she replied stiffly. "I have some work I need to get done."

Zeb looked at the woman standing before him and could hardly believe she was the same person he had been with Saturday night. Today there wasn't even a hint of warmth in the eyes hidden behind large square-rimmed glasses. Instead of a fancy bridesmaid dress she was wearing a plain charcoal-gray blazer with a long straight skirt and running shoes. Her blond hair was parted on the side in a short bob, and except for a hint of red on her lips, she wore no makeup.

She was all business, and he longed to catch a glimpse of the woman he had held in his arms on Saturday. "I think it would be a good idea if you and I talked before the meeting this morning," he told her.

She hesitated only briefly, then said. "Very well. Why don't I have some coffee sent up here?" She reached for the phone as he seated himself in one of the two leather chairs on the other side of her desk.

Zeb had to admit that he was equally impressed by Meridee's calm confidence and professionalism. The vulnerable creature he had taken home yesterday morning was nowhere in sight.

"Did you find everything you needed?" she asked, getting up to walk over to a narrow closet built into the wall.

"Yes. Your files are in excellent order," he answered, watching her untie her running shoes and slip into a pair of black pumps. He was reminded again of

Saturday night, when he had watched her remove her shoes in an unconsciously seductive manner.

"We have a good system of checks and balances," she stated confidently, bringing his thoughts back to the present.

After slipping her purse into the narrow cupboard, she closed the door and returned to her desk. She sat down and folded her hands in front of her. "Now, Mr. Far...Zeb, what do you wish to discuss with me?"

She was looking at him as though they were meeting for the very first time, as though she hadn't kissed him in a very thorough and intimate fashion. Or spent the night in his hotel room. She was looking at him as though she found his presence merely tolerable, and he longed to remind her that under different circumstances, they could be more than professional associates.

"For one thing, I thought you might appreciate my returning these privately rather than in front of the entire staff." He reached into his pocket and pulled out a pair of earrings.

For just a moment he thought he saw some of her composure slip, but her flash of vulnerability disappeared as quickly as it had arrived. "Thank you," she said politely, extending her hand palm up so that he could give her the rhinestone earrings.

He noticed that today she wore no earrings at all, or any other jewelry for that matter, except for a ruby ring.

"Did the bride and groom get away on their honeymoon?" he asked with polite interest.

"Yes, they're gone," she answered crisply.

"I noticed the wedding was mentioned in the paper yesterday."

"That's because my stepfather's the police commissioner," she told him.

"Now you tell me," he said with a wry grin. "After I crashed the party." She didn't return his smile.

"I'm sure you didn't come in early so that we could talk about my sister's wedding," she said. "We both know why you're here. Krystalene's been operating in the red and you've been sent here to straighten out the mess, right?"

He began to think that her reputation was well deserved. "Is there a mess?" he asked, steepling his fingers beneath his chin.

"I think you'll be surprised at what you find here," she said, choosing her words carefully.

"Maybe," he said noncommittally.

She sat forward and said, "Why don't you tell me what you expect from me."

"I expect cooperation," he answered smoothly.

She nodded in agreement and spread her hands slightly as she said, "You've got it, although judging by the amount of paper you just slipped into your briefcase, you appear to have accomplished quite a bit yesterday without my help."

"As I recall, you weren't in any condition to help had I needed it," he reminded her, and her cheeks turned a light pink.

"Just what is your point?" she asked directly.

"The point is this. During the next few weeks we're going to be working rather closely together. I appreciate that you have your work, and I'll try not to set unrealistic expectations when it comes to evening and weekend hours.'' His eyes gazed into hers without wavering. ''I want the lines of communication to be kept open. It's important that we're candid and above board with each other, that we work toward a common goal.''

''Which is?''

''Incorporating Krystalene into Denton Diversified with the least amount of resistance.''

''And if that's not possible?''

''Nothing's impossible, Meridee,'' he told her with a confident smile. ''The key to fixing problems is to negotiate reasonable compromises wherever they're needed.''

''And what about the nonnegotiable items?'' She arched one eyebrow.

''Everything is negotiable. I'm sure you're aware that I have the authority to do whatever is necessary to make Krystalene a viable part of Denton Diversified.''

Despite the image she was trying to project, Zeb could see that she wasn't as in control as she wanted him to think, for she was fidgeting with a pencil and looked as though she might break it in two. Her next words confirmed his suspicions.

''There's not an employee here who doesn't understand you have the power to eliminate any job you choose.'' Her eyes were flashing with scorn.

''I'm not some kind of Simon Legree,'' he told her, annoyed. ''I'm simply an efficiency expert, Meridee. You know that there are problems with the company or it wouldn't be operating at a deficit.''

''And it's because we are having financial problems that Denton was able to swoop down like a vulture on the buy-out. You say you want to be straightforward with me, Zeb. So tell me, are there any plans to save this company or are we simply going to be another tax write-off?''

Zeb stared at her for a moment before answering. She was a gutsy little thing and he couldn't help but admire her for it, yet he couldn't let her get the upper hand in their relationship.

"That's what I'm here to find out. It would be a lot easier for me if you'd change your attitude and not fight me on this."

"You've come to eliminate a couple of hundred jobs—including mine—and you want me to make it easier for you?''

"I don't want to see the jobs eliminated any more than you do. Hopefully that number will be kept to a minimum."

She eyed him warily. "I'm not naive, Zeb. I know what happens in a corporate takeover."

"I said I was going to be open with you, Meridee, and I am. Right now, the CEO in New York believes that the advantage to taking over Krystalene is in the patents and the tax write-offs."

A look of agony crossed her face, evoking sentiments in Zeb that he didn't want to acknowledge.

"Then we're right to be concerned over losing our jobs, aren't we?" she said with a defeated laugh. She shook her head. "I knew once you saw the figures it would be all over."

Suddenly it was important that he reassure her. Despite his initial impressions that New York was right, he found himself saying, "It's far from being over.

After spending yesterday going over the year-end reports, I'm not so sure.''

"Then there's a possibility the plant won't be closing?'' she asked, hope lighting her face.

"If you can convince me Krystalene can be profitable manufacturing soaps and shampoos, I'll recommend it remain open.''

"You want *me* to convince *you?*'' she asked.

"I want you to help me,'' he confirmed. "Why is that so difficult for you to believe? We do work for the same company.''

"For now,'' she added wryly.

"Can I count on your support?''

Meridee didn't know what to say. Normally when it came to business decisions she was comfortable relying on her intuition. But right now her intuition was telling her that she should tread carefully when it came to Zeb Farrell. The problem was, she wasn't sure if that was because of personal or professional feelings.

"It depends on what you mean by support,'' she said cautiously.

"As I said, cooperation is the key to this whole operation. You're well respected in the company. Work with me. Show the rest of the employees it's to their advantage to do the same.''

Again Meridee felt apprehensive. "I think you're overestimating my influence.''

"I want you on my side, Meridee,'' he said, staring directly into her eyes, a challenge in their depths.

The way he was looking at her made her wish she could tell him to get lost. He was too damned attractive, and he knew exactly what effect he was having on her.

"I guess I don't have much choice," she said, refusing to respond to his charm. "Of course, it would be much easier if I had Ingrid's help."

They stared at each other for a long moment, their eyes doing silent battle. "All right. Ingrid can come to the meeting," Zeb conceded with a sigh.

Meridee smiled smugly. "Thank you."

A knock on her office door announced the arrival of the messenger with their coffee. Zeb got to his feet and took care of paying for the delivery. As soon as they were alone again, he set a plastic cup down in front of each of them, then lifted his cup in a mock toast. "To finding solutions."

"To expediency," she added, hoping that Zeb Farrell was a fix-it man who would quickly right the problems of the company, then disappear from her life.

MERIDEE WAS WILLING to do just about anything to expedite Zeb's job at Krystalene, including starting early in the morning and working late in the evenings, which was the routine she fell into that first week. Although she hated to admit it, he was a natural at unsnarling messes, and she couldn't help but admire his perseverance.

On Friday evenings, Meridee often met with a small group of her female coworkers for what had come to be known as Chicks' Chow. It was a way to unwind at the end of the week, as well as a chance to commiserate about the trials of working in the corporate world.

"So what gives, Meridee? Is there something going on between you and the amazing Mr. Farrell?" Ginnie Sands asked as four women huddled around a table in a trendy restaurant in downtown St. Paul. "We've hardly seen you all week."

"He's working me to death—that's what's going on," Meridee answered dryly, tearing apart a hard roll. "The guy's a workaholic."

"Gee, I wonder why those words sound familiar," Ingrid pondered aloud in a teasing tone. "Could it be because I talked to your mother the other day?"

"I may put in long hours and work hard, but I'm not obsessed with work the way *he* is," Meridee insisted, reaching for a pat of butter.

Ingrid didn't say a word. She didn't need to—her expression said it all.

"I'm not!" Meridee repeated emphatically.

"Of course you're not," Ingrid said in a maternal voice.

"At least you took time out for Chicks' Chow. I bet he's still at the office," Ginnie surmised.

"He has a sort of 'damn-the-torpedoes, full-speed ahead' attitude, doesn't he?" remarked Laurie Phinney, the fourth member of their group. "With any other man you'd resent such self-assurance, but with him, it's kind of inspirational."

"You think he's inspirational?" Meridee shot her a look of disbelief.

"What surprises me is how easily he's won everyone's confidence," Ginnie added. "Before he came, all you saw were gloomy faces while everyone waited for a pink slip. Now the mood around the company is much more optimistic. It's as if people believe he will save their jobs."

"Yeah, but the question is, should we be putting our trust in this guy?" Laurie wanted to know. All three pairs of eyes looked to Meridee for an answer.

"I think there's a possibility that the plant will stay open, but that doesn't mean there won't be layoffs. Restructuring usually brings about the loss of somebody's job," she answered cautiously.

"I don't know about anyone else, but I'm sending out my résumés. I'm not taking any chances," Laurie stated pragmatically.

"You're not looking for another job, are you?" Meridee looked at Ingrid with a mixture of surprise and alarm.

Ingrid shook her head. "I haven't yet, but I have a feeling that Zeb Farrell's critical eye is on me. I thought you were going to fight this merger business," she said, looking at Meridee.

"We can't fight it," Meridee answered. "It's going to happen with or without our help."

"Wouldn't you know Denton would send a man to decide whether we close or stay open?" Ginnie remarked dryly. "It's because of male management the company's in the red in the first place."

"Ain't that the truth?" Laurie drawled. "Here we are making products that are bought and used primarily by women, yet with the exception of Meridee, no female has been able to crack the upper-management team."

"If I were the head of marketing, I bet I could make Krystalene a household word in no time," Ginnie boasted confidently.

"You *should* be head of marketing. You're more qualified than Ferguson and you've been with the company longer," Laurie remarked.

"Yes, well, Ferguson plays squash with Griggs. I don't," Ginnie said soberly.

Laurie lifted her glass to propose a toast. "I say we drink to the demise of the good-old-boy network." All four women clinked their glasses together.

"Maybe we should just drink to the demise of men and be done with it," Ginnie suggested with a twisted grin. "I mean, all they do is complicate life, right?"

"Oh, oh. That sounds as though there's trouble in paradise," Laurie speculated. "Did you and Brian have a fight?"

Ginnie laughed sardonically. "Only our usual difference of opinion on the subject of marriage. Brian's not sure deep commitment and true love are possible in the post-feminist age of shifting roles."

"In other words, he doesn't want to get married," Laurie deduced.

"Bingo," Ginnie confirmed.

"If I were you, I'd dump him, Ginnie. He'd never be able to handle your success if you moved ahead of him either financially or figuratively."

"Yeah, and he's definitely not the type to stay home and take care of the baby while you work," Meridee seconded. "Laurie's right. Dump him."

Ginnie looked at Ingrid. "What's your vote? Thumbs-up or thumbs-down?"

"I'm abstaining," she said, raising her hands defensively. "I'm not one to be giving anyone advice when it comes to men."

"I really shouldn't be, either," Meridee admitted. "Look at me. I was dumped for some bimbo who wears purple nail polish and violet mascara." She shook her head reflectively. "The funny part is, I didn't want to marry Richard, yet I was hurt when he didn't want to marry me."

"That's because deep down inside you're really looking for security and attachment," Ginnie philosophized. "All women are. I read it in one of those self-help books."

Meridee dismissed her statement with a wave of her hand and grimaced. "Don't say stuff like that. It's too depressing."

"Yeah, especially when men don't seem to have the same domestic urges we do," Laurie agreed. "They want to play the field. I actually met one guy who told me he likes to date a different woman every night of the week."

Sounds of disapproval echoed around the table.

"For a man that's acceptable, but can you imagine what everyone would say if a woman did that?" Meridee asked.

"Who's got the time? Most of the men and women I know are staying late at the office trying to get ahead in their careers," Ginnie pointed out.

"Personally, I don't want to be tied down or have to answer to anyone," Laurie insisted. "I'm seriously considering becoming one of those women who looks at relationships as flings."

"Flings?" Meridee raised her eyebrows.

"In this day and age, is that safe?" Ginnie asked critically.

"There's no need for you to wrinkle your noses. I didn't say I was going to be promiscuous. I'm simply going to stop looking at every date as marriage material. I'm going to have fun dating."

"Somebody get the thermometer out. I think this girl's running a fever!" Ginnie exclaimed, thrusting her fingers onto Laurie's forehead. "Fun dating?"

"It's a good thing her roommate left when he did," Ingrid remarked. "I think he was a bad influence."

"Peter was a great guy," Laurie said defensively.

"A great guy doesn't tell you you're the right woman for him, then move out because he wants to make sure there aren't any other right women roaming around," Ginnie remarked.

"Well, I'm not making that mistake again," Laurie said. "No more long-term relationships for me, just joyous romps."

"Romps?" This time Meridee made a face. "You know I'm not exactly an advocate of happily-ever-after and till-death-us-do-part, but I do think there should be more to a relationship than physical attraction."

"Why?" Laurie demanded. "Physical pleasure can be completely fulfilling and worthwhile in itself."

Again there was a chorus of groans.

"That may be, but studies have shown that sexual attraction is really very low on the list when it comes to factors contributing to a committed, workable relationship," Meridee pointed out.

Laurie grimaced. "Have you ever thought that maybe that's why those committed, workable relationships don't work? Let's face it, all of us have been in that type of situation, and are any of us still basking in the bliss of happily-ever-after?"

"She does have a point," Ginnie conceded grudgingly.

"I don't think I have a 'fling' personality," Meridee confessed. "It just doesn't seem right somehow."

"Men do it all the time," Laurie reminded her. "They date women for no reason other than to have a good time—no strings attached."

"Whether it be male or female, it still doesn't seem right," Meridee insisted.

"I figure as long as both parties agree, what's the harm? Actually, this type of relationship is more honest than the ones we were involved in. At least you enter it knowing that it's only temporary," Laurie stated.

"So are we going to have to start calling you 'Love 'em and Leave 'em Laurie'?" Ingrid asked with a cheeky grin.

"Go ahead and laugh about it. I think I'm being practical."

"Practical?" Meridee burst out laughing.

"Meridee, you of all people should understand the rationale here. You're always saying you don't want to get married."

"Well, that doesn't mean I want to have a series of relationships where all that matters is whether we're good together in bed," Meridee responded.

"I don't think I'm a romper, either," Ginnie said with regret.

"Me, either," said Ingrid.

Laurie shrugged. "Have it your way. Me, I think it beats getting emotionally involved with someone who's going to break out in a cold sweat the minute he hears the word commitment."

"I still think you're feeling that way because of Peter," Ginnie insisted. "I bet it'll take only one or two 'romps' and you'll give up on the whole idea."

"In the meantime, while Laurie's off finding erotic fulfillment, the three of us will be having fantasies about that rare man who doesn't believe that independence and ambition are unattractive in a woman," Ingrid proposed with a wry grin.

"I think if we're going to do any fantasizing, it should involve climbing the corporate ladder, not finding love and romance," Meridee suggested.

"That's assuming there is a ladder left for us to climb," Laurie said. "How long do you think it'll be before we get the news?"

Meridee shrugged. "Who knows? Every time I think Zeb has all the information he could possibly use, he comes in and asks for something else. I'm hoping he'll be out of here in a week or two. Otherwise, I'm going to be in a hospital being treated for exhaustion."

BED NEVER HAD FELT so good, thought Meridee as she slid between the covers later that night. She couldn't remember the last time she had worked as hard as she had the past week. And it wasn't just the physical fatigue. She was mentally exhausted from the constant stress she experienced whenever she was in the same room as Zeb Farrell.

She was grateful it was the start of the weekend. She needed the time away from the troubleshooter and the office. If she hadn't asserted herself, she doubted she'd be sleeping in on Saturday. Zeb hadn't looked too pleased when she had announced she wouldn't be working tomorrow, and she wouldn't have been surprised if he had asked her to work Sunday, as well.

She buried her head in the goose-down pillow and thought how ironic it was that she was the one who didn't want to go to work on a Saturday. She had just drifted off to sleep when the phone rang, awakening her with a jolt. The voice on the line seemed to come from a great distance.

"Oh, good, you're home. I've been trying to reach you all night."

"Zeb?" Meridee could hardly believe what she was hearing. She squinted as she looked at the digital clock radio on her nightstand. "It's after midnight," she protested sleepily. "Why are you calling me?"

"I was finishing up my audit of the capital expenditures and I found a discrepancy in the—" he began.

"You're still at work?"

"Yes, but I'm not going to be able to go any further here without your help. I need the adjusted figures from the equipment leases."

"I don't have any figures," she said irritably.

"Isn't your personal computer on line with the system here?"

"No!" she said, growing crabbier by the minute.

"What about a fax machine? Do you have one of those at home?"

"No. You're just going to have to wait until Monday morning to discuss this. Good night, Zeb."

Meridee stared at the telephone for several minutes after she'd hung up, feeling a bit guilty over ending the conversation so abruptly. Yet what did the man expect at midnight on Friday night?

She punched her pillow with her fist and tried to get comfortable once again, but despite her fatigue she felt wide awake. As she shifted around in the big bed, Vanna whimpered, unhappy about having her sleep disturbed.

"Shhh. It's okay, baby," Meridee murmured to the dog. But just when she was close to drifting off to sleep again, the doorbell rang. Since Vanna wasn't barking, Meridee thought it was probably Brenda. She often forgot her house keys, especially when she had a date and didn't need to take her car keys.

With a groan, Meridee climbed out of bed and hurried down the stairs. She peeked through the narrow strip of glass on the side of the door and gasped. Standing on her doorstep with briefcase in hand was none other than Zeb Farrell.

CHAPTER FIVE

WHEN MERIDEE OPENED the door, she was barefoot and wearing an olive-green trench coat she had snatched out of the front hall closet so that Zeb wouldn't see that she was wearing sheer-cotton shorty pajamas. Beside her, Vanna was running around in circles yapping at the stranger on the other side of the door.

"I'm sorry about coming over so late, but I brought those figures that I wanted you to look at," he said, gesturing to his briefcase. "It may just be what we've been looking for."

"You want me to look at them now?" Meridee asked him through the screen, wishing that the sight of him on her doorstep didn't make her pulse rate escalate alarmingly.

"It'll only take a few minutes. Were you on your way out or something?"

"If you must know, I was in bed," she said irritably.

"You were?" His eyes raked up and down her figure.

"Yes, I was," she stated firmly. Then she did something totally out of character. She flashed open her coat so that he could see she was in her pajamas.

Zeb cleared his throat and said, "If you'll just give me fifteen minutes, I promise I'll be on my way and you can go back to bed."

They eyed each other silently for a moment, locked in another war of wills. This time Zeb was the victor. "Wait here for a minute. I need to put Vanna in the other room or she'll jump all over you," Meridee grumbled.

When she bent down to pick up the dog, Zeb opened the screen door and said, "It's all right. She won't bother me." As he stepped inside the house, Vanna leapt out of Meridee's arms and headed straight for his legs, yelping and jumping excitedly.

"Vanna, down!" Meridee commanded, but the bichon paid no attention. "Vanna, down!" she repeated more forcefully, but the dog continued to frisk like a playful puppy.

Zeb crouched low to pet the hyperactive animal. "Well, aren't you a friendly little thing," he said as Vanna whimpered and begged for attention.

"She bites," Meridee warned, but Zeb continued to scratch the area behind the dog's ears.

"I think she has something in her mouth—something metal," he observed, holding Vanna's head still.

"Oh...those are her braces," Meridee explained.

"Braces?"

"Yes, braces," she said defensively, reacting to the look on his face.

"You've got to be kidding! You put braces on a dog?" he asked with a mixture of amusement and disbelief.

"I had to. Her teeth were improperly aligned. Dogs' teeth are supposed to be at an angle, but hers were straight up and down," she explained, unaware that her blue eyes softened whenever she spoke about her pet.

"I'm sure angled teeth are a must in the canine world," he said, trying to hide his amusement.

Meridee wasn't fooled. "It wasn't a cosmetic decision." She gave him a stern look. "Every time she chewed, her teeth hit the roof of her mouth and made little holes. It was quite painful for her."

"Little holes in the roof of her mouth, eh?"

"You don't believe me, do you?"

He grinned. "Hey, who am I to question the wonders of modern veterinary medicine?"

Meridee practically yanked Vanna from his arms, annoyed by his attitude. She should have known he would never understand. Few men did.

"Why don't you wait in the living room while I put Vanna upstairs?" she said, crossing the foyer to switch on a light in the adjacent room. "When I come back down I'll make a pot of coffee and we'll get down to work."

Zeb watched her climb the carpeted stairs, then poked his head into the living room, taking in the contents with one sweeping glance. Wicker furniture with soft floral cushions gave the room an informal, comfortable feeling. But what caught his attention was the number of plants she had. Everywhere he looked there were healthy green houseplants.

Instead of taking a seat on the wicker sofa, he drifted around the room, curiously eyeing photos artistically

arranged on tabletops and bookshelves. He remembered seeing several of the faces at the wedding last
weekend and assumed that they were family photos. He
liked the fact that she came from a close-knit family
and that she valued those ties.

Actually, there were quite a few things he liked about
Meridee. Unfortunately, they were things he wasn't
getting paid to like—such as her quirky sense of humor and her uncanny ability to know just what it was
he was looking for before he did.

In the short time they had worked together, she had
managed to earn his respect and admiration for the way
she managed people and for her tenacity. For the first
time in his career he felt as though he had met someone whose attitude toward work was the same as his.

If it weren't for the sexual attraction between them,
they would make a great team. Normally he had no
trouble working with female executives. He certainly
had come across his share of attractive women in the
professional environment, but never had he met one
like Meridee, who seemed to be able to distract him
with very little effort. Ever since that night of the wedding, when they had aroused feelings better left un-
provoked, he had had great difficulty ignoring the
primitive urges she stirred in him.

Although he doubted she would admit it, he knew
that she felt the sexual tensions too. It was the reason
she was so antagonistic toward him and why he often
found himself snapping at her. Despite her attempts to
look professional and downplay her femininity, she was
one sexy woman, and he was only fooling himself if he
pretended he wasn't attracted to her.

Hearing her moving around in the kitchen, he decided not to wait for her to join him in the living room, but took his briefcase and went to find her. She was at the sink filling the glass carafe for the coffee maker when he walked into the brightly lit kitchen. Instead of the green trench coat, she was wearing a blue-and-white-striped T-shirt dress with snaps down the front. On her feet were a pair of white tennis shoes, and she was wearing her tortoiseshell glasses.

After seeing her in professional dress all week, Zeb was a bit taken aback by her casual appearance. Gone was the crisply dressed, self-assured woman who had made an astounding board presentation earlier in the week. In her place was a small, delicate woman with a waifish charm. His thoughts drifted back to the night of the wedding and the way she had looked in the strapless dress. With the memory came a tightening deep in his loins, and he found himself wishing that it wasn't company business that had brought him to her house.

From the way she was scowling, it was apparent she didn't want him at her house at all—business or otherwise. "You don't have to bother with the coffee," he told her.

She gave him a wry look. "I need it if I'm going to stay awake."

"I'm sorry about the time. I would have come over earlier, but you weren't home," he said in his own defense, noticing that as in the living room, there were green plants everywhere. They hung from the ceiling, they sat on the counters, they were on the windowsills, and even on top of the refrigerator.

When he sat down at the soda-fountain-style table, she said, "It'll be easier to work in the other room. This table's rather small."

He would have set his briefcase down, but in the center of the small table there was ivy growing out of a teapot. "You must like plants," he commented as she moved the ivy to the countertop. "I noticed you have quite a few in your office, as well."

"I like clean air." She returned her attention to the automatic coffee maker. Plants help me breathe better."

"You think so?"

"It's true. They absorb toxins from the air and replace them with oxygen and moisture." She gave him a look that challenged him to contradict her. "They make the air purer."

"You must have the purest air in St. Paul," he said, glancing around the kitchen.

She let a cupboard door shut with a bang. "You can snicker all you want, but recent research from NASA proves that having fifteen to twenty leafy green plants in a home will clean the air. All the unwanted pollutants—you know, stuff like benzene, formaldehyde and carbon monoxide—can be eliminated by the miracle of photosynthesis." She smiled smugly as she turned to face him, folding her arms across her chest as she leaned against the island of cupboards.

"Not only is she an accounting whiz, but an environmentalist as well," he said softly, admiration in his voice.

"Maybe you ought to tell me what you want this 'accounting whiz' to look at," she suggested in the no-nonsense tone he was coming to expect from her.

Zeb opened his briefcase and pulled out a manila file folder, which he handed to her. "When I was going over the capital expenditures I found that these figures hadn't been accounted for on the year-end reports."

Meridee frowned as she opened the folder and gazed at the papers inside. After only a few moments of scanning the numbers she said, "I don't understand. I entered these figures myself. I know I did."

He pulled a computer printout from his briefcase and passed it to her. "Look at this and you'll see that there's a discrepancy."

After perusing the papers for several minutes, she looked at him. "You're right. Something's missing." She ran a hand across her forehead. "I don't understand how this could have happened."

"Someone who has access to the files could have accidentally deleted the figures," he speculated.

She eyed him suspiciously. "What are you trying to say? You know that only Ingrid has the password. She would never have made such a mistake and not told me about it."

"Maybe she didn't realize it had happened."

A frown wrinkled her brow. "You do think it was Ingrid, don't you?"

He could see that he had upset her and calmly answered, "It's a possibility."

"No, it's not a possibility." Her eyes sparkled as she came to her friend's defense. "Ingrid is too meticulous in her work to make such an error."

He leaned back, tilting the chair so that it balanced on its rear legs. "What is it with you and Ingrid, anyway? You've created a position for her...."

"I didn't create a position for her," she cut in hastily. "Krystalene has always had a senior accountant."

"You don't need one. All you have to do is delegate more work to the CPAs."

She shoved her hands to her hips. "Is this one of your cost-cutting suggestions? You want me to get rid of Ingrid?"

"I didn't say that. It's just that I'm having a little trouble figuring something out here."

She gave him a skeptical look. "You, the fix-it man?"

A grin spread across his face. "I've been working with you all week and I can't find fault with the way you operate."

His compliment sent a warm feeling flooding through her, and she forced herself not to succumb to the flattery. "Then what's the problem?"

He shrugged. "Maybe there isn't one, but I'm wondering why a bright, efficient executive would pass over qualified accountants and give an administrative position to someone who has had less background in accounting. She'd only completed a night course as a CPA a month before you promoted her."

"You checked into Ingrid's background?" she interrupted angrily.

"I've been through all of the personal files—not just Ingrid's."

"Information on paper doesn't always tell the whole story," she argued. "Ingrid is just as bright—if not brighter than—the other accountants in the department."

"And that's why you promoted her? Because she's so bright?"

"Yes." She met his steady gaze, then looked away, threading her fingers through her hair. No matter how long she talked, he would never understand her reasons for giving Ingrid the job. "Why are we arguing about this? I thought you wanted to find the discrepancy in the capital-expenditures figures."

The front legs of his chair came down with a small thud, and he reopened his briefcase, pulling out more computer printouts. "Be my guest," he told her, setting them down with a thump.

Meridee looked at the stack of reports and sighed. "Are you sure this can't wait until tomorrow?"

"You said you weren't coming in tomorrow," he reminded her.

Reluctantly, she pulled the reports over to her side of the table. "Maybe we'd better go into the living room where we can spread these out on the floor," she said in resignation.

Several hours later, after consuming the entire pot of coffee and poring over reams of computer printouts, they were about to give up when Meridee made a little sound of discovery.

"I think I've found it," she said, shifting to her knees. "Does this explain things?" she asked him, her pencil circling a column of figures on one of the data sheets.

Zeb studied the figures, a slow grin spreading across his face. "That's it. That's exactly what we've been looking for," he said with a satisfied sound.

She gave a tiny whoop of delight. "And I was just about to call it quits," she confessed with a smile, letting her pencil drop to the floor.

"The Krystalene accounting whiz comes through again," he said. "I have to admit that even I was getting tired."

Meridee glanced at her watch and fell back against the sofa, rotating her head to ease her aching neck muscles. "I can't believe we're finally finished. How do you keep working at this pace?" she asked him, rubbing her hand across the back of her neck.

He shrugged. "I love what I'm doing. It hardly seems like work."

"Don't you ever sleep?" She took off her glasses to massage her aching temples.

"Of course I do. Don't you remember?" he answered, alluding to last Saturday.

She deliberately turned her attention to the papers scattered on the floor and began gathering them together. "You know, I'm beginning to think you're a workaholic."

"Now that's a rather interesting observation coming from someone who gets more excited about her work than she does about anything else in her life," he commented shrewdly.

"That's not true!" she said emphatically.

He didn't say anything, but silently helped her gather the spreadsheets. As he put them back in his briefcase, he said, "This might come as a surprise to you, but I bet there isn't an employee in your department who doesn't think you're a workaholic.''

"Well, I'm not," she said again.

"Good, because I'm not, either."

She didn't comment, but lifted one eyebrow.

"You think I am, don't you?" he said in an accusing tone.

"What makes you think you're not?" she countered.

He lifted a shoulder. "Didn't you see that article in this morning's newspaper?"

"You mean the profile of work addicts?"

"Yup. According to that article, there's a fine line between working hard and being a workaholic."

"Didn't it say that work addicts were perfectionists and there was no pleasing them?"

He nodded. "Tell me, does this face not look pleased that you found the discrepancy in the capital expenditures?"

She couldn't hide her grin. "Look what we went through to find it! And what about the other signs associated with compulsive workers? Like rarely working a forty-hour week? I bet you seldom work nine to five."

"Do you know of anyone in a management position who works eight-hour days and takes weekends off?" he asked realistically.

She sighed. "Maybe we're all a bunch of workaholics. I have to admit, I did answer yes to several of the questions."

"I bet I know which ones," he challenged her. "You take work home with you on weekends, right?"

She nodded. "I have to to keep up."

"And I bet your family has given up expecting you to be on time?"

"Or to show up at all," she admitted grimly.

"And you believe it's okay to work long hours because you love what you're doing?"

"I *do* love my work. Don't you?"

He nodded. "Do you work or read during meals?"

"Only when I'm alone," she confessed. "But I don't have an obsessive need for control, and I'm not discontented if I don't have several projects going on at once."

"And I don't think either of us has difficulty relaxing or having fun, do you?"

She shook her head, not wanting to admit that she didn't relax and have nearly as much fun as she knew she should.

"What about the part about having difficulty with relationships?" he posed, giving her a long, measuring look.

"Difficulty with relationships?" she repeated cautiously.

"Uh-huh. According to that article, if you're a workaholic, excessive work interferes with intimate relationships. You have little energy left over for anything else."

"I don't put all my energy into my work," she answered, not wanting to admit that Richard had often complained that he was in hot competition with her career.

"Does that mean there's someone special in your life?"

She met his cool, intense stare with one of her own. "If you don't mind, I'd rather not discuss my personal life." She reached for the empty coffee cups and set them on the silver serving tray beside the glass carafe. "I prefer to keep my professional and private lives separate."

He was annoyed by how easily she could switch from friendly to frigid. He found himself wishing that he could see more of the person he'd caught a glimpse of last Saturday night.

"We're going to be working together for the next few weeks. It's only natural that we get to know each other," he reasoned.

"I don't see the point in discussing my personal life with you. It isn't exactly pertinent to our business, is it?"

"Not everything has to be business, Meridee." He leaned closer to her. "We work well together, but as I recall, we got along quite nicely last Saturday night, both on and off the dance floor."

"I thought we agreed to forget Saturday night ever happened." She gathered the remainder of the computer printouts from the floor and handed them to him.

"Maybe I don't want to forget," he told her, grabbing her wrist. "All week long I've been waiting to see more of the woman I held in my arms that night, but I can't seem to find her. Where did she go, Meridee?"

"She doesn't exist," she said weakly, her heart racing at his nearness.

"I don't believe that." He leaned even closer, watching her steadily.

"Zeb, you're a representative of Denton," she protested.

"No, I'm a man and you're a woman."

The way he said the words caused a pleasant sensation deep in her abdomen. She tried to pull her wrist away from him, but even though his fingers held her loosely, she felt powerless to escape. Despite what her logical mind was telling her she should do, she didn't really want to be free of his touch. The gentle pressure on her wrist became a caress as his thumb gently rubbed circles on the soft flesh.

"Isn't it time we stop trying to deny that fact?" His voice was low and husky, stroking Meridee's emotions just as his thumb caressed her flesh.

"What fact?" she asked, his nearness playing havoc with her senses.

"The fact that you're a woman. I'm a man." The look on his face spoke volumes.

Meridee stared at the sharp, firm lines of his mouth, and a tremor of desire shot through her as she remembered what it had been like when he kissed her. She could deny it all she wanted, but the truth was, she wanted him to treat her like a woman. Ever since she had first set eyes on him, she had wanted to be in his arms, to let her senses take over and leave logic behind.

She lifted her eyes to his. They were staring at her in a predatory way that left little doubt about his desire for her. Everything feminine inside her wanted to respond. Instinctively, she sagged toward him, her lips parting in silent invitation.

"I've been wanting to do this all week long," Zeb said. His mouth covered hers in a kiss that swept them both along on a tide of passion. He pressed her back until she was lying on the floor, her fingers tangling in his hair as all else faded into oblivion.

Over and over he kissed her as she moaned and murmured softly. Her hands found the firm muscles beneath the crisp white shirt; his fingers slid up the smooth skin on her thighs as they crept beneath the cotton knit dress.

Engrossed in each other's bodies, with hands exploring unfamiliar territory, they were speeding headlong to a place they'd never been before. Just how far they would have gone, Meridee didn't know, for Brenda came home.

"Meridee?" she said, stunned as she stood watching Meridee and Zeb roll around on the floor. "Excuse me—I...I didn't realize you had...company," she stammered as the couple unlinked themselves and looked in her direction.

Before Meridee could find her voice, Brenda had fled up the stairs. When Meridee glanced at Zeb, she saw that he was tucking his shirt back in his pants. She blushed as she realized that she was the one who had pulled it out in the first place.

A glance down at her own dress revealed it was open to the waist. With trembling fingers, she refastened the snaps, trying to avoid Zeb's eyes, which seemed to penetrate through to her soul.

"Feel like having some breakfast?" he asked, his voice as shaky as her composure. "I noticed you have one of those twenty-four-hour pancake houses not far from here.

"Now?"

"Why not? Since I kept you up most of the night, the least I can do is buy you breakfast."

Her fingers fumbled with the last snap on her dress, and she laughed nervously. "I probably shouldn't. I seldom eat breakfast, anyway," she said uncertainly.

"Make an exception," he pleaded in a husky voice.

She made the mistake of looking at his face. The desire she saw written there made her say, "All right. Just give me a couple of minutes to freshen up."

It was with shaky legs that Meridee climbed the stairs to the second floor. She knew she was crazy even to consider going to breakfast with him. She was breaking one of her cardinal rules and allowing her emotions to enter into a professional relationship. Yet how could she refuse when her whole body was still aflame from his kisses?

As she passed by Brenda's room, she saw the door was open.

"Zeb and I are going to go get something to eat," she announced, poking her head inside.

"I'm sorry about walking in on you like that. I didn't realize that you were... well, you know..." she trailed off awkwardly.

"About what you saw..."

Brenda quickly cut her off. "Let's just forget it, okay? I guess if we're going to be living together, we should set up a system of letting each other know when we have men in the house."

"Well, I usually don't have men in the house. Zeb is here on business."

Brenda gave her a look of total disbelief. "I suppose you're going to tell me you were balancing the budget when I walked in on you."

Meridee stepped into the room and closed the door behind her. "All right. So I was kissing Zeb Farrell in the living room. That doesn't mean you should jump to conclusions."

Brenda rolled her eyeballs. "Meridee, last Saturday you didn't come home until after dawn. Tonight I walk in and find the two of you rolling around on the floor practically tearing each other's clothes off. Do you really expect me to believe nothing's going on?"

Meridee heaved a long sigh of frustration as she watched her sister walk over to the armoire and pull out a pair of pajamas. "Nothing is going on!" she denied vehemently.

"If you say so," Brenda said with a shrug.

"Look, I really don't appreciate your attitude," Meridee said irritably. "You're a fine one to be questioning my behavior. You were supposed to have been home hours ago, yet you never called to tell me you were going to be late."

"Well, *excuse* me," Brenda said sarcastically. "Maybe it would be better if you worried about your love life and let me worry about mine." She slammed the door shut on the armoire.

"That's fine with me," Meridee agreed, moving toward the door.

"I just hope you know what you're doing. If people find out you and Zeb are having a thing, they might lose some of their confidence in you. After all, he is the enemy."

"He is *not* the enemy, and we are *not* having a thing." Meridee said as she sighed in exasperation. "And I'd appreciate it if you kept what you saw this evening to yourself."

"I'm not going to say anything," Brenda said petulantly, insulted that Meridee had even suggested the possibility.

"Good." Meridee walked toward the door.

"How did Zeb end up here, anyway? I thought tonight was Chicks' Chow."

"It was. He only stopped over because we had some important business to discuss," Meridee said, her hand on the doorknob.

Again Brenda looked at her skeptically. "I know he's one good-looking guy, but aren't you the one who's always saying you shouldn't mix business and pleasure?" she asked.

"I'm not. It's strictly business between Zeb and me." Even to Meridee, the words sounded weak, and they echoed in her mind a minute later as she ran a comb through her short hair. Staring at her reflection in the mirror, she chastised herself for her behavior.

It hadn't been easy, but all week long she had worked at keeping her relationship with Zeb on an appropriate business level. Despite his attempts to draw her into personal conversations, she had refused to be anything but professional. She was determined that the only part of her Zeb would know well would be her mind.

Now she had to go back downstairs and face him, knowing that his hands had touched parts of her she had never dreamed she would share with a business associate. What was worse was the lingering sensation of his lips on hers. She could still taste him, warm and sweet, as she applied a covering of red to her swollen mouth.

Just the thought of being with him again was enough to cause her nipples to harden. Disgusted, she pulled on a bulky cotton sweater, not wanting to be sitting in the middle of a restaurant and draw attention to herself whenever Zeb looked at her with that sexy gaze of his.

But all the anxiety she suffered while getting ready was for naught. When she went downstairs, she found Zeb on the sofa—asleep. Meridee felt a mixture of relief and disappointment. Not that she could blame him. She was sure he had worked day and night since he had arrived in St. Paul.

Asleep, he had a boyish charm that made her want to cover him up and turn out the lights. She did just that and went up to bed herself.

MERIDEE DIDN'T SEE ZEB again until Monday morning. As she expected, he was gone by the time she went downstairs on Saturday morning. Since Brenda didn't comment about finding him asleep on the sofa, Meridee could only assume he had left before either of them had gotten out of bed.

When she arrived at the office on Monday, there was a memo on her desk announcing a company meeting to be held that afternoon in the employee cafeteria. The topic of discussion was to be the merger of Krystalene and Denton Diversified. Zeb was in charge of proceedings.

"Have any idea what it's all about?" Ingrid asked, entering Meridee's office with the memo in her hand.

Meridee shook her head. She was reluctant to tell Ingrid about Zeb's visit on Friday night. She was also a bit annoyed that he hadn't confided in her about the meeting.

"Rumor is he's going to be announcing changes in personnel," Ingrid said with a somber expression.

"Maybe that's why I haven't heard about it. Maybe I'm one of the changes," Meridee said in an uncharacteristically pessimistic tone.

"Well, if you're gone, I'm definitely out of here, too," Ingrid said gloomily.

Meridee recalled the conversation she had had with Zeb regarding Ingrid and felt a surge of anger. She crumpled up the memo and tossed it into the wastebasket. "I refuse to believe that, and so should you." She straightened in her chair and reached for the phone, punching in Zeb's extension. His line was answered by Mr. Griggs's secretary, who told Meridee that the troubleshooter was in the conference room.

Meridee got up from her desk and started for the door.

"Where are you going?" Ingrid asked.

"You wait here, Ingrid. I'm going to make sure there aren't any surprises coming our way this afternoon."

CHAPTER SIX

MERIDEE'S ANGER was evident in her stride as she marched down the hall and into the conference room. Although she told herself her fury was a result of Zeb's withholding information from her, deep in her soul she knew that part of her ire was due to the fact that she hadn't heard from him since he had fallen asleep on her sofa. There had been no note left for her and no telephone call, making her question just what he was feeling regarding their passionate interlude.

"Be objective, stay calm," she told herself when her heart began to beat in triple time at the sight of him. He was perched against the large oval conference table, studying a transparency projected onto a screen at the far end of the room. At the sound of the door closing, he glanced over his shoulder. When he saw her, he turned around, a smile spreading across his face.

"Well, good morning," he said in a lazy, seductive way that threatened to interfere with Meridee's objectivity. He was minus his suitcoat, and the sleeves on his white dress shirt were rolled back, revealing a light dusting of dark hair on his forearms. It was obvious from the way he was looking at her that he was very glad to see her.

"Good morning," she said primly, squaring her shoulders as she walked toward him, determined not to allow his devastating smile to affect her. "I think we need to talk."

He flicked off the overhead projector and shoved his hands into his pockets. "It's funny you should say that. I've been thinking the same thing, especially after Friday night."

He was looking at her as though they were intimate friends instead of business acquaintances, and she had the impression that had she not stiffened as he leaned toward her, he might have kissed her.

"I'm not here because of Friday night. I'm here because of this." She waved the memo in the air as though it were a piece of hate mail. "Why wasn't I informed of this meeting?"

"You didn't get a copy of the memo?"

"A copy of the memo?" she repeated disdainfully. "I think I deserve a little bit more than a memo. You're the one who said you were going to keep the lines of communication open, that you would be direct and straightforward with me, yet I have to hear from Ingrid that you're handing out pink slips...."

"Now, wait just a minute," he interrupted her, holding up his hands. "I am not calling everyone together so that I can give out layoff notices. You've been working at my side for the past week. I thought you'd have a better understanding of the way I operate."

She knew what he was doing. He was trying to turn the tables on her, and she wasn't going to let him do it. "Then why are you having the meeting?"

"To let the employees know what's going on. Do you think I don't know the uncertainty and speculation that's permeating this place? I told you, Meridee, my job is to incorporate Krystalene into Denton Diversified in the smoothest way possible."

"Until these people know whether the plant is going to stay open or closed, the uncertainty's going to be there."

"I realize that. That's why I've decided to recommend that the company continue its operations—at least for a probationary period."

Meridee stared at him in disbelief. "You are?"

"It's only a preliminary recommendation, but I'm confident that if management can show that Krystalene not only holds some valuable patents, but can operate as a profitable business, the plant will stay open."

Meridee was not usually a demonstrative person, but after months of anxiety concerning the status of the company, she found she couldn't stop herself from throwing her arms around him and proclaiming joyfully, "But that's wonderful!"

"I'm glad you approve," he said, grinning.

"Of course I approve. These people need their jobs," she said ardently. "Oh, Zeb, thank you!" Suddenly aware that she had literally thrown herself into his arms, she tried to step back from him, but he had her in his grasp and wasn't about to let her go.

There was a funny look in his eyes as he stared at her. "Don't thank me yet. I said the plant would stay open. I can't guarantee there won't be any jobs lost. I'll be interviewing everyone before making any decisions," he said, looking into her eyes. "Of course, the union workers will get a good settlement whatever happens since they're protected by contracts.''

"But management isn't," she said. "Does that mean that Denton will be sending in replacements?" she asked in her usual direct manner, aware that his hands still held her by the waist.

"There's always that possibility," he admitted.

"It's more like a probability, isn't it?" she stated cynically.

"There might be one or two new people coming in, but you don't need to worry about your future with the company."

"I don't?" Doubt wrinkled her forehead.

He let his hands fall away from her waist and reached for her hands. "You don't. Even if the plant were to close, Denton would find a place for someone with your skills."

His touch was doing strange things to her, and she deliberately pulled away from him. "Now that you've decided to recommend that the plant stay open, will you be returning to New York?" she asked, turning her attention to the plastic transparencies spread out on the table.

"Are you anxious to be rid of me?" His intimate smile made her breath catch in her throat.

"I probably should be, but I'm not," she admitted candidly.

He moved closer to her. "Good."

She didn't retreat, even though her brain was telling her she was treading on dangerous ground. "I like working with you, Zeb."

"We make a pretty good team. Must be because we're a lot alike, you and I."

"Two almost but not quite workaholics?" she quipped, trying to keep things light.

"I think it's more than that. I'm sorry about falling asleep on you the other night," he apologized, his dark eyes studying her face.

She shrugged. "At least now I know you're human like the rest of us," she teased, trying to ignore the sudden sensitivity in her nipples.

"I can think of better ways of convincing you I'm human than by falling asleep," he said, leaning even closer to her. "Can I make up for breakfast by taking you to dinner this evening?"

Every hormone inside her was screaming yes, but Meridee refused to listen. "I'll take a raincheck if you don't mind. Now, I think I should get out of your way here so you can finish preparing for the meeting." She gave him a polite smile and started toward the door.

"Meridee, wait." He stepped in front of her, blocking her exit. "About Friday night."

She shrugged. "What about it?"

Zeb stared at her in disbelief. Was she really such a cool number that she could stand there and look at him as though nothing out of the ordinary had happened between them? "Don't you think we should talk about what happened?"

Again she lifted her shoulders. "It was late, we were both tired, and we got a little carried away..."

"A little carried away?" he repeated.

"All right. A lot carried away. Considering the circumstances, I don't find that so unusual. I think we both know that ever since we met there's been a tension building between us."

"And that's what you think happened Friday night? We released our tensions?"

"Yes. It's unfortunate, but it happened."

"Why is it unfortunate?"

"Because we're business associates and..."

"You make it a policy to never mix business and pleasure," he finished for her in a flat tone. "Look, I don't make a habit out of getting involved with women I work with, either, but in this case, maybe we both should make an exception."

Meridee shook her head vehemently. "It's not a good idea, Zeb. We do work well together, but that's not going to be the case if we allow emotions to enter our professional relationship."

"Aren't they already there?" he asked.

"They shouldn't be," she said. "Zeb, I didn't get to where I am by letting my emotions rule my head."

"I'm not asking you to let them run rampant over your common sense," he chided, annoyed that she could so easily dismiss what had happened between them. "But what harm can there be in two people enjoying each other's company?"

"The point is, we don't need to enjoy each other's company. We're supposed to be working together, not sleeping together," she said bluntly.

Her coolness took him by surprise. After the way she had responded to him on Friday night, he never expected she'd be so unemotional about their relationship. He leaned back against the table, crossing his arms over his chest. When he spoke again, his voice was cold. "If that's the way you want it, you've got it."

There was an uneasy silence, as though she were having second thoughts about what she wanted, and he dared to hope that she was going to change her mind. But then she glanced at her watch and said, "I've got to go. Is there anything you'd like me to do for the meeting this afternoon?"

He shook his head. "No. Everything's all set."

"Good." She walked over to the door. "I really am grateful for your decision to keep the plant open," she told him, one hand on the doorknob.

"It was a professional decision," he reminded her shortly. He watched her disappear through the door, wondering why he found her gratitude so annoying.

He didn't need to look far for the answer. He wanted more than gratitude from Meridee Osborne. Normally he was the one setting the tone in professional relationships, but in this case, he had no choice but to defer to her wishes.

"Well, we'll see how long you can keep business business, Ms. Osborne," he said aloud to himself, a smile curving his lips as he thought of the work that still lay ahead of them.

DURING THE WEEKS that followed, Meridee found it increasingly difficult to ignore her attraction to Zeb. Although they did have dinner together, it was strictly business, and she found herself wishing they could be talking about his life back in New York rather than discussing spreadsheets and returns on investments.

The longer she worked with him, the more she wanted to know about his background, what he did for fun when he wasn't working for Denton—although observing his work habits, she was beginning to wonder if there *was* anything else in his life.

But more than anything, she wanted to know if there was a woman in his life. Often, as they sat side by side working, she'd look at him and wonder about the women he dated. Did he go for the hothouse-flower variety? The kind of woman who never carried cash because she figured that's what men were for? Someone who always had impeccably polished nails and wore high heels with everything—including her jeans?

She knew he wasn't married, but maybe there was some dependable Dorothy waiting for him. Someone who didn't care that he spent nearly every waking moment of his life working. Someone who loved him.

A prickly sensation washed over her as she remembered what it had felt like to be in his arms. Few women would turn down the opportunity to feel like they were on a fast train to paradise, even if it meant the train only came at distant intervals.

But she *had* turned it down. And not a day went by when she didn't question that decision. Zeb made no further attempts to alter their relationship, though she often caught him staring at her with a mysterious look in his eyes. She was tempted to ask him what was on his mind, but she was afraid he'd tell her and that it would be the same thing that was on her mind. Sex.

As someone who had always been disciplined in her approach to her work, Meridee had difficulty dealing with the unexpected distraction of Zeb's physical presence. For the first time in her life, she found she had trouble staying focused, and she was beginning to daydream about flying off to some romantic island in the Caribbean where no one mentioned profit margins and capital budgets.

"Meridee. Meridee. Are you there, Meridee?" Her secretary's voice crackled over the intercom system, startling her out of her reverie.

"Yes, I'm here. What is it?"

"Your mother's on line one. She says if you're too busy, she'll call back."

Meridee hesitated for a moment. There were two reasons why her mother called her at work. One was because she was worried that she was working too hard; the other was because she was worried about Brenda.

"No, I'll take it." Meridee punched another button on the phone. "Mom, hi. What's happening?" she said cheerfully.

"Am I taking you away from something important?" Kate asked.

Meridee looked down at the piece of paper in front of her that was empty except for several large Z's scribbled across it. "No, I was just about to take a break. I'm glad you called," she said, crumpling up the paper and tossing it into the trash. "How's everything with you and Donovan?"

"We're fine."

"You don't sound fine. You sound worried."

"That's because I'm concerned about Brenda."

Meridee stifled a groan. She didn't feel like listening to her mother complain about her younger sister. She knew she'd regret asking, but she found herself saying, "What's she done now?"

"Nothing specific. It's more of a problem of lack of communication. She doesn't listen to anything I say."

Meridee smothered another groan. "She listens, Mom. She just doesn't follow your advice."

"I realize that she's entitled to her privacy, but I'd like to know what's going on in her life. You seem to be the only one she talks to."

"That's because I haven't imposed any restrictions on her," Meridee said pragmatically. "She's free to come and go as she pleases as long as she follows the rules of the house."

"That's something I wanted to talk about with you. Is it true that you don't have a curfew for her?"

"Mom! Brenda's twenty years old. You can't honestly expect me to set a curfew for her," she said indignantly.

"Requesting that she come in at a decent hour is hardly unreasonable. It's common courtesy between roommates. Meridee, your sister's at an impressionable age. She needs guidance." There was censure in her mother's tone, and Meridee became defensive.

"You don't want me to give her guidance, you want me to impose restrictions. Mom, Brenda and I are getting along relatively well. That's not going to be the case if I have to start acting like her keeper."

"I don't think it's illogical to set a time when you expect her to be home—for safety reasons if nothing else."

"We have an agreement that she always lets me know where she is and what time she'll be home. If she's going to be late, she calls me. That way I don't need to worry." She ignored the little voice that reminded her Brenda seldom remembered their agreement.

"She's awfully young to be given as much responsibility as she has."

"She's doing all right. She has a job, she's paying her share of the expenses, and we're getting along quite well." Meridee swung her swivel chair in a 180-degree turn. "Things could be worse. She could still be trying to get into modeling and waiting for her 'big break.'"

"Have you talked to her about going back to school this fall?"

Meridee sighed. "Of course I have, but she gets all defensive with me the same way she does with you whenever you bring up the subject."

"Registration for fall quarter is just around the corner. I was hoping she'd change her mind and decide to return to the university."

"I don't think that's going to happen," Meridee said flatly.

"Donovan thinks I'm pushing too hard on this college issue."

"He may be right. It's something Brenda has to want for herself."

"Will you at least mention that registration for fall quarter is approaching?"

Meridee sighed. "All right. I'll mention it to her, but I will not impose a curfew. She's not wild and reckless, Mom. She's just a typical twenty-year-old."

"That's why I'm worried. Do you know much about this Steven she's been seeing?"

"He seems to be a nice guy. He's a student at the university. That ought to be a point in his favor," Meridee said.

"I'd feel better about her going camping with him if I knew his family."

"She's going camping with him?"

"This weekend. A group of her friends are going up to the Boundary Waters. She probably wouldn't have told me about it if she hadn't needed to borrow a sleeping bag."

"If it's this weekend, she probably wasn't planning on telling me at all," Meridee said thoughtfully.

"Why do you say that?"

"Because the Krystalene company picnic is Saturday. She's supposed to be going with me."

"Oh, dear. This isn't going to cause trouble between the two of you, is it?" Kate asked apprehensively.

"Don't worry, Mom. I can handle Brenda."

MERIDEE KEPT REMINDING herself of those words when she arrived home that evening to a sink full of dirty dishes and the scattered remains of several large pizzas on the table. It looked as though Brenda had entertained and left without cleaning up—breaking one of the house rules they had agreed upon when she had moved in.

Juliet had warned Meridee that living with their younger sister would be the equivalent of one of the labors of Hercules. At the time Meridee had thought it an exaggeration, that Juliet, being extremely neat, hadn't been able to understand that not everyone considered dust balls to be public enemy number one.

Now, after a month of sharing a house with her sister, Meridee understood why Juliet had complained so often. Even though she wasn't a neatnik like Juliet, Meridee didn't like coming home to a mess created by another person. Consequently, when Brenda arrived home later that night, she was not in a very good mood. In fact, she was downright ornery.

"Where have you been?" she asked sharply, her hands immersed in soapy water.

"It's Wednesday. I had a softball game—like I do every Wednesday evening," Brenda replied innocently.

"What did you do? Invite the team over for dinner first?" Meridee jerked her head toward the empty pizza boxes stacked next to the garbage.

"There were only four of us. I didn't think you'd mind," Brenda said, reaching into the refrigerator for a soda.

"What I mind is the way you left this place. It was a mess when I got home."

"I'm sorry. I would have cleaned up, but we were running late." She set her can of soda down on the counter and held out her hand. "Give me the sponge and I'll finish."

"I'm nearly finished now, so I might as well do the rest," Meridee grumbled, holding the sponge out of her reach.

"You don't have to be so touchy about it. I said I was sorry," she said insolently, dropping down onto a chair.

"Brenda, I've been putting in sixteen-hour days. What I don't need is to come home to a dirty kitchen."

"I would have cleaned it up when I came home." She propped her feet up on the other chair and massaged her calf.

"But that's my point. I don't want this mess sitting here half the night. And another thing. There are two bathrooms in this house. One down and one up. I've asked you repeatedly to stash all your personal items in either one or the other, yet I continue to find your things in both places. This morning I almost used your toothbrush."

"Well, *excuse* me." Brenda got up from the table and started toward the door, but Meridee stopped her.

"And don't forget that this is your weekend to clean house," she reminded her.

"I know it is," she snapped impatiently. "I'm going to do it."

"When? Before or after your camping trip?"

Brenda's cheeks turned pink. "How did you hear about that?"

"Mom told me. What were you going to do? Sneak off without telling me you're not going to the company picnic on Saturday?"

Her blush deepened. "I told you I'm not exactly the picnic type."

"You don't have to sneer at it. Just because it's employees and their families doesn't mean it's going to be boring," Meridee contended.

"Well, it doesn't exactly sound like thrills unlimited," Brenda replied.

"It's a chance for everyone to get together and have some fun," Meridee said, exasperated.

"I've heard about how much fun it is from the guys in shipping and receiving," Brenda said sarcastically.

"It *is* fun!" Meridee declared. "And most of the employees appreciate the company's gesture of good-will. I think you'd enjoy yourself if you went."

"Well, I think I'd rather be camping with my friends."

"Who all's going?" Meridee asked.

"There will be ten of us."

"All women, or are men going along?"

Brenda gave her a look that said it was a ridiculous question. "Five guys and five women, but we're not going as couples."

Meridee raised a skeptical eyebrow. "Sounds like thrills unlimited to me."

"Real funny, Meridee."

"Who aren't you coupled with?"

"Steven. I suppose Mom's worried because she hasn't met his family, right?" They exchanged knowing looks.

"It's your life, Brenda, but would it hurt to bring him around a little more often? We don't know much about him, except that he's a student at the U." Curious, she asked, "What's his major?"

"Mortuary science," Brenda said with a straight face. "He likes to cut dead people open." She laughed wickedly and made several ghoulish sounds.

"Cute, Bren. What does he really study?"

"English lit."

"How serious is it getting between the two of you?"

Brenda put her hands on her waist. "What is this, anyway? Twenty questions? You're worse than Mom and Gran."

Meridee sighed and tossed the sponge into the soapy water. "It's scary, isn't it? The closer I get to my thirtieth birthday, the more I sound like Mom."

"I think you're stressed out over your job. I don't know why you're killing yourself for Zeb Farrell. You're probably going to end up getting laid off, and then what good will all those long crazy hours have done you?"

"Brenda, no one's going to get laid off. You heard what Zeb said at that meeting."

"Maybe that was simply his way of keeping company morale up. Lots of people think the pink slips will be handed out as soon as the company picnic is over."

Concerned, Meridee asked, "Where do you hear this kind of talk?"

"It's all over the plant."

"Well, I hope that in the future you will squelch such rumors. Zeb is doing everything he can to save jobs."

"You sound as though you're on his side."

"There aren't any sides, Brenda," she said wearily. "We all work for the same company."

"I hope you'll be saying that when Zeb goes back to New York."

"I will," Meridee said with more confidence than she was feeling. "If you're going to go camping, will you at least leave me the name of the campground where you'll be staying?"

"Yes, Mother," Brenda said with a sigh.

"It's only for emergency purposes," Meridee retorted.

Brenda turned to leave, then looked back at Meridee, her blue eyes softly appealing. "You're not mad at me because I'm not going to the picnic, are you?"

Hiding her disappointment, Meridee answered, "Of course not. Although I was looking forward to going with my sister."

"Why don't you take Zeb?"

"He's going to New York for a few days, and even if he were here, it's not my duty to escort him to the picnic."

"Your duty?" Brenda stared at her and slowly shook her head. "You, big sister, I will never understand."

MERIDEE DIDN'T UNDERSTAND her relationship with Zeb, either. She had thought that when he left for New York she would be relieved and able to concentrate on her work again. Instead, she found his absence disturbed her more than his presence, and she was grateful when Mr. Griggs requested her assistance with some of the administrative duties for the picnic.

If Meridee had been expecting any of her friends from Chicks' Chow to be disappointed that she would be judging relay races rather than joining in the fun, she needn't have worried. Ginnie had made other plans for the day, Laurie had come with someone Meridee could only guess was her latest "fling," and Ingrid, much to Meridee's dismay, arrived with her ex-husband.

What didn't come as a surprise was the way Ingrid managed to avoid her throughout the day. Only once did they have the opportunity to talk, and that was when they ran into each other at a refreshment stand.

"Is everything all right?" Meridee asked, her glance straying to where Ingrid's ex-husband waited for her under the shade of a maple tree.

Ingrid smiled weakly. "Everything's fine. It's a nice picnic, isn't it?"

Meridee nudged her away from the small crowd waiting to get soft drinks and said, "Ingrid, why is Ed with you?"

She glanced uneasily in his direction. "The boys wanted him to come along."

"The boys?"

"Yes. This is supposed to be a family picnic. They wanted their dad here." There was a defensiveness in her tone Meridee had never heard before.

"I thought he had given up all his rights with regard to the boys," she said, concern in her face.

"It isn't that simple, Meridee," Ingrid answered, anxiety on her face.

It was obvious that talking about the subject was upsetting her, and Meridee didn't know what she could do to help. "Are you sure you're okay?"

"Yes, I'm sure," Ingrid snapped impatiently. "Tommy and Ed are entering the father-son horse-shoe competition." She looked over to where her sons were tossing a Frisbee not far from their father. "The boys want us to be a family."

"But is this what *you* want?"

"It's only for one day. He's talking about moving to Idaho to look for work." Ingrid glanced nervously in

Ed's direction. "Look, I'd better go. Don't worry about me. I'll be fine."

But Meridee did worry. She tried to keep an eye on her friend, but the Golden Meadows Recreation Area was a large facility, with baseball diamonds, riding stables, picnic tables, and a swimming beach, where all sorts of games were being played. There was no way Meridee could keep tabs on Ingrid and oversee her picnic duties as well.

As soon as prizes had been awarded for the first round of children's games and relay races, Meridee headed over to the food pavilion, hoping to find Ingrid sitting at one of the tables covered with red-and-white tablecloths. As she waited in line for bratwurst and potato salad, her eyes scanned the crowd gathered under the striped awning.

"Looking for anyone in particular?" a familiar voice said close to her ear.

Without even turning around, Meridee knew that Zeb was standing behind her. A delicious feeling traveled through her entire body and made her smile with genuine pleasure.

"Aren't you supposed to be in New York?" she asked as she turned to face him.

"I finished early and decided my time would be better spent back here. Must have been the 'near workaholic' in me." He handed her a plate as they reached the serving line and said, "This is work, isn't it?"

Meridee stared at him for a moment, taking in every inch of his masculine body. It was the first time she had seen him in casual dress. Instead of a white shirt and tie, his broad shoulders were covered with a mint-green crew-neck T-shirt that was tucked into a pair of khaki shorts. Seeing the dark hairs covering his muscular legs reminded her of what he had looked like in his underwear, and she grew warm at the direction her thoughts were taking.

"Bratwurst or Polish sausage?" the man in the white apron on the other side of the table asked her.

"Polish—with kraut," Meridee answered, relieved to have to turn her attention to the food.

"Griggs said you really are working today," Zeb commented, following her lead and selecting Polish sausage—only two instead of one.

"I'm an official hostess." She pointed to the large round button pinned to her salmon polo shirt that read Got A Question? Ask Me.

"I do have a question for you." He waited for her to move her plate to the next food server, who was waiting to plop a scoop of potato salad on her plate.

"Uh-uh," she protested. "I am not discussing finances today, Zeb. In this heat and humidity, all I'm capable of doing is judging three-legged relay races and supervising an egg toss."

He grinned. "Relax. This isn't about business."

That only piqued her curiosity.

She was about to ask him just what it was about when the next food service worker asked, "Do you want a pickle?"

She started to shake her head, but Zeb leaned close to her and said, "Take one for me."

So instead of pulling her plate out of reach, she watched as a big, fat, juicy gherkin landed next to her potato salad.

"I'll take an extra cookie for you in exchange," Zeb whispered conspiratorially.

"That's all right. One's enough for me," she told him as she held her plate out for a slice of watermelon.

He chuckled and said, "Who are you fooling? I've seen that stash of cookies you keep in your drawer."

They had reached the end of the line, where an assortment of cookies was arranged on a serving platter. "All right. You can take one for me," she told him as she eyed the sugary confections. "But make sure it's chocolate."

After selecting beverages—she a glass of iced tea, he a cup of coffee—they went in search of an empty picnic table.

"How's this?" She looked at Zeb for approval as they found an unoccupied table.

"It's far enough away from everyone else," he commented, lifting his feet up and over the bench seat.

"I'm not good in cramped quarters," she admitted.

"Me, either. I need elbow room," he said with a grin. They ate in companionable silence until he said, "Judging by the number of people, I'd say your picnic's a success."

"It's going really well," she told him, acutely aware of how attractive he was and how happy she was that he had returned.

"You look different today," he observed in between bites of his Polish sausage.

"So do you," she countered.

"I wasn't sure how to dress. I've never been to a picnic in Minnesota before."

A woman walked by in a halter top and a pair of biker shorts, accompanied by a man in jogging pants and a T-shirt. "As you can see, anything goes," Meridee said.

Suddenly she was suspicious about his motives for being here. Had he come because he thought the annual company event was something that could be eliminated to save money?

"Are you ready for my question?" he asked.

"Sure. Ask away," she answered warily.

As if he were inquiring as to the location of the nearest phone booth, he asked, "How come you aren't married?"

Meridee's reaction was less casual. She nearly choked on her iced tea.

CHAPTER SEVEN

"WHAT KIND OF QUESTION is that to ask a picnic hostess?" she demanded.

In between bites of his sausage he said, "As I look around here and see all these families gathered together, I can't help but wonder why you aren't running around with a couple of kids clinging to you...or at least a husband."

Meridee tried to swallow a lump of potato salad that didn't want to slide down her throat. "You want an honest answer?"

He quirked an eyebrow. "Do you ever give any other kind?"

She couldn't hide her smile. Normally she would have steered the conversation away from the personal, but she was beginning to feel strangely comfortable with Zeb.

"If you were to ask my mother, she'd tell you my ambition keeps me from finding the right man. However, the truth is, I've never met anyone untraditionally oriented enough to interest me in making that kind of commitment."

"What's your definition of 'untraditional'? Are you looking for someone who'll stay home and be Mr. Mom while you work?"

"Who says I'm even looking?" she asked, then added, "If I were, I guess it would be nice to find a man who would wash my socks and cook dinner for me. As for babies..." she trailed off with a shrug of her shoulders.

"They're not in your career plan?"

"I guess I don't see how a woman with a demanding career can be both a successful mother and a successful businesswoman." She took a sip of iced tea and said, "Motherhood can be a full-time job. My sister Juliet has two little girls, and I've seen the work involved." She shook her head. "I already work fifty to sixty hours a week. Where would I find the time for children?" She didn't expect him to answer, but went on to ask, "What about you? How come you've never married?"

"I came close—once. I had a 'significant other' for a while," he admitted, his face revealing none of his feelings on the subject.

"You did?"

"Yes. Is it so hard to believe anyone would want me around twenty-four hours a day?" he asked with a grin.

"Not really, but you strike me as the type for whom it would be all or nothing in a relationship—marriage rather than living with someone."

He shrugged. "As it turned out, what we had wasn't enough for a marriage. She washed my socks and cooked dinner for me, but..."

"Not enough significance, eh?" Meridee said dryly.

"It's not what you think." Zeb's expression became serious. "We were engaged. The reason we moved in

together was to see if we could make it work. It was
sort of a trial marriage. As it turned out, it was a good
experience for both of us. We realized we didn't want
to spend the rest of our lives together."

"Did it sour you on marriage as an institution?"

"I don't think so," he said thoughtfully. "But
you've seen the hours I put in. Couple that with the
fact that I earn more frequent-flyer coupons than I'll
ever be able to use, and you don't exactly have a life-
style that's conducive to family life."

"Some people manage both...successful career and
a loving family."

"The question is, are they people like us?"

She smiled and shook her head. "Probably not.
Maybe we really are a couple of workaholics."

"Uh-uh. I don't buy that."

"You don't?"

"Nope, and I think I know a way I can prove to you
we're not."

She lifted one eyebrow inquisitively. "What do you
have in mind?"

"According to the experts, workaholics are restless
when they're away from their work. They have difficulty relaxing and having fun, right? Look at the people around you."

Meridee took a quick inventory of the picnic pavilion. It was a jovial crowd with lots of carefree, smiling
faces. As her glance moved out across the grassy
meadow, where a game of softball was being played,
Zeb said, "Do you think anyone's thinking about their
work?"

"They don't appear to be, do they?" she mused, a slight smile on her face.

"We can do that." His voice was low and tempting.

"Do what?" she asked.

"Have a good time. We can forget about capital expenditures and operating costs and anything that has to do with the merger."

Doubt chased the smile away. "Do you really think that's possible?"

"For one day? Sure we can. We'll be picnickers like everyone else. What do you say? Want to help me prove a point?"

There was a challenge in his eyes and Meridee responded. "Why not?" She reached into her pocket and pulled out a piece of paper. "Here's the schedule of events. What should we do first?"

He set down his fork and peered at the yellow slip of paper. "What are wheelbarrow races?"

"You know, one person walks on his hands and another person holds him by his feet," she explained. "They're for kids. You need to look on the other side. That's where the adult activities are."

He flipped the paper over. "Horseshoe tournament, softball games, hayrides, water balloon fights." He looked up at her. "Water balloon fights are for adults?" he asked in disbelief.

She shrugged. "Everyone says they're fun."

He glanced at his watch. "We have about fifteen minutes if we're going to try it."

"You want to be in the water balloon fights?" she asked, surprised.

"I've never pitched horseshoes, and when it comes to softball, my skills are marginal at best, but water balloon fights..." He wiggled his eyebrows mischievously. "Is it every man for himself or do we work in teams?"

"You get a partner."

"Good. I pick you." He speared her pickle from her plate and held it between his lips as though it were a cigar.

"Me? What if I don't particularly care to get drenched?" she inquired in a sugary-sweet voice, her hands on her hips.

"You're the one who said it was fun. Besides, what makes you think you'll get wet?" He chomped on the pickle. "Only the losers get wet."

"Maybe we should try bingo instead," she suggested as he got up to dump his empty plate in the trash receptacle.

"Uh-uh. The more I think about it, the more the idea of a water balloon fight appeals to me."

"You're really serious, aren't you?" she asked as he disposed of her empty plate as well.

"We'll be able to release our aggression," he told her, reaching for her hand. "And it'll be fun."

Meridee had never seen him in such a playful mood. For weeks all she had seen was the serious, businesslike troubleshooter. That man had been a threat to her emotional stability. This man was downright dangerous.

"Zeb, wait. You may not be working, but I did tell Mr. Griggs I'd be available to..." she began.

"Griggs can find somebody else to do whatever it is you volunteered to do," he said, leading her out onto the footpath that wound through the park.

"How did you know I volunteered?"

"Griggs showed me the picnic plans last week, and your name wasn't on the list of workers. Knowing you, I figured as soon as Griggs mentioned he could use some extra help, you'd offer." His arm shot out protectively as a young boy on in-line skates went whizzing by them.

"I'm here alone. I figured it would be easier for me to give up my time than it would be for someone who brought a family along," she said reasonably.

"Well, you're no longer alone, and whatever you have left to do you can delegate to Warren." Meridee looked up to see one of the firm's CPAs walking toward them. Before she knew what had happened, her "Got A Question?" button was on the pocket of Warren's plaid shirt and he was hustling off to check on the horseshoe tournament.

"See. You delegate very well," Zeb told her as he steered her toward the area of the park roped off for the games. "Don't look so apprehensive. This is going to be fun."

And it was fun, Meridee thought some time later when she and Zeb sat side by side on a park bench sipping soft drinks, their clothes still damp from the water balloon fights. Tiny blue ribbons hung around their necks, their reward for taking first place in the competition. Between them sat a picnic basket, a trophy for winning the three-legged race. On top of the straw basket were two travel mugs, the prizes they had claimed for coming in second in the canoe race.

"Not bad for a couple of workaholics who don't know how to have any fun, eh?" Zeb said, his arm resting across the back of the picnic bench.

"It was fun," Meridee said with a contented sigh, watching the crowd thin as people slowly made their way to the parking lot. "This picnic is such a nice tradition. I hope this won't be the last one."

"Uh-uh-uh," he warned, wagging his finger. "You're not allowed to talk about work today."

A couple of employees walked by carrying equipment that had been used to rope off the various sections of the park, and Meridee said, "I suppose I should find Mr. Griggs and see if he needs help with the cleanup." She began to rise to her feet, but Zeb stopped her with a hand on her shoulder.

"The last time I saw Griggs he told me you could consider yourself finished with your hostess duties," he told her.

She gave him a suspicious look. "Are you sure?"

"I think that's the third time you've asked me that question today. You never question my authority at the office. Do I look like I don't know what I'm talking about when I'm wearing shorts or something?"

"No, but you're different today. You're like a kid playing hooky from school."

"And you think I'd deliberately get you into trouble?" he asked, a mischievous glint in his eye. He reached for her hand and captured it within his. "I won't lead you astray."

"Well, that's a comfort," she replied, resisting the instinctive urge to pull her hand back.

"Hasn't it been kind of fun playing hooky with me?"

She couldn't help but grin. "Yes. And look what I have to show for it. A blue ribbon, an insulated travel mug and half a picnic basket."

"I'll make a deal with you. If you'll give me a ride back to the city, I'll give you my half of the basket," he offered, gently caressing the back of her hand with his thumb.

"You didn't drive here?"

"I came with Griggs." He leaned closer to her and said, "But I thought maybe you could give me a ride back...if it's not an inconvenience."

"No, it's no inconvenience," she told him, wondering if the tingling she was experiencing was due to her damp clothes or to the thought of spending the evening with him.

As soon as she was seated behind the steering wheel of her red Geo Prizm she had her answer. Never before had she had such difficulty concentrating on her driving. Although she focused her attention on the highway, Zeb's lean, muscular legs were a constant temptation to look in his direction.

Because their clothes were still slightly wet, the air in the car had a damp smell that only made her more aware of him sitting beside her. Talk was general: Zeb commented on the scenic landscape the farmlands made; she did her best to answer his questions about the area.

The tone of the conversation had changed from a carefree, playful banter to a more subdued, question-answer format, with Meridee playing tour guide. As countryside gave way to urban housing, sunlight began to fade, and soon the lights of the city dotted the horizon. With the dusk came a feeling of intimacy, and it seemed only natural that again the tone of the conversation should change.

"I really had a good time today, Meridee," Zeb said in a seductively low voice.

"Me, too. Do you think we proved we're not a couple of workaholics?"

"We got a pretty good start on it. But if we're going to finish the job, maybe we shouldn't stop now."

"Are you saying you don't want to go back to the hotel and work on the audit figures?" she asked in exaggerated disbelief.

"I'd rather spend the rest of today with you."

They had reached the city limits. As they stopped at a red light, Meridee looked over at him and asked, "Doing what?"

He shrugged. "Doing whatever it is you do for fun on a Saturday night."

"Well, we could go to the Glam Slam—that's a nightclub where Prince often goes—but I don't think they'd let us in dressed like this." She glanced down at her wrinkled shorts.

"I'm not up for the nightclub scene, anyway. What's that coming up on the right?" Zeb asked, looking at a string of flashing lights that lit up the boulevard.

"That's an outdoor fun center. They have go-carts, batting cages...those kinds of things," she explained, not expecting that would interest him.

"Do they have miniature golf?" he asked eagerly.

"Yes. Do you want me to stop?"

He grinned. "We're wearing the right kind of clothes, aren't we?"

The smile came naturally to her lips. When the light turned green, Meridee moved over into the right-hand lane and took the exit leading to the brightly lit outdoor recreation center.

"This is great!" Zeb enthused as she parked the car in the lot next to the miniature golf course. "Look! They even have bumper boats!"

Zeb's enthusiasm was contagious, and for the next hour and a half they were like two kids in playland. After hitting golf balls through revolving windmills and across castle moats, they headed for the go-cart area, where they drove midget cars around a figure-eight asphalt track with a dozen other drivers—most of them teenagers. Next they donned batting helmets and stepped inside large wire cages where automatic pitching machines fired fastballs at them.

"Now aren't you glad we didn't enter the softball game?" Meridee asked after she had swung at half a dozen softballs without making contact with any of them.

"You're swinging too late," Zeb told her, watching as the other half dozen balls sailed past her. He reached into his pocket for more change and dropped it into the pay slot. "Try it again," he said, walking over to where she stood, poised for action.

"Now," he called out, but again she missed. "Here.
I'll show you."

She thought he wanted her to give him the bat so that
he could demonstrate, but instead of taking it from her,
he wrapped his arms around her, placing his hands over
hers as they rested on the wood. The ball had barely
popped out of the machine when she felt him swing.
The sound of leather hitting wood signaled success.

"You have to find your rhythm," he told her as together they belted several more balls out into the far
corners of the batting cage. "Keep your eye on the
ball."

It was the only thing Meridee dared look at. She was
afraid that if she were to glance at his face, which was
dangerously close to hers, he'd see the effect his nearness was having on her. When he stepped back to allow her the chance to swing on her own, she found
herself feeling suddenly bereft.

"Damn!" she said as she missed the next three balls.
Glancing over her shoulder at Zeb, she tried to concentrate on making contact with the ball, but all she
could think of was how good it had felt to have his
arms around her.

"Want to go again?" he asked when the final ball
had been pitched.

Meridee removed the batting helmet and shook her
short blond hair. "I'll watch you."

Zeb selected one of the heavier bats and stepped up
to the plate. Instead of softballs, he opted for base-
balls, and Meridee watched him swing at the high-
speed pitches. He missed all but one, giving her a rather
sheepish grin when he was finished.

"Now you know why I didn't want to play ball at the picnic." He returned the bats to the rack and hung up their helmets. "Are you ready for our final adventure?"

"You mean the bumper boats?" She glanced over to the rectangular pool, where a line of people waited for a turn on the self-propelled rubber inner tubes.

Zeb nodded eagerly and ushered her over to the ticket stand.

"We're going to get wet," Meridee told him as she watched riders exit the chain-link fence with water dripping from their clothing.

"We're used to it, aren't we?" he asked, handing her a ticket.

If Meridee thought she had gotten wet during the water fight, it was nothing compared to the drenching she received as other riders deliberately crashed their boats into hers, splashing water up and over the thick rubber tubing.

She couldn't believe the childish glee that lit up Zeb's face as his boat overtook hers and he managed to force her under the tiny waterfall in the center of the pool. By the time they were finished, they both looked as though they had been caught in a heavy downpour.

"Now what?" she asked, half laughing, half groaning, as she stared down at her wet clothes.

"How about something to eat?" he suggested, wringing the bottom of his shirt between his hands.

"Looking like this?" she shrieked, holding up the edges of her soaking-wet polo shirt.

"Could go to a drive-in and get a couple of burgers, fries . . . all that good fattening stuff."

"Or we could pick up a pizza and take it back to my place," she offered, surprising him as much as herself.

"Your place?" he raised a speculative eyebrow.

"My place," she repeated, ignoring the tiny inner voice that said she was asking for trouble. "If you'd rather not..."

Zeb put his hand on her shoulder. "Pizza always tastes best when it's late at night."

Meridee smiled weakly and hoped that it was only pizza Zeb was planning on tasting.

THEY STOPPED AT an Italian restaurant not far from Lake Como for what Meridee promised Zeb would be the best deep-dish pizza in St. Paul. The easy camaraderie they had established followed them back to her kitchen, where they sat at her tiny table, reflecting on the events of the day.

Just when the tone of their conversation changed from friendliness to awareness, Meridee wasn't sure. All she knew was that suddenly Zeb was looking at her with a recklessness that made her feel as though she were about to step off a precipice into infinite space.

Apprehensive, she got up and cleared the dishes from the table. Zeb rose, too, following her over to the sink.

"I'd say you did a pretty good job of accomplishing your objective today," she said, trying not to notice how close he was. "We definitely had fun."

"That was only part of my objective," he said from behind her, but she wouldn't turn around. She couldn't; there was something in his voice that warned her if she did, she would be lost.

When he took her by the shoulders and slowly turned her toward him, she knew without a doubt what the other part of his objective was.

"Zeb, I..." She never got to finish her sentence—his mouth covered hers, driving all thoughts from her head and leaving her clinging to him languorously.

When he lifted his head, he said, "When are we going to stop pretending that we don't want to go to bed with each other?"

She tried to pull away from him, but he pinned her against the cupboards.

"You wanted me to be straightforward with you," he reminded her, holding her eyes with his.

"I was talking about business," she said weakly.

"There's more between us than business, Meridee." He placed his hand on her thigh and began stroking the exposed flesh. "It's something we both knew the first night we met, and it's not going to disappear because we pretend it doesn't exist."

"We agreed to keep our relationship professional," she murmured with difficulty as delightful tremors raced through her.

"We didn't agree," he contradicted her. "You told me it was going to be that way." His fingers worked their way up her inner thigh to her shorts.

"It has to be that way." Her words lacked conviction.

"No, it doesn't." His fingers slid inside the shorts and then her briefs, making her gasp. "In the past seventy-two hours I've had a total of about ten hours' sleep, and it's not because I'm a workaholic. The reason I worked like a madman was so I could get back to

St. Paul, because I couldn't stand to be away from you."

Meridee groaned as his fingers blazed a hot trail in the most sensitive area of her body. "This is going to complicate things," she said as he ignited a flame of desire she no longer wanted to smother.

"It'll be worth it," he promised, supporting her as her body shuddered in ecstasy. He bent his head, pressing urgent kisses across her lips and her face. "Come back to my hotel with me," he urged her as his mouth traveled down her throat.

"Not necessary," she murmured, arching instinctively as heat swept through her like a bolt of electricity. "Brenda's gone for the weekend." Her voice trembled with anticipation. "We can go upstairs."

An overwhelming feeling of desire welled up inside Zeb, a meltdown of energy that had him caressing her with hungry eyes as she led him up the stairs to her bedroom. Never had he felt such an ache for a woman or wanted to get so close.

When they reached the doorway to her room, she flipped on the light and they heard a tiny howl. There in the center of the queen-size bed, nestled comfortably in the spot where Zeb wanted to be, was a whimpering Vanna.

With an apologetic smile, Meridee said, "She doesn't like to have the light on when she's sleeping."

Zeb watched her pick up the dog and cuddle it as though it were a child.

"I'll be right back," she told him before disappearing with Vanna.

While she was gone he made a quick survey of the room. It was not what he expected of a high-tech, efficient businesswoman who deliberately kept people at a distance. Nearly everything was white, from the thick plush carpet to the lace-trimmed curtains. The only color came from the floral-print accent pillows on the bed and the lush green plants that appeared to be thriving in the pristine environment.

It was a very feminine room, a very romantic room, and Zeb wasn't sure if that was because of the ruffles and lace or because he could detect a hint of the scent he was coming to recognize as hers.

When Meridee returned, he was examining a white wicker étagère that held an assortment of dolls, most of them appearing to be untouched by any child's hands. There was one, however, that was obviously a sentimental favorite. The checkered cloth arms and legs had been mended numerous times, the once rosy cheeks were faded, and the thatch of golden hair was as stiff as straw.

"That's Red Baby," she told him when she saw that he was holding the tattered rag doll. "She was my very first doll."

"There's something special about the first one of anything," he said as he replaced the doll on the shelf.

"I'm sorry about Vanna," she said with an apologetic smile. She took off her glasses and set them on the nightstand beside the bed before slowly turning to face him.

Zeb could have told her that if the house had caught fire, it wouldn't have distracted him from his purpose. The taste of her still lingered on his lips, and the sight of her standing before him, ready for him, made his heartbeat skyrocket.

He wanted her so much he was afraid he was going to seem like a frenzied teenager. He wanted their first time together to be a slow, deliberate seduction, but doubted whether he would be able to control his desire long enough for finesse.

"This is a little different from the last time we went to bed together, isn't it?" A slow smile spread across her face, and she began to unbutton her shirt.

"Let me help you with that," he offered, his eyes gleaming wickedly. He removed her shirt and stood mesmerized by the enchanting picture she made in her satin-and-lace bra. "This is going to be a *lot* different from the last time we went to bed together," he told her, his eyes roving over her figure. She was all soft, fragile curves and creamy, white skin. "I had forgotten how small you are," he mused aloud.

Meridee immediately crossed her arms over her breasts. Zeb reached for her hands, pulling them away from her chest.

"I meant small-boned," he told her, wrapping her in his arms. "You walk around the office in suits with big shoulder pads and carry a briefcase that weighs almost as much as you do. A man can forget that underneath that professional facade there's a very sexy and delicate lady." His gaze fell to the swollen mounds of flesh spilling forth over the lacy cups of her bra.

Meridee chuckled softly. "No one's ever called me delicate before." Caught up in the moment, she twined her arms around his neck and pressed her hips against him so that she could feel his arousal.

"Maybe that's because no one's ever seen the uniqueness I see in you." His fingers traced the outline of her lips, then he bent his head and touched her beautiful mouth, kissing her as though she were the most fragile creature on earth.

Then the kiss changed, becoming deeper, more intimate. A husky cry escaped from Meridee's throat when his hand slipped inside the satin demi-bra and cupped a breast. With barely restrained passion, he kissed her and caressed her, loving the feel of her.

"I like your size," he said with a ragged breath. He lifted his mouth from hers to ease his own shirt over his head.

Next he disposed of his khaki shorts, revealing a pair of boxers covered with ducks. "Surprised you, didn't I?" he asked, amusement dancing in his eyes at the expression on her face.

With the boldness he was coming to expect from her, she reached out and ran her hands across the dozens of tiny ducks dotting the fabric. When she touched the hard length of him, she said, "I always liked the feel of knit cotton, but these feel ... ah ... pretty good to me, too."

Zeb swelled beneath her touch. He swallowed with great difficulty as her hands sent tremors of delight through every nerve in his body. "They're my souvenir of Minnesota," he said raggedly.

"Then we'd better take good care of them," she told him, running her fingers inside the elastic waistband in a teasing manner. As she slid the boxers down over his hips, her fingers grazed his manhood and he shuddered.

Uncaring whether he looked like a teenager or not, he discarded the shorts in the merest blink of an eye and turned his attention to taking off the rest of her clothes. Again she was ahead of him, her fingers pushing her shorts down over her hips. He watched her kick them off and send them somewhere in the vicinity of his boxers.

Wearing only the skimpiest pieces of lingerie he had ever seen, she looked like a goddess to him. She turned to pull back the white comforter trimmed with eyelet lace, and the sight of her cheeks peeking out beneath the bikini briefs was more than he could resist.

He grabbed her from behind, wrapping his arms around her as they tumbled to the bed. When her bra came undone or how her briefs were disposed of, Meridee wasn't sure. Caught in his embrace, she drew him even closer, her entire body growing hot as his hands traced an erotic path across her flesh.

He reached for his pants to retrieve some protection, but she stopped him with her arms. "It's all right," she told him, unwilling to wait any longer.

Clasping her face between his palms, he kissed her hungrily, greedily. Effortlessly, they turned and tumbled until she was astride him. She looked down into his eyes and smiled as she felt his hardness pressing against her softness.

"You Tarzan, me Jane?" he asked as she straddled him.

Meridee gave him a wicked smile and opened up to him, her soft folds accepting his presence, tightening as he moved into her, welcoming him with a warmth that made him groan in bliss. Embraced in her womanhood, he closed his eyes, savoring the exquisite sensation. They fit together with a perfection that made him want to stop time.

He wanted this moment to last forever. He wanted to love her slowly and tenderly. But her muscles were clinging and releasing, pulling him deeper, tempting him to move against her inner flesh. Back and forth she guided him in a rhythm that was ancient, in a rhythm that was elemental. No longer did his body belong to him. It was hers, and it was vitally important for him to know that she felt the same burning pleasure that was sending him over the edge.

It was like nothing he had ever experienced, he realized moments later, when the shock waves of pleasure had subsided and they lay shivering in the wild aftermath of climax. With a small moan of regret, Meridee rolled to his side, settling into the arm he crooked for her.

He took her mouth in a slow, savoring kiss, his hands sweeping over the elegant line of her spine. "You're quite a Tarzan," he said huskily.

"You're not a bad Jane yourself," she said, brushing her lips over his in a teasing gesture of satisfaction.

"What a way to end a perfect day," he said with a contented sigh. His fingers lazily circled her breast, causing her to shiver suddenly when he tugged gently on the tip.

"You were right. It was worth the complications," she murmured huskily, tracing a line down the center of his body.

The feel of her fingers sliding over his skin made his breath catch. "There don't have to be complications."

He closed his eyes and enjoyed the sensations as her hands moved closer to his thighs.

"Mmmm...maybe," she said sleepily, continuing to explore his body.

He opened his eyes and looked at her, loving how uninhibited she was when it came to sex. "There won't be as long as we're honest with each other." His lips covered hers, conveying a promise, the taste of her rekindling the pleasure they had shared. "We're good together, Meridee...so good I don't want it to be over."

"I'd say it's far from being over," she murmured, her leg sliding between his in a lazy, sensual movement. "Wouldn't you agree?"

Zeb's body immediately reacted to her provocative gesture. He answered her by pinning her flat on her back and lacing his fingers in her hair. "Oh, I agree. Only this time it's me Tarzan and *you* Jane."

CHAPTER EIGHT

ZEB AWOKE THE NEXT morning to find himself alone in a strange bed. A glance at the rumpled covers and the indentation in the pillow beside his head reminded him that he had not slept alone.

Not that he needed a reminder. He could recall every waking minute he had spent with Meridee in this wonderful white bed, the memory of their lovemaking sending a delicious feeling of satisfaction through every part of his body.

He sighed as he stretched his stiff limbs, wondering just how much of his soreness could be attributed to yesterday's activities and how much was due to their wild night of lovemaking.

One thing he knew for sure. Nothing in his experience had prepared him for a woman like Meridee. She was a strong, self-confident and sensual female who wasn't afraid to explore the secrets of her body, and he was captivated by her.

After their night of passion, he wouldn't have thought he'd have the energy for anything but getting dressed and going back to the hotel this morning. He soon discovered he was wrong, for as he rolled over and caught her scent which still lingered in the linens, he felt a familiar quick jolt of excitement. He wanted her again. If anything, his craving for her was even more intense than it had been last night, for now he knew the warmth and softness of her body and the passionate potential of her soul.

He wondered where she had gone, why she wasn't lying beside him. He was about to haul his naked body out of bed when she walked into the bedroom.

"Oh, good. You're not dressed," she said with a lazy grin, which only made his blood pump faster. She was wearing a pair of denim shorts and a sweatshirt the color of watermelon, her face scrubbed clean of any traces of makeup, her blond hair softly framing her face.

Zeb's eyes widened in surprise, but before he could respond to her statement, Vanna came tearing into the bedroom and jumped up onto the bed.

"Easy does it," Zeb called out, trying to corral the energetic animal, but Vanna paid no attention and raced back and forth in a frenzy, barking at the man intruding her territory. "Hey. Settle down, girl. I'm not going to hurt anyone."

Within seconds Meridee had grabbed hold of the white tornado, calming her with a soothing tone of voice. "Now you be nice," she warned the tiny dog, then turned to Zeb and said, "She's not used to me having guests."

Zeb found her statement comforting. He didn't like to think of anyone else taking his place between Meridee's sheets.

"I can see why she's so territorial. This is quite a bed." A smile slowly spread across his face as he propped his back against the brass headboard.

You'll look like a million dollars when you wear this elegant necklace! It's a generous 20 inches long and each link is double-soldered for strength and durability.

HARLEQUIN'S

With a coin — scratch off the silver card and check below to see how many gifts you get.

YES! I have scratched off the silver card. Please send me all the books and gifts for which I qualify. I understand that I am under no obligation to purchase any books, as explained on the opposite page.

334 CIH AEGC (C-H-SR-02/92)

NAME

ADDRESS   APT.

CITY   PROVINCE   POSTAL CODE

Twenty-one gets you 4 free books, a 20" necklace and mystery gift

Twenty gets you 4 free books and a 20" necklace

Nineteen gets you 4 free books

Eighteen gets you 2 free books

DETACH AND MAIL CARD TODAY

Business Reply Mail

No Postage Stamp
Necessary if Mailed
in Canada

Postage will be paid by

**HARLEQUIN READER SERVICE
PO BOX 609
FORT ERIE, ONT. L2A 9Z9**

"You slept well, then? No complaints?" she asked, looking at his lips and remembering what it had felt like when they'd kissed every inch of her. She couldn't control the heat that flushed her cheeks at the memories. She had responded to his touch as she had to no other lover, giving herself to him without any restraint or reservation. Just the sight of him this morning made her aware of needs she thought had been more than satisfied.

"Not a one, except maybe that my bed partner is wearing clothes and I'm not," he said with a wicked grin.

"That's because I had to take Vanna outside," she answered, wishing his smile didn't have such a devastating effect on her.

"You can still take your clothes off and come back to bed," he suggested in a husky, teasing voice, his fingers playing with the edge of her sweatshirt.

"I don't think I'd better. My muscles already ache," she confessed.

"I know what you mean, but it was worth every twinge, wasn't it?" he asked seductively.

"Definitely," she agreed, unable to resist leaning over to kiss him. What began as a simple brush of her lips across his deepened and promised to become much more satisfying until Vanna came between them. Chagrined, Meridee grabbed the bichon and said, "I think she's a little jealous."

"Why don't you put her downstairs and come back to bed," he whispered close to her ear, his hand finding its way inside her sweatshirt. "I know some excellent techniques for soothing aching muscles."

"My brain tells me that's not such a good idea," she said, her breath growing ragged as his hand caressed her breast.

"Other parts of you would disagree," he said, rubbing the turgid nipple.

Meridee looked at him openly, honestly, wondering how he could so easily generate desire after everything that had happened last night. "I have a plan of my own. I'll put Vanna downstairs, then come back and show you." She scooped up the whimpering bichon and walked toward the door. "Don't get dressed," she called over her shoulders.

"Not a chance," Zeb mumbled to himself, folding his arms across his chest and smiling smugly. In another part of the house he could hear doors slamming and water running, and he pictured Meridee running around—nude. When she returned, she wasn't naked, but she still looked every bit as sexy as she had when they had tumbled in the sheets.

"My arms ache," she remarked, flexing her muscles. "It must be from paddling that canoe yesterday."

"Lots of my body parts ache, but it's not necessarily from canoeing." He patted the pillow beside him. "If you come back to bed, we'll get rid of one big ache."

She clicked her tongue disapprovingly. "I'm going to help you get rid of *all* of your aches," she told him, offering him a hand.

"And how do you plan on doing that?" he asked as she led him down the hallway.

When they reached the bathroom she pushed open the door and motioned for him to enter. "Ever try a carbonated bath?" she asked as they both stepped into the ceramic-tiled room.

"Blue water that fizzes?" he asked as he stared at the bathtub. "What is it? Some magic potion?"

She pulled a couple of fluffy white towels from the vanity. "Go ahead. Try it. It's full of muscle-relaxing minerals."

Zeb climbed into the tub, easing his large frame down into the blue water. With a groan he leaned back and closed his eyes.

"Well? What do you think?" she asked.

He opened his eyes and grinned devilishly. "I think it would feel just like a hot-spring spa if I had you in here with me." He stretched out a hand toward her. "As my mother always said, a pleasure shared is a pleasure doubled."

"You haven't told me anything about your family," Meridee commented as she stripped off her clothes.

"There's not much to tell. I have two brothers and one sister, parents, grandparents, aunts and uncles."

"You come from a big family, then?"

"Umm-hmm."

Meridee climbed in at the opposite end, but Zeb gently urged her toward him, lowering her carefully into the water so that she was sitting between his legs with her back up against his chest.

"Are you close to them?"

"As close as an almost workaholic can be to his family," he answered. "Ah," he said as he pulled her close to him. "Now this is more like it." He positioned her so that her head rested next to his chin and clasped his hands gently around her waist. "I can feel the minerals soothing me right this minute, can't you?"

Meridee playfully splashed water at him. Zeb retaliated by sliding his big strong hands up to cup her breasts, making her gasp with pleasure. As his hands gently caressed her, she closed her eyes, savoring his touch. While his fingers played with her nipples, his mouth was at her ear, nibbling at the sensitive flesh.

"I've never taken a bath with a woman before," he murmured, his breath hot against her flesh.

"Not even your significant other?" she asked, suddenly feeling very possessive of him.

He chuckled. "Hardly. She wasn't as uninhibited as you are."

"You think I'm uninhibited?" she asked, twisting her neck to look up at him.

"Wonderfully so," he growled, catching her mouth beneath his.

"It's nice to know my efforts are appreciated," she said softly when he freed her.

"Maybe I should show you just how appreciative I am," he suggested huskily, one hand on her breast, the other plunging beneath the water to rest on her thigh.

"We're supposed to be soothing our muscles, not exercising them," she said, her breath catching in her throat as his fingers found the hair at the apex of her legs.

"We'll do both," he told her, pressing kisses along her neck.

Familiar sensations filled her with a delicious sense of anticipation. She was about to take another intoxicating journey to a place where her body would no longer belong to her alone.

The thought was exhilarating. Her body was responding to his, ready for another trip to enchantment when he became very still and said, "You locked the front door, didn't you?"

Confused, she sat forward. "Of course I did. Why?"

"I thought I heard someone come in." They both sat quietly, listening for any sound that would indicate someone was in the house.

Meridee's stomach plummeted. "I hope it's not my mother." She quickly climbed out of the tub and began toweling the moisture from her skin. "She has a key, but I can't believe she'd just walk in. She always knocks or calls first," she said, her voice a frantic whisper as she clumsily pulled on the sweatshirt and denim shorts. "I'll be right back," she told him before slipping out the door.

As soon as she reached the top of the stairs Meridee knew that it wasn't her mother rambling around in the house. Sitting next to the front door were a backpack, a sleeping bag and a cooler. Brenda was back from her camping trip.

With a silent curse, Meridee hurried down the stairs. She found her sister in the kitchen removing a cup of hot chocolate from the microwave.

"What are you doing home?" Meridee asked, trying not to sound as frustrated as she felt.

"The weather was so lousy we decided to come home early," Brenda explained as she carried the hot chocolate over to the table. "All it did was rain."

"But I wasn't expecting you to come back until to-night." Meridee couldn't hide her disappointment.

"If we had stayed any longer, our stuff would have floated away," Brenda said. "Don't worry. If you're planning on working today, I promise I won't get in your way." She pulled out one of the metal chairs and sat down at the table.

Work? Work was the furthest thing from Meridee's mind at the moment. She was still thinking of Zeb's naked body immersed in blue water.

"Ummm, this tastes good," Brenda remarked after taking a sip from the stoneware mug. "The only thing that would make it better would be a French pastry dripping with butter."

"Sorry, the closest we can get to that is day-old bran muffins," Meridee said discouragingly.

"I know it probably looks silly to be drinking hot chocolate in the middle of summer, but you wouldn't believe how cold it was up in the Boundary Waters." Brenda shivered at the memory. "And it didn't help that all my clothes were wet."

"I have the air conditioning on in here. Maybe you ought to sit outside in the sunshine," Meridee said, hoping she could get her sister out of the way long enough for Zeb to leave.

"Are you kidding? I can't go outside looking like this." She made a face as she glanced down at her wrinkled jeans and T-shirt. "I slept in this outfit, and I haven't put on makeup or washed my hair since I left."

"You're not supposed to when you go camping. That's why it's called roughing it."

"It's disgusting is what it is," Brenda said with a snarl. "I'm not going to do that again." She took another sip of the chocolate, then added, "At least not with any guys. It's too primitive."

"If your sleeping bag's damp, you should probably hang it outside on the clothesline," Meridee told her, wondering how much longer she could keep Zeb's presence a secret. "And I still think you should go sit on a lawn chair and soak up a few rays. It'll chase the chill away."

"I will in a little bit." She drained the remains of her hot chocolate, then rinsed out the cup in the sink. "Before I do anything, I want to go upstairs and soak in a nice hot bath."

Meridee nearly sputtered, "You can't."

"I can't take a bath?" Brenda shot her a puzzled look.

"Not right now. I'm using the bathroom upstairs. Why don't you take a shower in the bathroom down here?"

Brenda eyed her suspiciously. "I don't want to take a shower, Meridee. I want a nice long soak in the tub."

Suddenly Vanna, who was confined to the laundry room, began whining, and Brenda looked around inquisitively. "Where's Vanna?"

"She's in the laundry room. I put her in there because I have a guest and she was being difficult."

"You have a guest?" Brenda walked over to the staircase and gazed upward. "Meridee, do you have a man upstairs?" she asked incredulously.

"Yes, and it would be less awkward for me if you would make yourself scarce until he's gone," Meridee said quietly, an appeal in her eyes.

Unfortunately Zeb chose that moment to make his appearance, coming down the stairs in the clothes he had worn yesterday. Clothes that had at one time looked laundry-fresh now looked as though they had spent the night in a crumpled heap on the floor—which is exactly what had happened. The stubble of a beard darkened his chin, and there was no way to disguise the fact that he had spent the night with Meridee.

Brenda's eyes raked over Zeb's disheveled appearance, and then she turned to Meridee, accusation written all over her face. "So much for house rules," she mumbled under her breath.

Meridee couldn't prevent the color that darkened her cheeks, but she was determined not to be intimidated by her sister.

"Good morning," Zeb said as he stepped off the bottom riser.

"Good morning, Mr. Farrell," Brenda recited in a proper office manner.

"Brenda came home early from her camping trip because it was raining," Meridee explained, trying not to act as uneasy as she was feeling.

"Got washed out, did you?" Zeb didn't seem to be the least bit discomfited by the situation.

Brenda, on the other hand, was obviously disconcerted. "Yeah...ah...look, maybe I ought to return the sleeping bag I borrowed from Mom." She walked over to the front door and was about to pick up her camping gear when Meridee's voice stopped her.

"Mom's probably at church. Why don't you set the wet things outside in the sun and leave the rest of the stuff for now?"

Brenda looked apprehensively from her sister to Zeb. "I suppose I could," she said with a shrug.

"While you do that, I'm going to take Mr. Farrell back to his hotel," Meridee said in her no-nonsense tone of voice. She turned to Zeb and said, "I'll get my keys and be with you in a minute."

Seeing him nod, she hurried up the stairs to her room where she slipped on a pair of canvas shoes, then pulled the door shut as she left, not wanting anyone else to see the disarray after her night with Zeb.

Before she went downstairs, she stopped in the bathroom to make sure there was nothing that would indicate she and Zeb had shared a bath. By the time she got downstairs, Zeb was sitting outside on the wooden glider in the sunshine, gently rocking to and fro.

"All set?" he asked when he saw her.

She simply nodded, and he followed her to her car. After driving several miles in silence, she finally spoke.

"I'm sorry about Brenda showing up like that," she apologized.

"So am I," he agreed. "But probably not for the same reasons."

"Why do you say that?"

"Because I think you're more upset that your sister knows I spent the night than you are about being interrupted in the middle of what was turning out to be a very romantic morning," he answered, eyeing her carefully. "Am I right?"

"I admit I was a little embarrassed, but that doesn't mean I wasn't disappointed that we didn't get to finish our bath." She shot him a look that told him she, too, was frustrated with the outcome of their morning.

He sighed. "I'd much rather have those hands of yours on my body than clasped around that steering wheel." He reached over and stroked her shoulder. "We still can spend the day together."

"You want to work today?" she asked, deliberately misunderstanding him.

He chuckled. "Work is the last thing on my mind, and you know it."

His words sent a shiver of excitement through her, but she forced herself to remain levelheaded. "Unfortunately, that's the problem."

"Why is it a problem?"

"Because we're supposed to be working. That's the reason we're together."

"Wrong. Want me to prove how wrong you are?" he asked seductively, his fingers teasing the flesh of her neck.

She playfully pulled away from him. "That's exactly what I'm talking about. Now that sex has entered our relationship, it's going to complicate things."

"Not necessarily."

"You just said you wanted to spend the day together and it had nothing to do with going over financial statements," she reminded him.

"It's Sunday. We shouldn't be working."

"And what happens tomorrow when it's Monday and we don't want to be working?" she asked.

"We're two professionals, Meridee. We'll work when we're supposed to work," he assured her, leaning closer to her as he talked. "You and I are so much alike. One of the things we have in common is that we keep our emotions tightly reined. We use our heads when it comes to professional decisions, not our hearts. It's one of the reasons why we're so attracted to each other."

Meridee wanted to believe him, but right now she was dangerously close to letting her heart rule her head. The line between emotion and logic had never seemed so fuzzy as it did this morning.

She searched for the right words to explain how she felt about what had happened between the two of them, but she honestly didn't know what to say. For the first time in her life she felt as though she might not be in complete control of her emotions, and it was a frightening experience.

When she didn't respond right away, he added, "You're not sorry about last night, are you?"

She looked at him then, her face as honest as the daylight. "No, I'm just not sure where we go from here."

"Why don't we take it one day at a time?" he suggested.

It sounded reasonable, but then she remembered that his days in St. Paul were numbered. A slight frown creased her brows as she said, "I'm afraid there'll be gossip around the office."

"Because of Brenda?"

She shook her head. "She won't say anything if I ask her not to. But someone's bound to find out or guess that we're seeing each other. I've worked in an office too long to know you can't keep some things quiet."

"Do you want to keep it quiet?"

From the tone of his voice, he sounded as though he didn't care whether anyone knew about them or not. "I'm not worried about what other people say as long as it's true," she said a bit defensively. "The problem is that gossip often is the product of someone's imagination."

"And you'd rather not be the subject of that gossip. I understand that," he told her, his fingers caressing her earlobe. "We'll be discreet. I promise you, these hands won't even come close to your body while we're in the office. I'll sit three feet away from you if you want me to."

She wished that she could tell him that their professional relationship was the only one they should have. But the truth was, she wanted to be with him, and she was too honest to pretend she didn't.

"You're right. We'll just have to be careful around the office. Our private lives are our own," she stated unequivocally.

"Good attitude," he said.

She flashed him a smile. "Why is it that we always seem to think alike?" She didn't wait for an answer, but went on to say, "You know, I'm going to miss you when you're gone."

When I'm gone? Suddenly Zeb was reminded that his work with Krystalene was nearly finished. Soon he would be moving on to another project in another city. The smile faded from his face. After what had happened last night, he didn't want to think about moving anywhere, not even back to New York.

He rubbed his chin thoughtfully. Maybe he could stay and oversee operations until everything was running smoothly. He was sure he could convince New York to let him do that. Only one thing worried him. What if, when things were running smoothly, he still didn't want to leave?

"YOU MUST HAVE HAD a good weekend," Ingrid remarked as she carried two mugs of coffee into Meridee's office on Monday morning.

"What makes you say that?"

"You were humming when you stepped off the elevator." She set one of the mugs on Meridee's desk, then sat down in the leather chair across from her.

"I was not," Meridee denied with a chuckle. "I never hum."

"That's what has me worried," Ingrid said warily. "That and the fact that you're wearing makeup."

"That's because my face is sunburned. I'm trying to cover it up," she said, reaching into a drawer for a mirror.

"Sunburn? You who have sworn off rays?"

Meridee glanced at her reflection in the mirror and grimaced. "Good grief. I look like Rudolph."

"I don't know. I think you look healthy. You have the kind of skin that would tan beautifully," Ingrid commented, a hint of envy in her tone.

"Well, I prefer healthy, untanned skin," she said, shoving the mirror back into her drawer.

"So where did you go to get that sunburn?"

Meridee avoided eye contact with her, concentrating on the papers that were on her desk. "The same place as you. The picnic. I think it turned out well, don't you?"

"It was nice," Ingrid agreed. "I didn't get to see much of you, though. Must have been because we spent most of our time at the children's games."

"Then it worked out all right with Ed?" Meridee asked cautiously.

"He was real good with the boys," Ingrid answered evasively. "It's been a long time since the five of us felt like a family." There was a wistful expression on her face.

"Is he living close by?" Meridee asked.

"He's been staying with his sister over near Maplewood. He's trying to get his debts paid off and his life put back together, but it isn't easy for anyone in his situation."

Meridee thought she detected a hint of sympathy in Ingrid's voice, and she wondered if Ed had come back because he was hoping to get money from his ex-wife. The thought was disturbing, and she felt compelled to speak candidly to her friend.

"No, and it wasn't easy for you, either. Ingrid, you don't need to feel responsible for Ed's troubles. Look what you had to go through to get your own life back together. You're not thinking about trying to help him out financially, are you?"

Ingrid blushed and Meridee knew she had already given him money.

"Look, I know it's none of my business, but don't let him persuade you to do things you don't want to do out of guilt," Meridee warned her.

"It's not the way you think," Ingrid said uneasily. "Maybe we should change the subject."

There was a brief pause before Meridee asked, "Did the boys win any prizes at the picnic?"

Ingrid nodded. "Tommy won a baseball glove, and Matt got two tickets to a Twins game. I told him he had to take Jeff since he didn't win anything."

"That sounds like a reasonable request," Meridee said.

"I heard you won a few prizes yourself. Is it true that you and Zeb Farrell were a couple?"

Meridee almost choked on her coffee. "A couple? Ingrid, you sound like my mother. Just because Zeb and I teamed up for a few of the games hardly makes us a couple."

"You know how the rumor mill works around this place. Put two single people in the same room and everyone will swear they only have eyes for each other."

Meridee looked her directly in the eye. "It's not like you to beat around the bush about things."

Ingrid looked at her over the rim of her mug, slowly sipping her coffee. After a couple of seconds she said, "I called your house yesterday, and Brenda told me you were with Zeb. When I called here, there was no answer."

"That's because we weren't here," Meridee answered matter-of-factly. "I decided to show him around St. Paul. You know the hours we've been putting in these past few weeks. Well, I thought that for one weekend it would be nice to relax instead of work."

"Humming on the elevator, relaxing instead of working..." Ingrid eyed her curiously.

"I'm only human," Meridee retorted dryly. "And when it's as beautiful a summer day as it was yesterday, I do human things." When Ingrid didn't comment, she felt compelled to say, "It was simply too nice a day to spend indoors."

Ingrid shrugged. "You won't get an argument from me." She took another sip of her coffee. "So where did you go?"

"Zeb wanted to see some of the landmarks in this area, so I took him on a minitour of the city, including a couple of the lakes." She didn't mention that they had walked hand in hand through the Como Park Conservatory or that they had picnicked in the park and watched the sun set over the water of Lake Phalen, cuddled on a blanket in a private corner of the beach.

"He's already been looking for you this morning," Ingrid told her.

As hard as she tried, Meridee couldn't prevent another blush. She turned around to open a file cabinet. "That's typical, isn't it? Today it's all business again."

"Were you expecting it to be any different?"

"Of course not."

Meridee was relieved when the phone rang. It was someone from marketing. She smoothly answered her questions, giving Ingrid a brief explanation when she was through. From that point on, their talk centered on business, and as soon as they had gone over the schedule for the day, Ingrid rose to her feet.

"Don't forget we're meeting with Lowell Perkins and Evelyn Young at nine-thirty," she reminded Meridee as she walked toward the door. "What about lunch? You want to try that new deli over on Sixth Street?"

"I can't today." Meridee was reluctant to tell her that she had already ordered lunch from the deli—an alfresco lunch for two, with paté, cheese, fruit, French bread and sparkling water. She and Zeb had decided to spend their lunch hour at one of the parks they had visited yesterday.

However, Ingrid seemed to expect an explanation, and finally Meridee said, "I'm having lunch with Zeb."

"Look, it may be none of my business, but you're not thinking about getting involved with this guy, are you?" Ingrid asked, concern in her voice.

"I like being with Zeb. He's fun," Meridee said defensively.

"Fun? Are we talking about the same man?" Ingrid wrinkled her face in disbelief.

"What is it about him you object to?" Meridee asked. "Ever since he came here you've been wary of him."

"You want an honest answer?"

Meridee hesitated, not sure she wanted to hear any criticism of him, but because of her friendship with Ingrid she felt compelled to say yes.

"He's been dangling a pink slip over my head since the day he arrived. I'm afraid the only reason he hasn't let me go is because he has feelings for you, and I can't help but wonder what's going to happen when his work is finished here and he returns to New York. When he's no longer worried about impressing you, will I be out the door?''

"Zeb wouldn't do that!" Meridee said vehemently, not wanting to think that their relationship could mean anything to anyone but the two of them.

"I hope you're right. I need a job, and I'd hate to think of him using you."

"What makes you think I'm not using him?"

"Because you never hum on Monday morning and this is the first time I've ever seen you sunburned," Ingrid said on her way out.

CHAPTER NINE

THE FOLLOWING WEEKEND Meridee brought Zeb to Sunday dinner at her mother's. She knew it was a risky undertaking, especially since her grandmother would be at the backyard barbecue and would undoubtedly interpret Zeb's presence as a sign that her granddaughter was finally getting somewhere in the game of finding a husband.

It was something Meridee and her sisters had come to expect. Whenever any of them had brought a date to a family gathering, Gran began hearing wedding bells and did everything in her power to make sure that the unsuspecting man heard them, too.

Since Zeb had already met her grandmother and been subjected to one interrogation, Meridee hoped his appearance wouldn't create quite the sensation it otherwise might have. Unfortunately it did.

Not only did Gran ask him embarrassing questions regarding his background, she took it upon herself to tell Zeb that he had reached an age where he should be looking for a nice girl to settle down with. All Meridee could do was smile weakly and retreat to the kitchen, where her mother was putting the finishing touches on their food.

"Need any help?" Meridee asked as she stepped inside the air-conditioned kitchen and saw Kate stirring a pitcher of lemonade.

"Oh-oh. Gran must be giving your Zeb the treatment if you're offering to help in the kitchen," Kate said with a smile, stepping over to the refrigerator for some ice.

"He's not exactly *my* Zeb, Mother, and I wouldn't have brought him over today if I'd thought Gran was going to ask him how much life insurance he carries and whether or not his medical coverage can be converted to a family plan."

"Oh, it's not that bad," Kate chided gently, setting the crystal pitcher and six tall glasses on a serving tray.

"No, it's worse," Meridee said with a moan, dropping onto one of the padded stools at the eating counter.

"Tell me, dear, why did you bring him?" Kate asked, setting a stack of plastic picnic plates in front of her.

"Because I thought it would be nice for him to experience a little of our Minnesota hospitality. I'm sure by now he's probably tired of hotel food."

"And that's the only reason?"

"That and the fact that he loves barbecued ribs, and you, mother dear, make fantastic ribs," she said, giving Kate an affectionate grin. She knew her mother was fishing for information regarding her personal relationship with Zeb, but she didn't offer any.

"Well, whatever your reasons are, I'm glad he's here, because it means I get to see you. It's nice to know that for once you're not spending your Sunday

SWINGING ON A STAR   173

working," Kate told her as she opened the refrigerator and pulled out a bowl of freshly cut fruit. "Brenda says you've been putting in some long hours because of the merger. I hope you're not overdoing it."

Meridee shrugged. "It hasn't been that bad."

"Can I assume that if Zeb is here, you're no longer concerned about losing your job?"

"Actually, my position in the company is rather secure, and I have Zeb to thank for that," Meridee told her, reaching into the bowl of fruit to snatch a cherry.

Kate looked at her in surprise. "That's quite a turnaround from what you were saying when he first arrived."

"I know. It's hard to believe I thought of him as my enemy," she reflected wistfully. "He's actually strengthened my position in the company."

"In what way?"

"Well, for months now I've been trying to get upper management to implement some critical changes in accounting procedures, but they wouldn't even listen to my suggestions," she explained while she wrapped place settings of silverware inside cloth napkins. "I don't know if it was because of my age or because I'm female, but they just didn't want to hear what I was saying."

"Maybe it was simply a case of fighting the good-old-boy network," Kate suggested.

Meridee shrugged. "Whatever their reasons, everything changed when Zeb arrived. Some of the very first recommendations he made were changes I had already proposed."

"So he made you look good?"

"He made me look very good," she said with a satisfied grin. "I never thought I'd say this, Mom, but this merger is a positive step forward for Krystalene."

Kate's face was pensive. "Have you told that to your little sister? She seems to think she has a reason to be concerned about layoffs."

"Brenda doesn't need to worry about her job, Mom," Meridee told her, sneaking another piece of fruit.

"Are you sure?"

"Yes. Some positions will probably be eliminated, but not hers. Look, if you want me to talk to Zeb about it, I will."

Kate shook her head. "No, I'm sure you're right." She smiled in relief. "The only reason I'm concerned is that Brenda's had so many ups and downs lately, I think it's important that she has some stability in her life. At first I was opposed to her taking the job, but she seems to be much happier working than she was going to school."

"She's fit in remarkably well, considering she hasn't had any training or experience," Meridee agreed.

"Then it works out—the two of you working together?"

"Work's not a problem. It's living together that seems to present the problems."

"It's not going well?"

Meridee held up her hand and wiggled it in a gesture of mediocrity. "So-so. It's been a bigger adjustment for me than it has been for her. I'm not very good at having to share my space."

"And we both know Brenda has a way of invading other people's space," Kate commented with a chuckle.

"No kidding. Mom, there are two bathrooms in that house and she has her stuff in both of them. I've told her she can take the bigger one upstairs because she has so many cosmetics, but no. She insists on behaving like a gypsy—moving her stuff from room to room. One morning I nearly put deep heating rub on my tooth-brush instead of toothpaste."

"She's a little disorganized," Kate said fondly.

"She's a lot disorganized," Meridee corrected her. "Now I know why she and Juliet were at odds so much of the time. You know the kind of housekeeper Juliet is. At least I'm gone most of the time, so there's less of a chance for us to get in each other's way."

"I wish you were home more often. I hate to think of her being on her own so much of the time," Kate said with a slight frown.

"I don't think she's exactly alone, Mom. She's been seeing an awful lot of Steven."

"He seems nice enough. I keep hoping that he'll be able to persuade her to go back to school someday. She might settle in better once she's had a chance to decide what she really wants to do with her life," Kate com-mented thoughtfully.

Meridee had a feeling her mother was about to launch into her crusade to get Brenda back to college and was grateful when Donovan stuck his head inside the back door to announce that the ribs were done.

"Come on. I'll help you carry all of this stuff out-side," Meridee told her mother, sliding off the bar stool and reaching for the tray with the lemonade.

As she stepped out into the bright sunshine, she was greeted by the aroma of barbecued ribs and the sight of her grandmother sitting beside Zeb, her hands moving animatedly as she talked. Seeing Zeb looking so at ease with her grandmother brought a smile to Meridee's face. As she crossed the patio, parts of their conversation gradually became audible, and she heard her grandmother say something about returning to New York.

Meridee deposited the lemonade on the picnic table and was about to return to the kitchen when she saw her grandmother pat Zeb's hand affectionately and say, "If you get a chance to come back to Minnesota, I want you to promise me you'll come see me."

If you get a chance to come back. For days Meridee had been avoiding thinking about what was going to happen when Zeb's work was finished in Minnesota. He had said they would take things one day at a time, and that had worked until now. Suddenly she realized that the end of his visit was near, and he hadn't told her if he would ever be back.

When she took her place beside Zeb at the picnic table, she did so with the realization that this would probably be the one and only time he would sit beside her for Sunday dinner with her family. It was a thought she didn't want to dwell on, yet she couldn't quite put it out of her mind as she noticed how well he got along with her family.

When dinner was over, Donovan showed Zeb his orchid collection while Meridee and her mother cleared away the dishes. A short while later, the barbecue became a pool party as Juliet and Ross stopped over with

Annie and Sara, and everyone decided it was time for a swim. Once again, Meridee was surprised by how easily Zeb fit in. Seeing him give Sara and Annie piggyback rides into the deep end of the pool, she couldn't help but wonder what kind of a father he would be.

That thought, like so many others that day, was extremely disturbing, and Meridee was unusually pensive as they took the long way home from her mother's later that evening.

"You're awfully quiet tonight," Zeb remarked as they walked hand in hand down the street.

"I'm sorry. I guess I'm tired," she said.

"There's no need to apologize," he said tenderly, making Meridee wish she hadn't used fatigue as an excuse. She had always spoken her mind instead of hiding behind polite responses, yet for the first time she found it difficult to tell Zeb what she was feeling.

Maybe because she didn't understand what was going on inside her. Ever since she had heard him say he was going back to New York, she had wanted to confront him and ask him what would happen to their relationship once he left. Instead, she had pretended nothing was wrong, smiling and laughing with the rest of her family as they frolicked in the pool. Even now, she didn't know how to bring up the subject.

"I like your family," he said, his thumb gently massaging the back of her hand.

"I'm sorry about my grandmother asking all those embarrassing questions," she said.

He gave her hand a gentle squeeze. "I didn't mind. Actually, she reminded me of *my* grandmother. She does the same thing to me. I've quit bringing female guests to any parties I know she's planning to attend," he confessed.

"I guess grandmothers don't understand that not everyone wants to get married," she said softly.

"I guess they don't."

There was a small silence, then he said, "You were right. Your mother does make the best barbecued ribs in town."

"What were the two of you talking about when she dragged you inside to show you the house?"

His mouth twisted into a grin. "You think she had ulterior motives?"

"Did she?"

He turned to face her. "No. I think she just wanted to reassure herself that you weren't going to lose your job."

"She talked about my work?"

"Only briefly. Actually, the conversation was more about your sisters. She told me how happy she is that Juliet's studying to be a dietitian and how she wishes Brenda would go back to the university. She's a nice lady, Meridee."

"I'm glad you like her, and I'm also glad that the weather cooperated for our family gathering. Now you'll be able to take some Minnesota memories back to New York."

"I'd rather take you." He brought her hand to his lips and pressed a kiss on her palm. "I'm going to miss you."

They had reached her driveway, where his rented Lincoln loomed in the darkness. Meridee's heart started to pound. "When are you leaving?"

"Next Sunday."

A hollow feeling started in her toes and quickly escalated to her heart. "Then you're finished here?"

"Unfortunately." He sighed. "They've already assigned me to another project in Cincinnati."

Meridee felt suddenly bereft. "I see," she managed to murmur. "Well, it's not as if we didn't expect it, is it."

He slipped his arm around her and pulled her close, lifting her chin with his finger. "I don't want this to be the end of us, Meridee. I want there to be more picnics in the park, more carbonated baths for two." He kissed her then, a long, slow kiss that made Meridee's insides tremble.

"I don't want to say goodbye, either, Zeb, but long-distance relationships can be tricky, not to mention expensive," she told him, finally finding the courage to speak.

"Are you saying you want to end it now?" His steady gaze held hers.

She reached up to run a finger along his jaw. "You know I don't, but . . ."

She didn't get to finish, for once more his lips were on hers. When the kiss finally ended, he said, "It doesn't have to be expensive. I'm the one with the abundance of frequent-flyer tickets."

"What about the tricky part? Traveling gets old fast—and exhausting."

"Then we'll spend lots of time in bed . . . resting," he said with a wicked grin. "Isn't it worth a try?"

He was so close that even in the moonlight she could see every wonderful detail of his face. She wondered if maybe it wouldn't be foolish to end something that felt so right. "All right. We'll try it."

He kissed her again. "Great. Now how about coming back to the hotel with me for a nightcap?"

"It's getting late..." she began, but Zeb started to trail burning kisses across her neck. "Let me just go inside and leave a note for Brenda," she said.

She turned to climb the steps to the back door, but before she could insert the key in the lock, a car pulled into the driveway. Brenda jumped out, slamming the door without so much as a glance at the driver.

The car reversed out of the drive with a squeal of rubber and was gone before Brenda had even climbed the back steps. As soon as Meridee saw her sister's face, she knew she had been crying.

"Are you all right?" she asked, as Brenda's slumped figure drew near.

"I'm f-fine," she stuttered, her voice laced with unshed tears.

"What happened?" Meridee demanded, taking a hold of her sister's arms. "You're trembling."

"I... I broke up with Steven," she said disconsolately, bursting into tears. "Oh, Meridee, it was so aw-awful."

"Come on. Let's go inside," Meridee said soothingly, handing Zeb the key so that he could unlock the door for them.

"I can't believe it's over. Everything seemed so right for us," Brenda said, sobbing.

Meridee led her over to the kitchen table and sat down beside her. "Tell me what happened."

"He told me . . ." Brenda stopped when she realized that Zeb was in the room with them.

"Look, I'd better get going," he said, clearing his throat. "I still have some calls to make this evening."

Meridee shot him a look of sympathy, her eyes expressing her gratitude for his sensitivity to Brenda's feelings. "I'll see you in the morning," she told him as she walked him to the door, not caring if Brenda saw her kissing him goodbye.

As she walked back toward the table, Brenda said, "I'm sorry about interrupting things between you and Zeb."

"You didn't interrupt anything," Meridee lied, trying not to think about what could have been. "He was getting ready to go back to his hotel, anyway. Now tell me why you broke up with Steven," she said, setting a box of tissues on the table as she sat down.

"I didn't break up with him. He broke up with me." She paused to blow her nose. "I was such a fool, Meridee. I believed everything he said. I really thought that he was the right one for me." She bit down on her lip, but she couldn't stop the steady stream of tears. "And now he's g-gone."

"Are you sure? Lots of couples have disagreements. It's part of any relationship. Maybe you can work it out," Meridee suggested optimistically.

"Uh-uh. It's over. He hates me," Brenda cried.

"I'm sure he doesn't hate you. You've disagreed, that's all."

Brenda shook her head vigorously. "He's going back to his old girlfriend . . . the one he went steady with during high school."

"Are you sure?"

She nodded. "All the time he's been seeing me he's been writing to her. It seems she's transferring from the community college up in Brainerd to the university down here, and guess who's going to be her roommate."

"Steven. Oh, Brenda, I'm sorry." Meridee got up and put an arm around her shoulders.

"I really thought this was it, Meridee," Brenda said, her voice cracking as she tried not to cry.

"You haven't known him all that long, have you?" she asked, remembering how her sister had insisted on more than one occasion that Steven was only a friend.

"Maybe not in actual weeks and months, but, Meridee, there was something special there. It was as though we clicked. You know what I mean?"

Meridee nodded in sympathy. She understood only too well, for it was exactly how she felt about Zeb after only knowing him a number of weeks.

"Oh, Meridee. I wish I were more like you," Brenda said, sniffling.

"Like me? Why?"

"You're so strong emotionally. You're always in control. When you and Richard broke up, you didn't fall apart."

"And you won't fall apart, either," Meridee said firmly. "You're hurting right now, but tomorrow you'll feel better, and each day it will get a little easier."

Brenda gave her a dubious look.

"It's true. I didn't fall apart over Richard, but believe it or not, I did cry, Brenda," Meridee told her, remembering how humiliated she had felt when she had discovered Richard's betrayal.

"You did?"

"Just because I don't always show my emotions doesn't mean I don't hurt like everyone else," she said quietly.

Brenda gave her a weak smile. "But you're always so together."

"I just try to stay focused on my goals. One of those goals is to be successful at my job. Another is not to assume responsibility for other people's feelings. We can't control how other people feel, Brenda. You make yourself vulnerable if you try. When a relationship's over, it's over."

Brenda closed her eyes and grimaced. "I just wish it didn't hurt so bad."

"I'm sorry, Bren. I wish there were something I could do."

Brenda blew her nose again, then heaved a long sigh. "I have to get to bed or else I'm going to look like a mess tomorrow."

"See? The healing process has already started. You're thinking about tomorrow," Meridee said, getting to her feet.

"Thank goodness I have my job." Brenda sniffled as she got up from her chair. "Do you know how awful it would be if I had to go to school and see Steven walking around campus with his arms wrapped around his old girlfriend?" She shuddered at the thought.

Meridee gave her a gentle hug. "Forget about Steven and concentrate on Brenda," she advised her. "Set some professional goals for yourself. You're bright and you have a good future at Krystalene."

"You really think so?"

"Yes, I do." Meridee walked over to the sink and filled the glass carafe for the coffee maker. "You're in an entry-level position now, but there's lots of opportunity for advancement," she said.

"That's what Judy in personnel said. She told me that once I pass my six-month probationary period, I'll be eligible to apply for other job openings that are posted . . . as long as I meet the qualifications."

"That's what's nice about Krystalene," Meridee said, setting the coffee maker's automatic timer. "They try to promote from within, which means there's room to grow."

"You don't think that's going to change with the merger?"

"Not a chance. It's a people-oriented company. That's one of the positives Zeb commented on when he first arrived."

"Is it true he's leaving at the end of the week?"

"Yes. He's done what he was sent to do. Now it's up to management to take his recommendations and keep things running smoothly."

"And what happens to you?"

Meridee shrugged. "My job won't change much."

"I wasn't talking about your job. I was talking about you and Zeb. I'd have to be blind not to notice what's going on."

This time Meridee denied nothing. "I like Zeb. It's nice to meet a guy who isn't intimidated by a successful woman."

"But isn't it going to be hard to say goodbye to him?"

"Zeb's going back to New York. That doesn't necessarily mean we're saying goodbye," Meridee replied with more confidence than she was feeling. She slipped out the kitchen door, calling over her shoulder, "Turn off the lights when you go to bed."

FOR THEIR LAST WEEKEND together, Zeb took Meridee to Stillwater, Minnesota, a picturesque little town situated on the St. Croix River just east of St. Paul. There they boarded the Minnesota Zephyr, an elegant dinner train that took them along the scenic woodland bluffs of the valley while they dined in four-course, white-linen style.

After the three-hour journey, they spent Saturday night in a stately three-story mansion that had once belonged to a lumber baron and his family but was now a bed-and-breakfast. In a room with a huge oak fireplace, they made love in a high walnut bed after relaxing in a double Jacuzzi.

Because Zeb's plane was scheduled to depart at noon on Sunday, they chose to forgo the inn's gourmet breakfast in favor of spending an extra hour in bed. Later, they ordered coffee and doughnuts from a roadside café and ate them in the car on their way to the airport.

"I guess this is it," Zeb said as they waited for the airline to announce boarding of his plane.

Meridee stared at his now-familiar face, feeling as though she had seen it a thousand times, yet every time she gazed at him, she saw something new. "I can see why they call you an efficiency expert. I never would have expected you to have gotten things straightened out this quickly."

"It normally takes me longer, but I had great help with this one." He reached for her hand and wrapped his around it. "We make a good team."

"Not bad for two not quite workaholics," she said with a grin.

"I think we definitely proved we know how to do other things," he said with a look that made her stomach tingle.

"When will Denton be sending in the new people?" she asked, needing to talk about business or risk becoming emotional over his leaving.

"They probably won't officially transfer here until September, but they should be out next week to meet with management and to look for places to live," Zeb answered.

"Are they male or female?"

"Male, but you're going to like them. Bob Maren's a computer genius, and Ted Lopez is a great people manager."

"We'll see," she said noncommittally. "Tell me something, Zeb, and I want an honest answer. Is Griggs going to be replaced?"

"Denton won't fire him, but my guess is that with all the changes going on, he'll probably be looking elsewhere for a job."

"And me?" she asked.

"No company in its right mind would let an employee like you get away," he said sincerely. "I just hope that as personnel changes occur, you won't get discouraged and want to jump ship, too.''

"Then there are going to be layoffs?'' she asked, a look of alarm on her face.

"We need to streamline if we're going to be competitive. I've already told you you don't need to worry about Ingrid's position. You were right about her. She's earned her position and she's good at what she does.''

Before Meridee could say another word, Zeb's flight was called. "I guess this is goodbye,'' he said, regret on his face.

"I hate goodbyes,'' Meridee confessed, trying not to act like a sentimental fool.

"I never dreamed it would be this difficult to leave St. Paul,'' he told her. He took her in his arms and hugged her tightly. "Do you think you'll be free next weekend?''

She couldn't answer, for tears threatened to break loose. She nodded, averting her head.

"Don't forget about me,'' he said, then put a finger under her chin to make her face him. He kissed her, a long, passionate kiss that Meridee thought could have sealed his memory in her mind forever. Then with a wave and a smile he was gone, and she was left gazing at a steady stream of strangers getting onto the plane.

Instead of leaving right away, she stood by the plate-glass windows, staring at the jumbo jet parked outside. It was only after it had taxied away from the terminal that she numbly started back to the parking lot. As she sat behind the wheel of her Geo, she realized she was lonely. For the first time in her life she truly felt all alone, and it wasn't pleasant.

She wanted someone to drive her back to her house in the city. She wanted someone to accompany her on walks around the lake. She wanted someone to discuss the *Wall Street Journal* with her every morning. She wanted someone to lie beside her at night. She wanted Zeb.

IT WAS BUSINESS AS USUAL on Monday morning, and had it not been for the empty office down the hall, there would have been no indication that Zeb had ever been at Krystalene. Meridee, however, noticed his absence the minute she walked into her office and saw there were no messages from him lying on her desk.

On Wednesday, Ted Lopez and Bob Maren arrived at Krystalene, and as Zeb had predicted, Meridee liked both of them. Acting as Zeb's messenger, Ted handed her a business-size envelope marked Personal, which she covetously clung to until she was back in the privacy of her office. There, she wasted no time in tearing open the flap. Inside was an airline ticket to New York for the following weekend.

> It's only been two days, and I miss you like crazy. Please come to New York this weekend. If the flight times are inconvenient, this can be changed.
>
> Z

New York for the weekend. The thought was a romantic one, and Meridee immediately phoned her mother to let her know that she would be out of town and make sure she could take care of Vanna and her plants.

Not that she didn't trust Brenda to look after the house in her absence. She did, to a degree, but there were some things she didn't take chances with, and Vanna's health was one of them. She also knew that her mother would welcome the excuse to check up on her youngest daughter.

Never had Meridee found it more difficult to concentrate on her work than she did on Friday. Generally not one to daydream, she found herself staring off into space, while her mind conjured up images of Zeb's smiling face.

Shortly after lunch, Brenda burst into her office. From the look on her face, Meridee knew that something was terribly wrong.

"What's up?"

"I thought you might be interested in seeing this," Brenda said angrily, slapping a piece of paper down on her desk.

Meridee carefully picked it up, her stomach tightening as she recognized the separation notice from Personnel. "You're being let go?"

"As if you didn't know," Brenda said accusingly.

"I *didn't* know," Meridee protested. "There must be some mistake."

"It's no mistake. Mr. Griggs told me my position is being eliminated as part of the consolidation efforts. He said it was part of the 'streamlining' process suggested by your precious Zeb."

"That can't be. Zeb would have told me if yours was one of the jobs being eliminated." She picked up the phone and started dialing. "It's Meridee Osborne. Is he in?" she said briskly into the receiver.

"Who are you calling?" Brenda wanted to know.

Meridee held her palm over the mouthpiece and said, "Mr. Griggs."

What followed was a brief but succinct conversation during which Meridee learned that her sister's position in the company was indeed one that had come under Zeb's restructuring plan. Although Mr. Griggs agreed that Brenda was bright and showed lots of promise, the bottom line was she was being released.

"See. I told you," Brenda whined as Meridee grimly set down the phone. "Now what am I going to do? I don't have a job, I don't have a boyfriend...."

Meridee flipped through her card file until she found Zeb's number in New York. Again she punched numbers on the phone. "I'm calling Zeb."

However, Zeb was not in the office, and Meridee had to leave a message for him to call her as soon as possible.

"I don't know what good you think it's going to do to talk to him," Brenda said. "He knew all along that I was your sister, yet that didn't stop him from getting rid of my job."

"Look, I'm going to get this straightened out, all right?" Meridee snapped impatiently. "Why don't you go back downstairs and I'll call you after I've talked to him?"

"I'm not going back downstairs. Everyone knows I've been canned."

"Then wait for me in the lunchroom. I have work to do."

Reluctantly Brenda left, but instead of focusing on the quarterly financial reports on her desk, Meridee kept hearing Zeb's voice telling her they should always be aboveboard with each other.

She had trusted him, thinking she had finally met a man who understood her, a man who would always be honest with her. She squeezed her eyes shut and dropped her head into her hands, muttering, "Why, Zeb, why?"

CHAPTER TEN

"WHEN DID MS. OSBORNE call?" Zeb asked his secretary when he returned from the board meeting that had kept him away from his desk all day.

"A couple of hours ago. Would you like me to get her for you?"

He glanced at his watch and grimaced. "She's probably on her way home by now." He rubbed a hand across the five o'clock shadow that was barely visible along his jaw. "She didn't say what she wanted, did she?"

"No, only that she wanted you to return her call as soon as possible."

Zeb had a strange feeling in the pit of his stomach. It was an uneasy feeling, the kind he always got when something wasn't quite right. "See if you can reach her, will you? I have to collect some things from my office."

He hadn't even opened his briefcase when his secretary appeared in the doorway. "I'm sorry, Zeb. Ms. Osborne has already left for the day. Would you like me to try her at home?"

Zeb couldn't banish the nagging feeling from the pit of his stomach. "Maybe you'd better."

Zeb was somewhat relieved when only a few minutes later his secretary reappeared and reported there was no answer at Meridee's home. He decided that she was probably on her way to the airport and his uneasiness was nothing but anxiety over seeing her again.

He still couldn't believe how she had invaded his life in such a short time. There had been other women who had occupied his thoughts on occasion, but never one who haunted him day and night. Meridee was everywhere... even at work, a place that had always been a refuge no matter what was going on in his personal life.

He quickly gathered the files he needed to look at over the weekend and tossed them into his briefcase, knowing full well that he wasn't even going to glance at them. Images of the luxurious hotel suite he had reserved flashed in his mind. When he said good-night to his secretary, there was such a broad grin on his face, he left her staring after him in bewilderment.

He had planned the perfect weekend. Theater tickets had been bought, dinner reservations had been made and the hotel had promised him a romantic weekend getaway. Now all he needed to do was wait for his perfect woman to arrive.

And wait he did. Several hours later, he stood at the airport gate with flowers in hand, frowning as an airline employee stuck a "delayed" tag beside Meridee's flight number. As he paced in the waiting area, he scolded himself for not bringing his briefcase and for not calling ahead to see if her flight was on time. He'd simply rushed to the airport in his haste to see her again.

So he sat down with the rest of the people waiting for passengers on flight 117 from Minneapolis/St. Paul and stared out at the sky, wondering where Meridee was in that mass of gray.

As it turned out, she wasn't in the skies over New York or any other state. She wasn't even in a plane. She was walking into a Mexican restaurant in downtown St. Paul, and no one was more surprised to see her there than Ginnie and Laurie.

"Meridee! Why aren't you on your way to New York?" Laurie asked.

"I had a change of plans," she answered as she settled onto the bench seat beside Ginnie.

Ginnie and Laurie exchanged inquisitive glances, but before either one could say anything, Meridee added, "I brought Brenda along tonight since Ingrid couldn't make it."

"Hi, guys," Brenda said as she slid in beside Laurie.

"I thought it was time she experienced Chicks' Chow," Meridee explained, giving their waitress a grateful smile as she added two more place settings.

"What she really means is she didn't want me sitting at home moping over losing my job. She's trying to cheer me up," Brenda said.

"You've come to the right place, then. There are times in a woman's life when nothing works but the company of us chicks," Laurie said with a grin, looking over the top of her menu.

As soon as the waitress had taken their orders and left again, Brenda asked, "So what do you guys talk about at these things?"

"Sex."

"Men."

"And more sex."

"And more men."

Ginnie and Laurie alternated their answers, then laughed together. "We're just kidding!"

"No they're not," Meridee said.

"Sometimes we discuss current events," Ginnie said seriously.

"Yeah, like who Kim Basinger's current boyfriend is," Laurie added.

Brenda laughed. "I get it."

"Actually, we talk about everything and anything, but even your sister will agree that at least once during dinner we discuss men," Ginnie told her.

"As far as I'm concerned, that subject can be skipped this evening," Meridee commented, her mouth twisting into a grimace.

"I didn't say we had to talk nicely about them. We can have a session of male-bashing," Ginnie answered.

"I'm up for that," Brenda said, dipping a nacho into the salsa. "My boyfriend just went back to his old girlfriend. I could bash both of them."

"I'd like to know how some women do it," Laurie stated, slowly shaking her head. "None of my ex-boyfriends ever come back."

"I wouldn't want any of mine back," Ginnie muttered. "They're all jerks."

"Speaking of jerks, is it true that Ingrid's seeing her ex again?" Laurie asked Meridee.

"She says she isn't, but I have a hunch that's why she's not here tonight," she answered soberly.

"Someone said they saw her at a restaurant with him," Ginnie remarked.

Meridee frowned. "I know he's been visiting the boys, but every time I've tried to talk to her about him, she clams up."

"I'm sure it can't be easy—especially because the kids want him around," Laurie added. "I sure would hate to see her end up in the kind of situation she was in when she came to work at Krystalene...living in a women's shelter." She shuddered at the thought.

"Ingrid has a good head on her shoulders. I don't think she'd make the same mistake twice," Ginnie said optimistically.

"I guess we can only hope she knows what she's doing," Meridee said.

"Do any of us know what we're doing when it comes to men?" Laurie asked.

"I thought you were the one who had the system figured out. Isn't the love-'em-and-leave-'em approach working?" Ginnie said flippantly as the waitress arrived with their beverages.

Laurie waited until they were alone again before saying, "I try to remain unattached emotionally, but something happens inside me when a guy kisses me. I feel vulnerable and I start having these fantasies of getting closer to him."

"Who was that cute guy you were having lunch with yesterday?" Brenda asked, swirling her straw in her cola.

"That was Derek, the newest employee in our department," Laurie replied, her eyes brightening. "And are you ready for this? He's never been married, he doesn't have a steady girlfriend and he's nice."

"They're all nice when they want to get to know you better," Ginnie remarked cynically. "It's not until after they've sunk their teeth into your neck that you see their true colors."

"Oh, don't be so cynical in front of this young lady here," Laurie scolded gently. "They're not all out for blood."

"It's all right, Ginnie," Brenda said. "I'm in a pretty cynical mood myself."

"And with good reason," Ginnie empathized. "But listen. Do not despair. Although we all do our share of male-bashing, we also know that there are good men out there."

"Sure there are," Laurie agreed cheerfully. "They're just not always easy to spot. If I were you, I'd experience life. Travel. Have some fun."

Although Meridee heard the conversation going on around her, her mind was a thousand miles away. It was not in her nature to leave conflicts unresolved, which is exactly what she had done with Zeb. She experienced a small pang of guilt at the thought that he might be waiting for her at Kennedy Airport. She wished now that she had told his secretary she might not be on the six o'clock flight, instead of sending a wire at the last minute.

Ever since Brenda had burst into her office with the news that she had been laid off, Meridee had been behaving imprudently. Feelings of betrayal and hurt had clouded any sensible decisions she might have made. She had gone to the airport with every intention of getting on the plane bound for New York. However, when the flight had been delayed leaving Minneapolis, her intuition had told her to stay home.

Now, having had some time to analyze the situation, she realized that she hadn't even given Zeb an opportunity to explain his reasons for letting Brenda go. Normally she confronted situations head on, yet instead, she had canceled her trip at the last minute. And all because of feelings she didn't know how to handle.

"Excuse me. I need to make a phone call," she told the others, sliding out of the booth just as the waitress was setting their dinners on the table.

"Meridee, your food's going to get cold!" Brenda protested, but she paid no attention and headed out to the lobby where a pay phone hung on the wall.

As she expected, there was no answer when she dialed Zeb's apartment. Another pang of guilt washed over her, and she quickly called to check that her message had been given to him.

It did little to ease her conscience, however, and she was preoccupied all through dinner.

"Meridee, your body may be with us but your spirit is definitely in another world. This thing with Zeb Farrell must be serious if it can distract you from food," Laurie said finally.

"Who's distracted?" she asked, turning her attention to the plate of chimichanga in front of her.

"That's one thing about Meridee. She always manages to keep her cool when it comes to men," Brenda told the other two women, admiration in her tone.

Meridee played with the food on her plate, a frown creasing her forehead. She had absolutely no appetite and felt like telling the three of them that right now she was anything but cool. However, the look on her sister's face stopped her.

"Well, if you can stay cool over a man like Zeb Farrell, you are one together lady," Laurie said, lifting her glass in a salute.

Meridee continued to push the food around on her plate.

"I second that," Ginnie added, raising her glass as well. "If a man like Zeb Farrell invited me to New York for the weekend, I'd have to be on my deathbed to stay home."

"He's not all that special," Brenda interjected. "Have you guys forgotten that he's responsible for the changes that are happening at Krystalene? Not everyone is happy with what's going on. In some cases, two positions have been made into one."

"And some good employees did lose their jobs," Ginnie added.

"Yeah, like me, and he didn't even care enough about Meridee to tell her he was going to get rid of me."

Brenda's words caused Meridee to cringe, yet she tried to keep her tone light as she said, "Well, he's gone now, and I doubt that he'll be back."

"You don't think Denton will send him out here to check up on things?" Ginnie asked.

"It's not likely. His job was to solve our problems, and I don't think he'd stay on to make sure things run smoothly even if Denton wanted him to," Meridee answered, wishing they would change the subject.

"Does that mean you won't be seeing him again?" Laurie asked.

"I'm not sure," Meridee replied with a weary shrug. "Look, if you don't mind, I'm going to make it an early night. I'm beat."

"You want to leave already?" Brenda protested, wrinkling her nose in disappointment.

"You don't have to go," Ginnie told her. "I can give you a ride home if you want to stick around with us for a bit."

"You don't mind, do you, Meridee?" Brenda asked.

"No, that's fine. I'll see you at home later," she said. She left some money for her share of the meal and headed for the exit.

When she walked into her house, she expected the phone to be ringing. It wasn't. After letting Vanna out and changing into her pajamas, she sat down and stared at the instrument, finally picking it up and dialing New York.

"Zeb, it's Meridee," she said when she heard his voice.

"What happened? Why weren't you on the plane? You're not sick, are you?"

He sounded worried, and her heart felt like a lump of clay. "No, I just didn't think I should come," she managed to say.

"Why not?"

She took a deep, calming breath. "Because of Brenda."

"Brenda? What does she have to do with this?"

"You mean besides the fact that she lost her job, a job that you never once indicated to me was in jeopardy." Anger had crept into her voice.

"Griggs decided to let her go?"

"You sound surprised. Wasn't it your recommendation?" A tiny ray of hope buoyed her spirits, but her optimism was short-lived.

"I didn't think her position would be eliminated at this time."

"Are you saying Griggs wasn't authorized to release her?"

"I made the recommendation, but he altered the time schedule for some reason."

"Then she can have her job back?" she asked eagerly.

Zeb sighed. "Sooner or later Griggs was going to have to let her go. She's in a position that should be consolidated with another one."

"Why didn't you tell me this was going to happen?" she demanded accusingly.

"If I had known you were going to be this upset, I would have." He began to sound defensive. "Your mother told me she wished Brenda would go back to college, anyway. This would be a good time for her to do that."

"Brenda doesn't want to go to college," Meridee snapped angrily. "That job was one of the few things in her life that had any meaning for her, and you just snatched it away from her. Don't you understand that this is my sister we're talking about?''

''I realize that, but don't let emotion cloud the issue,'' he warned her.

''She's not only my sister, Zeb. She's bright, enthusiastic, reliable and an overall asset to the company.''

''She is also underqualified and doing a job that should be consolidated with another position in the company,'' he reasoned.

Normally Meridee would have agreed with his logic, but she wasn't behaving in her usual pragmatic manner. This wasn't business she was discussing with him, but a matter of trust between the two of them.

''I thought union jobs were protected under the terms of the merger agreement?''

''Griggs and the union agreed that a limited number could be cut.''

''And Brenda's was one of them.''

''Yes. In the long run, this is probably going to help Brenda.''

''Help her?'' she repeated in disbelief. ''If that's what you call help, I think my family is better off not being the recipient of your benevolence.''

''Meridee, you're not being fair...'' he began.

''*I'm* not being fair?'' she repeated in disbelief. ''We agreed from the very beginning to be up-front and honest with each other.''

''I have been honest with you!''

''You helped to get Brenda fired!''

''I did my job, Meridee. Why is that so difficult for you to understand?'' Zeb sighed impatiently. ''You pleaded with me to give careful consideration to Ingrid's position, and I did. I considered everything you said and weighed all the alternatives and came to the conclusion that Ingrid is an asset to the company, one we shouldn't lose."

"But Brenda is expendable?"

"Yes, she is. You knew when I came that some jobs were going to be eliminated."

"Just because Brenda doesn't have three kids to raise doesn't mean she doesn't need her job."

"It's not a question of her needing a job, Meridee. What's gotten into you, anyway? Do you know that you are clearheaded and unemotional in everything involving your work except when it comes to your sister and Ingrid? Then you lose your perspective."

"Well, excuse me for caring about people," she drawled sarcastically.

"It's not a matter of caring. I care, too, but this is business, and unfortunately companies are successful because decisions aren't based on the needs of their employees. Don't take this personally. It's strictly business."

"Well, it's a little difficult for me to separate personal feelings from business in this case."

"You're angry with me for doing my job. I think in time you'll see that I had a good reason for doing what I did. You know, this could be exactly what Brenda needs in her life."

"Oh, sure," she said. "Standing in the unemployment-compensation line is just the dose of humility a twenty-year-old needs to make her appreciate the work ethic."

"That's not what I meant. The way I see it, if Brenda were to..."

"I don't think I care to hear what plans you have for my sister's life," she said. "You're right about one thing, though, Zeb. I shouldn't mix personal feelings with business. That's why I didn't come to New York tonight. And that's why it's probably a good thing we're finished working together. Because any way you look at it—personally or professionally—it isn't going to work anymore." And before he could protest, she hung up.

"HAVE YOU SEEN MY PILLS?" Brenda asked the following morning as she padded into the kitchen, where Meridee was reading the morning newspaper. Not waiting for an answer, she added, "Boy, you look awful. Didn't you sleep last night? You've got big dark circles under your eyes."

"Thanks, Brenda. That's just what I need to hear."

"I'm sorry," Brenda said with a contrite smile.

"For your information, I worked late last night," Meridee explained, flipping a page of the newspaper. "And what pills are you talking about?"

"My birth control pills."

"You're taking birth control pills?" Meridee asked, looking at her over the top of her glasses.

"I have to because I have trouble with my periods. I thought you knew that," her sister answered, opening the refrigerator and pulling out a carton of milk.

"No, you never mentioned it."

"You mean Mom doesn't tell you everything?"

"Hardly," Meridee said dryly. "Where did you leave your pills?"

"I put them in the drawer in the bathroom down here." Brenda pulled a glass from the cupboard and filled it with milk.

"What kind are they?" Meridee asked uneasily, fighting off a sinking sensation.

Brenda shrugged. "I don't know. They're birth control pills. My doctor changed my prescription because I was getting nauseated from the other ones. They come in a little round pink case."

"A little round pink case?" Meridee's face turned pale. She tossed the newspaper aside and rushed from the room.

Brenda went after her, following her into the small bathroom on the first floor, where she watched Meridee pull the vanity drawer open. Combs, brushes, makeup and hair clips rattled as she scrounged through the contents. Finally, she held up a round plastic case.

"That's them," Brenda said. She was about to take the case when Meridee snatched it out of her reach.

"Not so fast," Meridee told her, pulling the dispenser from its plastic case. "Meridee Osborne" was typed in bold-face letters along with her gynecologist's name on the prescription label. "Damn! These are mine."

"Yours? But where are mine?"

Meridee charged out of the bathroom and up the stairs to her bedroom with Brenda close on her heels. She opened her overnight case and pulled out an identical plastic case.

"Look familiar?" Meridee asked sharply.

Brenda examined the birth control dispenser, a puzzled look on her face. "What are you doing with my pills?"

"Damn!" Meridee swore again under her breath. "Don't you get it? I've been taking your pills!"

"And I've been taking yours?"

"Or maybe yours and mine. Who knows? What day is it?"

"July nineteenth."

Meridee rubbed her forehead. "I started taking mine right around the end of June. That means I should still have a week to go, yet there's only one left in here." She slipped the blister pack back into the plastic dispenser and gave it to Brenda.

She mentally calculated the difference between the number of pills she should have taken and the number of pills left in the dispenser. "I might have taken seven of yours, but how can we know for sure?"

"I don't see how you ended up with my pills, anyway."

"Because when I went to pack for my trip to New York, I grabbed the pink dispenser from the bathroom—*my bathroom*—downstairs and put them in my overnight case. I didn't realize they were *your* pills—and who knows how long I've been taking them?"

"No wonder I couldn't find them yesterday."

"Brenda, for these pills to be effective, you need to take them regularly," Meridee reminded her.

Brenda shrugged. "So I'll take two today. I've skipped before and nothing's ever happened."

"The problem is, we're off schedule," Meridee told her, her voice rising.

"You don't have to have a cow," Brenda drawled. "It's not like you weren't taking any."

"But I was probably taking the *wrong* ones. Don't you get it? There are twenty-one birth control pills and seven placebos," she said, shaking the dispenser at Brenda. "For at least two days I've been taking placebos instead of the regular pills."

"Oh-oh." A look of dawning understanding spread across Brenda's face. "That means I must have been taking the wrong ones, too," she complained.

"And whose fault is that? I told you to keep all of your stuff in the bathroom up here, but no. You wouldn't listen to me." She threw up her hands in frustration. "Now look what's happened!"

"What do we do?" Brenda wailed.

"How should I know?" Meridee snapped, unable to think of anything except the weekend she had spent in bed with Zeb. What if she'd had the wrong pills then? "Damn! This would never have happened if you had done as I asked you."

"I'm sorry, Meridee. I didn't think something like this would happen." Brenda's expression became thoughtful. "Maybe you can just double up your pills for the next few days. I'll call Mom and ask her to call Dr. Gilbert. She'll be able to tell us what we should do."

"Brenda, this is not a problem Mom needs to be concerned with," Meridee stated firmly. "I'll call the clinic myself."

Meridee walked over to the phone beside her bed and quickly punched in seven digits. "The nurse practitioner's probably not there because it's Saturday, but

I should be able to leave a message for a doctor to call me."

As it turned out, one of the clinic physicians returned Meridee's phone call within a few minutes and answered all of her questions regarding the mix-up.

As soon as Meridee had hung up the phone, she turned to Brenda and said, "Since neither of us knows for sure how long we've been taking the wrong pills, the doctor said to get our prescriptions refilled and start them up again on the fifth day of our periods—whenever that might be. We've probably got our cycles off track, so we'll just have to wait and see."

"I'm really sorry about the mix-up," Brenda said sincerely.

"I'd like you to be more than sorry, Brenda. I'd like you to get your stuff—all of it—out of the bathroom downstairs and put it in the bathroom up here. Understand?"

"All right, all right. You don't have to be so grumpy about it," she mumbled as she left the room.

Meridee looked again at the pills in her hand. It had been such a simple mistake, yet had she gone to New York this weekend, it could have had serious consequences. She would have made love with Zeb and possibly conceived a child. Maybe there was a silver lining in the cloud left from her argument with Zeb.

During the next two weeks, she not only worked long hours at the office, but took work home as well. She knew that everyone suspected she was trying to ease the pain of her breakup with Zeb by working harder than usual, but the truth was, not even work could take her mind off him for long.

When Mr. Griggs told her she was to fly to New York for a conference at Denton headquarters, Meridee's first thought was that she'd get to see Zeb. However, when she arrived at corporate headquarters, she discovered that he was not even in New York but assigned to another of Denton's subsidiaries that was in a financial crisis.

She wondered if he was getting involved with some female executive on the job there. Was he taking her miniature golfing and riding on go-carts? Were they spending weekends in some romantic bed-and-breakfast?

With difficulty, she concentrated on the information being presented at the conference, but she found it uninspiring. Normally she loved business conferences and welcomed the opportunity to meet with other professionals, but this time she only wanted to go home.

On the third and final day of her visit, she was considering skipping the afternoon session of the seminar and catching an early flight home when she saw Zeb. He was in the main lobby of the corporate headquarters when she and her breakfast companions entered the building. There was no way she could avoid talking with him, for several members of her group knew him and greeted him enthusiastically.

When it was her turn to say hello, she found her mouth had suddenly gone dry. "Zeb...hi," she said, offering him her hand. "I wasn't expecting to see you here. Your secretary said you were out of town." She cringed inwardly after the last statement. She didn't want Zeb to think she had been looking for him.

"I just got back," he said, holding her hand longer than necessary. "It's good to see you, Meridee." He had said the same thing to the others, but he was looking at her as a lover, not as a business acquaintance, and it caused her to fidget nervously. "I didn't know you were going to be here."

"I'm here for the management seminar," she said as evenly as possible, wishing the sight of him didn't stir so many pleasant memories.

Zeb glanced at his watch, then placed a hand on her elbow. "Then you'd better get upstairs. I'll ride up with you," he said, gently urging her toward the elevator.

Meridee would have liked to have said no, but the others had already started to drift toward the row of elevators, and she had little choice but to allow him to escort her.

"How are things at Krystalene?" he asked as they waited for a car.

"Fine. Bob Maren and Ted Lopez have been a big help."

"Good. I'm glad to hear that."

An elevator car arrived, but because of the number of people waiting to get on, Zeb steered her toward another car that had arrived at the end of the row. As they stepped inside, the doors quietly slid shut behind them and Meridee found herself alone with him. She reached out to punch the number twenty-seven, but Zeb was reaching for it, too, and their hands collided.

"Sorry," she said, snatching her hand back, a weak smile on her face.

"How have you been, Meri?" he asked. No one but him had ever called her that, and the name rolled off his tongue with a seductive charm.

She could feel his gaze on her, but she deliberately fumbled with her purse, pretending to be looking for a tissue. "Busy, as usual," she answered, trying to resist the pull of his eyes. She couldn't, and when she finally looked up, her heart skipped several beats.

In all of her dreams and fantasies, she had never imagined that he could be so attractive to her. Unconsciously, she licked her lips, and Zeb moved closer.

"I miss working with you, Meri. And I miss being with you."

He leaned so close Meridee thought he was going to try to kiss her, but the elevator doors whisked open and she quickly stepped out into the small crowd scattered outside the conference room. Zeb followed her.

"Looks like I'm just in time," she told him as the seminar attendees slowly began filing into the meeting room. She headed for the open double doors, but Zeb placed a hand on her arm.

"Will you have lunch with me?" he asked, when she looked up at him inquisitively.

"I'm sorry, but I'm not feeling very well," she told him, looking at a spot over his shoulder.

He laughed. "Is that the most original excuse you can come up with? You're not feeling well?"

She turned abruptly and started for the doors again. He followed, saying, "Are you still angry with me over Brenda losing her job?" When she glared at him, he said, "You are, aren't you?"

"Zeb, I'm here in New York on business," she reminded him in a steely tone.

"I have *business* I wish to discuss with you," he told her in an equally hard tone, his eyes darkening. "That's why I invited you to lunch."

"I told you, I don't feel much like eating today, but even if I did, I'm supposed to lunch with the seminar participants."

"Do you always have to do everything you're expected to do?" he asked testily.

"I thought that that was one of the things you admired about me," she said in a falsely sweet voice.

He grinned lopsidedly. "Not if it means sitting through a boring seminar on effective management when you've heard it all before, anyway."

"For your information, I'm skipping the afternoon session."

He lifted an eyebrow. "You are?"

"Yes. I've decided I'd rather catch an earlier flight home."

"You're leaving today?"

"At four-thirty."

"That doesn't give us much time."

"It gives *us* no time," she said and entered the conference room. She walked toward one of the tables at the back, but before she had a chance to sit, Zeb was beside her, pulling out her chair. He promptly sat down in the place beside her.

"What are you doing?" she asked in a low voice, conscious of several speculative glances in their direction.

"I'm going to sit in on the seminar. Maybe I can get a few tips," he answered innocently.

"Suit yourself," she mumbled and opened her briefcase to pull out her leather notebook.

"Are you sure you want to sit through this?" Zeb whispered in her ear as the speakers were being introduced.

"Don't you have someplace you're supposed to be?" she whispered back.

"Yes, I have business to discuss with a certain executive from Krystalene, but she refuses to see me," he replied.

Meridee ignored his remark and tried to concentrate on what the speaker at the podium was saying, but Zeb's knee was touching hers beneath the table. She could smell the scent of his after-shave, and it reminded her of so many things she didn't want to remember. By the mid-morning break, she had taken very few notes, yet she knew exactly how many times Zeb had inadvertently touched her arm.

"Had enough?" Zeb asked in a low voice as the seminar participants began filing out of the room.

Meridee knew he was referring to the lecture, not his presence, but she had indeed had more than enough of both. "It is a little repetitive, isn't it?" she admitted.

"It's good information, but you're beyond this stage of the game."

His compliment warmed her, but she was determined to keep her distance. She gathered together her notebook and handouts and slipped them into her briefcase, saying, "As usual, you're right, Mr. Farrell." She got up from the table and headed for the exit.

"Where are you off to now?" he asked, following her.

"Probably back to my hotel to pack," she told him.

"What about lunch? I know a place that makes great pizza." He looked at her with hope written all over his face.

Meridee truly wasn't feeling well, and the thought of food didn't sound inviting. "Zeb, I don't think it's a good idea for us to start up anything again," she finally said.

"Start up? Meridee, we never finished what we began in St. Paul." They had reached the elevators and were alone in the corridor. "I need to talk to you. I'm sorry about what happened with Brenda, but you never did give me a chance to explain how I felt."

She wanted to say yes, she wanted to be with him, but she was wary of giving in to her feelings.

"All I'm asking is a chance to talk to you. We'll have lunch, then I'll drive you to the airport. Just think of the hassle it'll save you."

There was such an honest appeal in his voice she found it difficult to say no. "All right," she finally conceded.

"Great." He smiled then, and she immediately felt too vulnerable to his charm. But before she could change her mind, an elevator car had arrived and the doors were opening. Zeb ushered her inside and held his finger against the button marked Door Open, saying, "I need to check in with my secretary. How about if I pick you up in say—" he paused to look at his watch "—an hour and a half?"

"That'll be fine," she replied. "I'm staying at the Plaza Hotel."

Zeb released the button and slipped back into the corridor. As the door slid shut, Meridee could see a look of satisfaction on his face, and as much as she hated to admit it, she was pleased.

CHAPTER ELEVEN

MERIDEE WAS WAITING for Zeb in the lobby when he arrived at her hotel, her carry-on garment bag at her feet. He was driving a red sports car, which she eyed suspiciously as she got inside.

Noticing her speculative gaze, he asked, "Don't you like my car?"

"It's nice, but it's not what I expected," she answered.

"You mean I look more like a dark luxury-car type?" he asked as he pulled out in the city traffic.

"Red seems out of character for you," she said.

"You drive a red car," he pointed out.

She shrugged. "Maybe I'm out of character, too. So where's this famous pizza place you're taking me to?" she asked, changing the subject.

"Over in the Bronx. They make it the old-fashioned way, with a thick crust and lots of cheese and sausage. I hope you're hungry."

Actually, Meridee wasn't hungry at all. Ever since she had woken up this morning, she had felt as though she might be coming down with the flu. "I told you I don't have much of an appetite today."

"Your appetite will surface once you step into Joe's Pizzeria, I promise," he told her confidently. "Few people can resist his pizza."

When they arrived at the pizzeria, there was a line of people waiting to be seated, and Meridee wasn't sure if she felt up to waiting for anything—especially food. But a dark-haired, ruddy-complexioned man wearing a white apron stepped out from behind the glass partition where four men were tossing dough into the air and headed toward them.

"Zeb! It's good to see you!" he said, rubbing his hand on his apron before offering it to his friend.

"Joe, I'd like you meet Meridee Osborne."

The owner of the pizzeria smiled and shook her hand before leading them to a booth in the back with a Reserved sign on the table.

"Do you want the usual or are you going to let the lady choose?" Joe asked Zeb when they were seated.

"I'm in luck, Joe. She likes the usual," Zeb answered with a grin, while Meridee tried to ignore the protest her stomach was making at the strongly scented pizzeria.

"And what do you want to drink?"

"A couple of beers?" Zeb looked for confirmation to Meridee, who shook her head.

"Make mine a cola," she requested, hoping the drink would settle her stomach.

"I'll have a cola, too," Zeb told Joe, who repeated their order and retreated behind the partition.

"So tell me, was this a good trip for you?" Zeb asked in a businesslike manner.

Meridee nodded. "It was interesting seeing Denton's operations, and the seminar had its highlights."

"Now that Denton's seen you, I'm sure you'll be getting the call to come out more frequently," he predicted.

"Maybe," she answered cautiously, wishing the aroma of cheese and garlic wasn't quite so strong.

Zeb continued to talk about business, making no reference to their personal relationship. Although Meridee wanted to hear what he had to say, she found herself having trouble concentrating. The queasiness in her stomach had been compounded by a slight lightheadedness. It was also extremely warm in the pizzeria, and out of a sense of self-preservation, she excused herself to go to the ladies' room.

Although it was cooler in the restroom, it didn't seem to help. Meridee splashed some cold water on her face, then dug deep into her purse to get an antacid tablet. She sat down on the vinyl-covered chair in the corner and willed her body to behave as though she were on land instead of at sea. It didn't, and she wished she had told Zeb she wasn't up to lunch.

The queasy feeling was even stronger when she returned to the booth and she saw Joe setting a pizza in the center of their table. It was covered in everything under the sun—from green peppers to anchovies—and Meridee wanted to run back into the ladies' room.

"You're just in time," Zeb announced as she sat down. "Doesn't this look great?"

Meridee forced a smile to her face. "Just great."

Joe appeared satisfied with her answer, giving them both a broad grin. "Enjoy," he said before leaving.

Meridee briefly rested her forehead on the palm of her hand and Zeb asked, "Are you feeling all right?"

"It's a little warm in here," she answered, not wanting to admit how bad she was feeling. She watched Zeb reach for a slice of the pizza and suddenly knew that she was not going to be able to eat any of it. Just the sight of the dripping cheese made her stomach churn.

Zeb was about to plop a piece onto her plate when she stopped him by lifting her hand. "I don't think I'd better eat anything."

He put the pizza on his own plate, then looked at her with concern. "You're really not feeling well, are you?" he asked with such tenderness she felt a tear threaten to fall from the corner of her eye.

"I'm sorry. I'm afraid that if I don't leave, it may be embarrassing."

Zeb signaled for the waitress and smiled. "We decided to take this with us instead of eating here. Could you box it for us?"

The waitress returned his smile, and to Meridee's relief she disappeared with the offensive pizza. "What about your friend?" she asked, glancing over to where Joe was happily tossing pizza dough in the air.

"He'll just think I wanted to have you all to myself. Let me say a few words to him and we'll leave, all right?"

She nodded in agreement. "Why don't I meet you outside? I could use some fresh air."

Although the air was hardly fresh, at least it was free of the odor of garlic and cheese. Meridee welcomed the gusty wind, but it did little to alleviate the heat, and she was grateful when Zeb appeared only a few minutes later, carrying a cardboard box in his hands.

"If you wait here, I'll bring the car around," he told her, then headed for the parking lot at the corner. He took the pizza with him, but when Meridee climbed inside the car, there was no evidence of it anywhere, and she could only assume he had put it in the trunk.

"Where are we going?" she asked as he pulled out into the flow of traffic.

"Someplace where you can lie down until it's time for you to catch your plane," he replied.

"But I've already checked out of my hotel."

"I realize that. Just lean back and relax for now, all right?" He shot a sideways glance in her direction.

Meridee removed her glasses and put them in her purse, appreciating the fact that he had the air-conditioning on maximum power. In what direction or how far they were going, she didn't know, nor did she care. All she wanted was for the battle in her stomach to cease.

It wasn't long, however, before the car came to an underground garage.

"We're here," Zeb said gently, stroking her shoulder, and she realized that she must have dozed off.

"Where's here?" she asked when he came around to her side of the car and opened the door.

"My place. How are you feeling?" he asked, his dark eyes filled with concern.

"Surprisingly, better," she answered, although her stomach still felt unsettled.

"Come on." He reached out a hand to her. "I'll take you inside."

He led her into a very elegant condominium with skylights and high, beamed ceilings that gave one the sense of vast open space and allowed lots of sunshine to brighten the rooms. None of the windows had drapes, only vertical blinds, and Meridee immediately noticed that there were no plants.

Zeb gently urged her beyond the marble entryway into the living room, where a sectional sofa wrapped around a good portion of the room. However, it wasn't the boldly patterned sofa or the big-screen television that drew her attention, but the model railroad display dominating the area that would have normally been used as a dining room.

"Is this yours?" she asked, pulling her glasses from her purse so she could take a closer look at the display, which included miniature mountains, rivers and a small town.

While Meridee gazed at the train setup, Zeb slipped into the kitchen to put the pizza into the refrigerator. "This is my hobby," he told her when he returned.

"Some hobby," she marveled, watching him flip a switch that sent several trains moving along the tracks. "Why didn't you ever mention this to me?"

"I did. Don't you remember the day we went to Bandana Square in St. Paul and I bought that loco-motive for my nephew?"

"You said you still had the original train set you had received for your ninth birthday. You never said you had anything like this." Her arm made a sweeping gesture to encompass the intricate setup before them as trains passed through mountain tunnels, across trestles and past blinking warning signals. "I don't think you got all of this for your ninth birthday."

"When I was nine, all I had was a single loop of track with a locomotive, a couple of boxcars and a red caboose. It's that one over there." He pointed to a train that was winding around a plaster-of-paris mountain. "I've acquired most of this in the past five years. That's when I moved here and finally had the space to indulge myself."

"Did you make all of the scenery?"

"With the help of a few hobby-shop kits."

She slowly walked around the rectangular layout, taking in all the details—the tiny town with its movie house, school and church, the road crew working on potholes, the telephone lines strung across the lush, green countryside. "This is incredible," she said in amazement. "You must have spent a lot of time putting this together."

"It's a hobby that keeps me busy," he admitted. "But you didn't come here to see my trains." He flipped the switches on the control panel and the lights were extinguished, the trains halted. "You should be resting. I'll show you where the bedroom is."

Meridee was going to tell him she didn't need to see the bedroom, she could quite easily rest on his sofa. But the thought of lying on a bed was too tempting, and she followed him into an elegantly furnished bedroom decorated in deep hunter green.

There was only one window and a skylight over the bed. Both had pleated fabric shades that Zeb pulled to darken the room. Next he tossed the green-and-gold-striped pillow shams onto a chair near the wall and pulled back the bed covers for her.

"Would you like me to get you something? Aspirin? Antacid?" He looked at her inquisitively. "Is it your head that's bothering you?" he asked as she removed her glasses and pressed fingertips to her temples.

"It's not throbbing. I just feel light-headed, and my stomach's upset. I'm probably overtired. A rest is all I need." She gratefully dropped down onto the bed, kicking off her black pumps.

"There's a bathroom through here," he told her, gesturing to a door to the left of the king-size bed. "Why don't I check on you in an hour?" he suggested.

She nodded as she stretched out on the bed, not bothering to remove her suit jacket or her skirt. If only the room didn't feel as if it were revolving.

"Would you like me to get you your luggage from the car so you can change into something more comfortable?" he asked. "You're going to get all wrinkled."

"It's all right," she mumbled, keeping her eyes closed.

Zeb was immediately at her side. "Here. Let me at least help you out of your jacket," he said, carefully easing the tailored garment from her shoulders. He also helped her out of her skirt, then placed both pieces on the valet in the corner. "Just holler if you need anything."

Meridee buried her head in the pillow, appreciating the feel of the cool cotton sateen against her skin. Now that Zeb was out of the room, she could grimace and make as many faces as she wanted, which was what she usually did when she wasn't feeling well.

She closed her eyes and forced her body to relax, not wanting the unrest in her stomach to have any embarrassing results. She knew that if she could just fall asleep for an hour, she would feel better.

She did sleep, and probably wouldn't have awakened if it hadn't been for Zeb coming into the room and gently nudging her shoulder. "Meridee, wake up."

"Has it been an hour already?" she asked him as he sat beside her.

"Actually, it's been two. I didn't want to wake you, but I was worried you might miss your flight." He reached across to the nightstand, where a mug of steaming brown liquid sat. "Here. I brought you a cup of coffee."

All it took was one whiff of the freshly brewed coffee and Meridee's stomach revolted. With a startled groan, she leaped out of bed and dashed into the bathroom, where she became sick. Zeb was immediately at her side, comforting her, helping her back to bed when she had finished.

"I'm sorry. This is so embarrassing," she said as he tucked her back into bed.

"Everyone gets sick, Meri," he told her in a soothing voice, perching on the edge of the bed. "You probably picked up some flu bug."

She could only groan and turn her face into the pillow. "Whatever it is, I'm not going to be able to make my flight home," she murmured unhappily. "I feel awful."

"You'll have to stay here for tonight," he said gently, smoothing her hair away from her face.

"I'm in your bed. Where will you sleep?"

"I have a guest bedroom."

"Why didn't you put me in there?"

"Because you're more than a guest. And I like the way you look in my bed."

"Please don't say things like that when I'm feeling so awful," she begged.

"We've always been honest with each other, Meridee."

She thought about Brenda and said, "Most of the time."

He sighed. "Look, you need to sleep. I'm going to leave the bedroom door open. Give me a call if you need me, all right?"

Meridee nodded, although she knew she'd have to be desperate to seek his help. It was bad enough that he had witnessed her being sick once. She'd get through the night without him, even if it meant crawling to the bathroom.

As it turned out, she didn't need to crawl anywhere. She slept until shortly after midnight, when she awoke with a dry mouth and an empty stomach. When she turned on the bedside lamp, she saw that Zeb had been in to check on her, for her luggage was at the foot of the bed.

Other than feeling a little weak, she appeared to be over the "bug" that had invaded her body. Her stomach felt hollow, and after washing her face, brushing her teeth and peeling off her pantyhose, she decided the feeling was actually hunger. Replacing her slip and silk blouse with a pair of satin lounging pajamas, she ventured out of the bedroom in search of something to drink.

It was dark in the apartment, except for the glow coming from the aquarium in the corner of the living room. When Zeb had brought her into the condo, she had been so fascinated by the model railroad, she hadn't noticed the fish. She carefully padded over to the glass tank and gazed at the beautiful aquatic life inside.

"Meridee?"

She heard Zeb's voice a moment before a light went on.

"Are you all right?" he asked, walking toward her.

He was only wearing a pair of briefs, and Meridee's body tingled despite her weakened state. "I'm fine," she said. "I'm sorry if I woke you."

"It's all right. I heard you moving around and I thought you might need me."

"I was just looking at your tropical fish. They're beautiful."

He stepped further into the room, eyeing her critically. "Are you sure you're okay?"

"Yes, in fact I think I'm hungry," she said almost shyly.

"Let me get dressed and I'll fix you something."

"I can do it," she insisted.

"No, it's all right." He quickly disappeared, only to return a few minutes later wearing a pair of denim shorts and a Mets T-shirt. "Come on into the kitchen and I'll see what I can do."

Like everything else in Zeb's apartment, the kitchen was elegantly designed with all the modern conveniences. It positively gleamed, and Meridee wondered if it was used very often.

"Are you sure you feel up to eating?" Zeb asked as she sat down on a tall stool at the eating counter.

"I think so. Maybe I should try some soda crackers and tea. That's what my mother used to give us when we were kids and we had the flu."

He reached into the cupboard and pulled out a box of crackers, setting them on the counter in front of her. "Sorry, but I don't have any tea. How about some ginger ale? That's what my mom always gave *us* when we had the flu."

"Ginger ale will be fine," she answered, opening a package of crackers.

Zeb filled two glasses with ice from the dispenser on the refrigerator door, then set them on the eating counter while he rattled around in a bottom cupboard. When he produced a bottle of ginger ale, there was a smile of victory on his face.

"I knew I had one of these down there somewhere," he said as he unscrewed the cap and poured the golden liquid over the ice in her glass.

Meridee sipped the bubbly beverage carefully. "Mmmm. This tastes good. Thank you."

Zeb perched himself on the stool beside her, grabbing a couple of soda crackers.

"If you want to eat real food, don't let me stop you," she told him.

He shook his head. "I already ate the cold pizza before I went to bed," he confessed. "Sorry. I wasn't going to mention that."

She grinned. "It's all right. Normally I love pizza, but..." she trailed off with a shrug.

"I canceled your plane reservations and rescheduled you for tomorrow morning," he told her. "You're on the nine-thirty flight."

"Thank you." She reached over and gave his forearm a gentle squeeze. "I appreciate everything you did for me today, Zeb, and I'm sorry I ruined your afternoon."

"You didn't ruin my afternoon."

She gave him a dubious look. "I'm sure you would rather have been working than nursing a sick woman."

"You didn't exactly allow me to nurse you, and what makes you think I didn't work?" he asked.

"Did you bring work home with you?"

"I *always* bring work home with me," he said with a crooked grin.

"I thought you were supposed to be in Cincinnati?"

"The boss called me home for a few days. I need to give a progress report." He poured more ginger ale into her glass and asked, "Would you mind if I brought out some salami and cheese?"

"No, not at all," she answered. "I'm really feeling much better. I don't know why I became sick, but whatever it was, it seems to have passed. Maybe it was one of those twenty-four-hour flu bugs."

Zeb got off the bar stool and walked to the refrigerator, where he pulled out a stick of salami and a wedge of cheese. "Tell me how things are going at Krystalene. Are Ted and Bob stabilizing things?"

"Yes, even Griggs likes them."

For the next half hour they discussed the changes that would be necessary if the company was going to prosper in the nineties. Although Zeb had outlined a plan that established procedures for its short-term success, it was now up to Meridee and the other managers to develop a plan for long-term investments. Despite feeling confident in her ability to make those decisions, Meridee was grateful for the opportunity to discuss strategies with Zeb.

"It sounds as though you have everything figured out," Zeb commented.

"I'm happy with the progress we've made," Meridee said thoughtfully. "It's good to hear that you approve of our plans."

"You have no reason to second-guess yourself. You're more than capable of developing a strategic plan that will make Krystalene prosperous now that the bugs have been worked out."

"Thank you for the vote of confidence." Meridee lifted her glass in a salute.

Zeb lifted his own glass and clinked it against hers. "Kind of seems like old times, eh?"

"We do work well together, don't we?" she said wistfully.

"I've missed you, Meri." He reached over and ran his forefinger across her cheek.

"Zeb, I . . ."

"Shhh. Don't say anything, please. Just listen to me, okay?"

She swallowed with difficulty, then nodded.

"Ever since I left St. Paul I've been thinking about you. I wanted to give you time to get over your anger about what happened with Brenda, but today when I saw you at corporate headquarters, I knew that I couldn't let you go back to Minnesota without telling you how I feel about you."

"How do you feel?" she found herself asking.

"As if I should be requesting a position with Krystalene in St. Paul instead of troubleshooting for Denton," he admitted candidly. "I've never met anyone who can make me feel the way you do." He took her hand in his. "I want to be with you."

"You wouldn't be happy working at Krystalene," she told him.

"What makes you say that?"

"Because you like solving problems. It's the challenge of rescuing a business about to go under that excites you. You'd be bored working with a company that's operating efficiently."

"You could be right, but the point is, I want to be with you. I want you to be part of my life."

She sighed. "I don't see how that's possible. You have your job, I have mine. Two near workaholics trying to make time for romance isn't such a great prospect," she said sadly.

"Maybe we're not destined to have the traditional kind of relationship other couples have, but there must be something that will work for us."

Meridee didn't answer right away, but stared thoughtfully at her glass.

"Can you honestly tell me you've been happy these past few weeks?" he asked, watching her steadily.

Meridee shook her head, her eyes downcast. "I've been miserable. I hate unresolved conflicts. I can't believe I've let this go on as long as I have."

"I don't want an unresolved anything between us." He put his arm around her shoulders and pulled her close. "I'm sorry about Brenda's job, but it was a business decision, not a personal one. Can't you understand that?" He lifted her chin with his finger.

"I want to, Zeb. In my head I know that you acted in a professional manner, but inside me I can't seem to stop feeling hurt," she admitted.

"I never meant to hurt you, Meri." His left arm was on the back of her chair, his right arm resting on the counter with his hand holding hers. "You're always so unflappable when it comes to your work, I never thought you'd react so emotionally to a professional decision."

"Neither did I," she said. "Maybe that's why I've always followed my intuition and kept my personal life separate from my professional one." She took a sip of the ginger ale.

"We're no longer working together. Shouldn't a personal relationship be easier now?" he asked.

She put her arm around his neck and said softly against his ear, "What if we're doomed to be unsuccessful at intimate relationships because we're workaholics?"

"*Almost* workaholics," he corrected her, then kissed her tenderly on the mouth.

"You shouldn't have done that," she said, when he lifted his mouth from hers. "You'll catch my flu bug."

"It's worth the risk." He kissed her again.

"Your lips could be considered lethal weapons to a woman in my weakened condition," she told him, clinging to him for support.

He looked at her flushed face and said, "You've been up long enough. Why don't you let me carry you back to bed?"

"Carry me?" She gave him a skeptical look.

"Me Tarzan, you Jane," he said with a sheepish grin.

She laughed and allowed him to sweep her up into his arms. "To the treetop, Tarzan," she commanded as he carried her past the aquarium and back into his bedroom.

He deposited her on the bed, then sat down beside her. "I'm glad you're feeling better." He pressed a light kiss on her lips. "Although if you were still sick, I'd have an excuse to keep you here with me. I don't suppose there's any chance that you could stay through the weekend?" he asked.

She shook her head. "I can't. Besides the fact that I have to be at work on Friday, we're having a family celebration. It's both my mother's and my stepfather's birthday." She paused for a moment, then beamed. "I know. Why don't you come to St. Paul?"

"What about your sister? Will there be a problem if I'm with you?"

Meridee hesitated only a second before saying, "No, I don't think so."

"Good. I'd like to come," he said.

"Then it's all set," she said. "You can stay at my house. I have a guest bedroom, too."

"It might be better for both of us if I had a hotel room."

Her face fell. "Why?"

"Because it isn't exactly easy to sleep in the same house in a room only a couple of feet from yours."

"I'm sorry," she apologized.

"It's not your fault. The only reason I'm not crawling in beside you right now is that you've been sick and you need rest more than you need me."

"And I can't have both?" she asked, running her fingers up and down his arm.

"As much as I'd like to stay, you do need your sleep." He reached for her fingers and slowly raised them to his lips.

"Thanks... for everything," she said as he slowly retreated from the room.

"If you need anything..."

"I'll be fine," she said with a smile.

And as she snuggled down into the covers, she thought that for the first time in weeks, she really was fine.

ALTHOUGH MERIDEE FELT much better in the morning, she still had a slight queasiness in her stomach and was grateful when Zeb insisted on taking her to the airport. The thought of riding on a hot bus or crowded shuttle wasn't a pleasant one, and sitting in Zeb's airconditioned car felt like a luxury.

To Meridee's surprise, tears fell from her eyes when she said goodbye to Zeb at the airport. Not one to show emotions readily, she attributed her instability to the fact that she was recovering from the flu. Zeb didn't seem to mind. He gently brushed away her tears and promised he'd be in St. Paul in less than forty-eight hours for a wonderful weekend.

Despite her assertion that everything would be wonderful when he came to Minnesota, Meridee couldn't ignore the tiny niggling doubt that kept surfacing all the way home. It was only when she arrived back at her house that she had to face the reason for her apprehension. Brenda.

She was stretched out on the sofa watching a soap opera, a fashion magazine propped against her knees. When she saw Meridee, she said in a flat voice, "Oh, you're home."

The scattered remains of lunch were spread out on the glass-topped coffee table. Shoes, a jacket and various other articles of clothing were strewn about the room, and the drapes were still drawn.

"Where's Vanna?" Meridee demanded, looking around the house suspiciously.

"She's out in the backyard."

"She's outside in this heat?"

"I had to put her out. She was crying by the door." She gave Meridee an obstinate look. "Trust me, she's still breathing."

Meridee choked back the scolding she felt like giving her sister and hurried to the back door, where she found the bichon stretched out in the shade of the back step, her tongue hanging out of her mouth.

"Come on, Mommy's home," Meridee cooed as she opened the door and the tiny dog bustled inside. After giving Vanna an abundance of affection and refilling her water dish, she went back into the living room.

"Didn't I tell you she was alive and well?" Brenda said sarcastically as the bichon jumped up on the couch next to her.

"Her coat looks a little matted. Have you been brushing her?" Meridee asked, a bit peeved that Vanna chose to sit next to Brenda.

"Yes, I've been brushing her and I gave her her vitamins and I put the lemon juice in her drinking water to keep her facial hairs white," Brenda said in a bored voice. "All I've done for the past four days is take care of your dog."

"You haven't had any luck finding a job?" Meridee asked, kicking off her shoes.

Brenda made a sound of disgust. "Most places want someone with at least a year's experience. As soon as they see I only worked four months at Krystalene before I was let go, they either offer me a filing position or reject my application." She cast an accusing glance in Meridee's direction. "How do they expect me to get experience if no one will hire me?"

"Something will turn up." Meridee tried to sound optimistic, but she was aware of the difficulties facing her sister when it came to finding a good job. It was one of the reasons why she had gone out of her way to procure a job for Brenda at Krystalene. Still, Brenda had to start somewhere, and Meridee couldn't help but feel she shouldn't turn down a job simply because it was another entry-level position.

She had picked up the stack of mail from the end table and was flipping through it when Brenda said,

"Your phone messages are on the bulletin board in the kitchen."

"Anything exciting happen while I was gone?"

"It's been pretty dull with the exception of Rodney's arrival."

"Donovan's son is visiting?"

Brenda nodded. "He came the day before yesterday."

"How long is he staying?"

She shrugged. "Who knows? With Rodney, anything goes. I think Mom's a little worried that he might decide to transfer to the university up here and not return to New Orleans."

"That's all we need—Rodney living behind us," Meridee said with a frown.

"Why don't you like him? I think he's kind of cute."

"He *is* cute, but he's also irresponsible and a big flirt." She looked at her sister curiously. "Don't go getting any ideas about him," she warned.

"Meridee! He's my stepbrother for Pete's sake! Besides, he brought a guest."

"He has a girlfriend?"

"Yeah, and she's surprisingly nice."

"I suppose this means they'll be at Mom and Donovan's birthday party this weekend."

"Which means you and I are going to be the only unattached women."

Meridee felt a twinge of guilt. "I'm not exactly going to be unattached."

"You have a date?"

"Zeb's coming to Minnesota and I invited him to Mom's party."

"You did what?" Brenda squeaked in disbelief.

"I invited him to the party," Meridee snapped, suddenly feeling annoyed about her sister's attitude. "And you might as well know, he's staying here instead of at a hotel."

Brenda jumped up from the couch. "I don't believe this! Zeb Farrell's the reason I lost my job. How can you even think about letting him stay here?"

"He feels bad that your job was one of those that were eliminated. . . ."

"Hah!" Brenda didn't let her finish her sentence. "What happened to you in New York? When you left you didn't want anything to do with the man. You spend three days with him and now you tell me he's coming to stay with us?"

"I didn't spend three days with him," she said. "I didn't even see him until yesterday. I got sick at the conference and he took me back to his condo until I was better."

"You weren't sick at all, were you? That was just your excuse to stay with him," Brenda said accusingly.

"I *was* sick!" she declared emotionally. "And if it hadn't been for Zeb, I wouldn't have had a place to stay, because I'd already checked out of my hotel."

"That was convenient. Are you going to tell me he 'nursed' you through your illness, too?"

"He *did* take care of me." Brenda made a sound of disbelief as Meridee gathered up her belongings. "I don't need to stand here and defend myself. Zeb is coming tomorrow night. He's staying until Sunday." She started toward the stairs.

"What about our house rules?"

"I've just changed them. Male guests are allowed at the discretion of the person who pays the rent on this place—me." She started up the stairs.

"I pay rent, too," Brenda called after her.

Meridee paused halfway up the stairs. "Mother pays your share of the rent," she retorted.

"That's because I lost my job thanks to *your* boyfriend."

Meridee would have liked to remind her that Kate had been paying Brenda's share of the rent long before she ever lost her job, but she didn't want to get into a verbal war.

"I don't have time to argue with you, Brenda. I need to get to the office," she said as she continued up the stairs. By the time she reached the top step the front door had slammed shut, and she could only shake her head in regret. She should have known that resolving her conflict with Zeb would create a new one with her sister.

"I'll straighten everything out with Brenda tonight," she told Vanna, who had followed her into the bedroom and was watching her owner change into a dark blue suit. "And when Zeb gets here he can talk to her. Everything will be fine." She wondered why, if that were so, she suddenly felt like crying.

"I will not cry over an argument with my sister," she said to her reflection in the mirror, sniffling back the tears. Vanna barked, as if in understanding, and followed Meridee as she made her way back downstairs. With one last glance at the disorder in the living room, Meridee slipped out the door.

CHAPTER TWELVE

ON HER WAY TO THE OFFICE, Meridee stopped at the florist to wire Zeb a philodendron as a way of saying thank you for the care he had shown her while she was in New York.

The first person she encountered when she stepped off the elevator in the Krystalene office complex was Ingrid, who looked surprised to see her.

"Oh! You're back. We weren't expecting you until tomorrow."

She looked uneasy and Meridee wondered why. "I know. Griggs told me I didn't have to come in this afternoon, but I wanted to get caught up so I can take the weekend off. It's both my mother's and Donovan's birthday." She opened the door and gestured for Ingrid to go in.

"You're looking a little pale," Ingrid commented, her hands folded across her chest as she eyed Meridee.

"I had the flu in New York, so I'm not planning on being here very long," Meridee told her, sinking down into her leather chair. "There are just a couple of things I need to do."

Ingrid didn't sit, but chose to stand, leaning up against the window ledge. "So other than that, how was your trip?"

"I enjoyed seeing Denton's headquarters, but the conference wasn't very inspiring. Even if I hadn't gotten sick I think I would have cut out early. The next time they have one of these things maybe I ought to suggest that you go," she said.

"I don't think that's going to work," Ingrid replied, shifting uneasily.

"Why not? If you want to advance in the company, you really should take advantage of the seminars they offer. Couldn't you get your mother to stay with the boys while you're gone?"

"That's not the problem," Ingrid said dully.

Meridee sat forward, fixing her with an inquisitive gaze. "Ingrid, what's wrong? Why are looking at me that way?"

"Because I have something to tell you and I don't want you to be upset with me." She took a deep breath and said, "I'm turning in my resignation tomorrow."

Meridee's eyes widened in disbelief. "You're quitting?"

Ingrid nodded weakly. "I'm sorry, Meridee."

Perplexed, she asked, "You don't need to be sorry, Ingrid. Just tell me why you're leaving."

Ingrid took another deep breath, then said, "Ed was offered a job in Idaho, and the boys and I have decided to go with him."

This time the sick feeling in Meridee's stomach had nothing to do with the flu. "You're getting back together with Ed?" She tried not to look horrified, but the truth was, the thought alarmed her.

"I know you don't approve, but he's changed, Meridee. He's not the same man he was two years ago when he walked out on us. He really cares about the boys and he wants us to be a family again." Her eyes pleaded for understanding.

"Ingrid, it's not my position to either approve or disapprove, but I'm concerned that you're doing this for the wrong reasons. Is this what you want? Or are you doing it because the boys want him back?"

"I'm not making some great sacrifice, if that's what you're worried about," she answered tersely.

"What I'm worried about is what's going to happen to you." Meridee got up from her chair and came around to the front of her desk. "I haven't forgotten the desperate conditions you faced because Ed couldn't control his drinking. He put you through hell—and not only you, but the boys, too!"

"Believe me, Meridee, I haven't forgotten, either. Living with an alcoholic is an experience one never forgets. I'm not even sure I can forgive him for some of the things that happened."

Meridee's fears were not alleviated by Ingrid's tentative smile. "Then why go back to him?" she asked, frustrated.

"Because I'm tired of being both mother and father to the boys. I'm tired of trying to make my paycheck stretch from payday to payday. But most of all, I'm simply tired of being alone," she said on a note of exasperation.

Meridee opened her mouth to speak, but stopped when Ingrid said, "Please don't tell me how strong I am and that I can stand on my own two feet."

"But you are strong!" Meridee declared fervently. "Look what you've been through these past two years."

Ingrid was shaking her head in denial. "I know you like to think that we're a lot alike, but you've always been so independent, so dedicated to your career. I only work to support my boys."

"But you have a wonderful career here."

"I don't want a career. I want to be able to stay home and take care of my boys. And I want a man in my life. I know you probably think that makes me sound wimpy, but it's the way I am."

Meridee's shoulders slumped forward and her eyes softened. "Ingrid, I'm not anti men. I just want you to be sure Ed is the man you want to be with."

"Ed is an alcoholic. That doesn't mean he isn't a good man. He has a disease, a disease he has under control."

"And what if it gets out of control again?"

"I don't like to admit that that's a possibility, but if it does happen, we'll deal with it," Ingrid said with the backbone Meridee already knew she possessed. "All five of us are in counseling trying to make this work."

Meridee didn't know what to say. It was difficult not to be concerned about Ingrid's decision.

"If you want to start over with him, wouldn't it be wiser to stay here in St. Paul?" she suggested at last. "You have a good job, your family's here, the boys are all in school. There must be something Ed could do here in the cities."

"He thinks it'll be easier to make a fresh start if we're not surrounded by people who know every detail of our past. And as for the boys leaving school, it hasn't been easy for them the past couple of years, especially not when Ed was in jail."

The reminder of all the pain Ingrid had suffered when her husband had been sentenced stirred Meridee's protective instincts. She felt compelled to make a final effort to dissuade her friend. "You're a strong woman, Ingrid. I know you think you need a man, but you *can* make it on your own."

Ingrid smiled. "Everyone needs to be loved, Meridee. Someday you'll discover that for yourself."

"So you do love Ed?" she asked softly.

"Maybe not the way I did when we were first married," Ingrid admitted. "All I know is that we share something special. He's the father of our boys. And as long as he stays sober, I'm convinced we have a chance to make our marriage work."

"Then you're going to get married again?"

Ingrid nodded. "Three weeks from Saturday. I'd like you to be there."

"Of course," Meridee answered. She smiled at her friend warmly, in spite of her reservations.

There was a brief silence, then Ingrid said, "I know I'm taking a risk, but anyone who's ever loved someone knows that love involves risks."

Meridee could only nod in understanding. "When are you leaving for Idaho?" she asked.

"My last day of work will be two weeks from tomorrow. Then it'll take us a couple of weeks to get packed."

Meridee bit down on a lip that was suddenly quivering. "That soon?"

Ingrid nodded. "We want to get the boys settled before school starts."

"It'll be a big change for them."

Again Ingrid nodded. "It'll be a big change for me. Look, Meridee, I don't know how to say this, but I want you to know how grateful I am for everything you've done for me. If it hadn't been for you taking a chance on giving me this job, I don't know what would have happened to me and the boys."

"You're a lot smarter and a lot stronger than you give yourself credit for. And you've been a valuable employee. That's why you're in the job you have now," Meridee said sincerely.

"You taught me a lot, and I'm not just talking about accounting procedures. You showed me how to think of myself as a success and not a failure. You wouldn't let me crumble, even though there were many days when I felt like crumbling, and...I want you to know, I'm going to miss you." Ingrid choked back a sob.

"I'm going to miss you, too," Meridee said, giving the older woman a hug. Hot tears stung the back of her eyes and for the third time in one day Meridee found herself overwhelmed by her emotions.

Between leaving Zeb, arguing with Brenda and hearing that Ingrid was resigning, she had had more emotional stress in one day than she usually encountered in an entire month. By five o'clock, she was exhausted both mentally and physically, and she wondered how she would find the energy to deal with Brenda.

Only it wasn't Brenda who was waiting for her when she arrived at home. Her mother was sitting on her front steps, a bunch of colorful zinnias in her hand. Meridee was immediately on the defensive. Kate bearing flowers was an omen of a scolding in the offing.

"Mom. What are you doing here?" she asked, trying not to look suspicious.

"I brought you a get-well bouquet," Kate said, handing her the purple-and-pink zinnias. "Brenda told me you'd been sick."

"Thank you." Meridee accepted the flowers, sniffing them appreciatively. "Have you been waiting long?"

"Just a few minutes. How are you feeling?" Kate's maternal eyes raked over her slender figure and Meridee could see that she hadn't passed muster.

"I'm fine," she answered.

"Are you sure?" Kate asked, studying her face. "You look awfully pale."

"I haven't exactly had the best of days, Mom. Why don't you come inside and I'll explain?" she suggested, pulling open the screen door.

"I can only stay a few minutes. Donovan's taking me to a concert at the Lake Harriet Bandshell this evening."

"That should be fun. It's a beautiful evening for it," Meridee commented as she unlocked the door and led her mother inside. "Come into the kitchen while I put these in water," she said, noticing her mother's eyebrows lift as they passed the messy living room.

"Is this what you had to come home to?" Kate stared distastefully at the dirty dishes sitting in the kitchen sink.

"Brenda hasn't been the easiest person to live with since she lost her job." Meridee bent down to get a crystal vase from under the sink. "If you feel like talking to her about it, be my guest," she said dryly, filling the vase with water. "I wouldn't object to you using your influence to get her to help keep this place clean."

"I'll talk to her about it," Kate promised, taking a seat at the table. "She came to see me at work today."

"Oh?" Meridee feigned a nonchalance she wasn't feeling.

"Is it true that you've invited Zeb to stay with you this weekend?"

Meridee set the flowers on the small table and looked directly at her mother. "Yes. Is there a reason why I shouldn't have?"

"Meridee! It's because of Zeb Brenda isn't working!"

"No, Mom, Brenda's the reason why she isn't working. She's been on dozens of job interviews, but none of them are offering what she had at Krystalene, so she won't take any of them. I'm sorry that she lost her job, but I'm not going to take responsibility for it. Have the two of you forgotten that I'm the reason she even had a job in the first place?"

"I'm not blaming you for Brenda losing her job. I'd just like you to be a little more considerate of her feelings."

"What about my feelings?" Meridee demanded, hanging on to her temper with an effort. "This is my home, and I want Zeb to stay here. I don't want to send him to some hotel."

"He doesn't have to go to a hotel. He can stay with Donovan and me," Kate offered.

"What about Rodney? Brenda said he's back and he's brought some girl with him."

"That's true, but we have room for Zeb."

"Uh-uh." She shook her head and folded her arms across her chest. "I'm not going to have Zeb staying in a house where some strange girl's running around."

"Rodney's girlfriend is leaving tomorrow," Kate assured her. "Brenda said you both agreed there'd be no overnight male guests as long as you were sharing a house."

"I'm almost thirty years old, and this is my house. I don't think it's unreasonable to invite guests to stay here," Meridee said testily.

"Nevertheless, Brenda does have a point. There's little privacy if there's a man in the house."

"She didn't worry about that when she allowed Steven to spend the night here," Meridee retorted, then immediately regretted her slipup when she saw the distressed look on her mother's face.

"Steven slept here?"

"He was on the couch, Mom. And if Zeb stays here, he'll be in the guest bedroom."

Kate was quiet for several seconds, then asked, "Are you in love with him, Meridee?"

"Love?" Meridee was taken aback by her mother's question.

Kate quickly moved her hand in a dismissive gesture. "Forget I asked that question. I promised myself I wasn't going to pry into your personal life, and I'm not going to. I think there are two alternatives in this situation. Either Zeb or Brenda has to stay at our place."

"You'd rather it were Zeb, wouldn't you?" Meridee said.

"It would be easier, considering that Rodney's staying with us." Kate lifted her eyebrows in a silent appeal.

Meridee groaned. "Let me think about it," she said somewhat impatiently. "I'm going to have a talk with Brenda tonight, and I'll give you a call tomorrow, all right?"

"All right, dear," Kate said with her gentle smile. She paused and looked at her daughter. "Are you sure you're feeling okay? You look a little pale."

Meridee sighed. "I'm fine, Mom. I'm just a little weak, that's all."

"Maybe you should have your blood checked. You could be anemic."

"I'll make an appointment for next week, I promise," she said, urging her mother toward the door.

"Would you like to come with Donovan and me to the concert? I've packed a picnic supper—a little fried chicken, potato salad..." She looked at Meridee inquisitively.

The thought of food was unappealing, and Meridee shook her head. "I'm not quite ready for real food, Mom. I'd better pass."

"If your stomach's still queasy, try a little broth and toast."

"I will," Meridee promised.

When Juliet called and asked if she could stop over, Meridee was tempted to tell her she was going to go to bed early, but her sister was eager to show her the wedding photographs she had selected. Meridee had just finished grooming Vanna's coat when Juliet showed up on her doorstep, photo album in hand.

"I thought you said you were feeling better," Juliet commented when she stepped inside the house.

"I am better," Meridee stated, tightening the belt on her robe.

"Then why are you in your pajamas at six-thirty?"

Meridee pushed her hair away from her face. "Because yesterday at this time I was flat on my back with a horrible case of the flu."

"Is your stomach still upset?" Juliet asked, noticing the bottle of antacid on the table.

"No, but I still feel nauseated. Actually, it comes and goes. It's so weird. One minute I feel good, the next minute I feel rotten."

"How long has this been going on?"

Meridee shrugged. "I don't know. A few days, I guess. I didn't actually get sick until yesterday afternoon. At first I thought it might be food poisoning, but now I think I probably picked up one of those twenty-four-hour flu bugs."

"Are you sure that's all it is?" Juliet asked suspiciously.

"What else could it be?" Meridee asked. "I haven't traveled to any exotic countries recently, so I don't think I have a tropical disease," she said, leaning her head back against the sofa.

"Do strong odors bother you?"

"Certain food odors do. Why?"

Juliet chewed thoughtfully on her lower lip. "Meridee, there isn't any chance that you could be pregnant, is there?"

"No!" she said vehemently. "For Pete's sake, Juliet, don't even suggest such a thing."

"I'm sorry. It's just that what you've been describing sounds exactly like how I felt when I was pregnant with Sara and Annie."

"Well, I'm not pregnant!"

"All right, all right," Juliet said quietly. "I didn't mean to upset you."

Meridee sighed. "I'm sorry. I shouldn't be so touchy, but you wouldn't believe what's been happening in my life."

"You want to talk about it?" Juliet asked.

Meridee shook her head. "I wouldn't know where to begin. I think the final straw was going into the office today and finding out Ingrid is quitting."

"She's found another job?"

"No, she's moving to Idaho with her ex-husband."

"Oh?" Juliet looked at her in astonishment.

"The irony of it all is that I fought long and hard to convince Zeb not to eliminate her job. That wouldn't be so bad except that I didn't even think of saving Brenda's job, and now she's the one who really needs one."

"Do you think Zeb would have kept Brenda on if you had fought for her job?" Juliet asked.

Meridee sighed. "Probably not. He doesn't make decisions based on emotions."

"Neither do you."

Meridee smiled. "Don't I wish." She grabbed the photo album and set it between them. "I think we should stop talking about me and look at the wedding pictures."

Although Meridee made all the appropriate comments when Juliet showed her the photographs, she was preoccupied with thoughts about the day she discovered that she and Brenda had mixed up their birth control pills. Halfway through the album, she looked at Juliet and asked, "What other symptoms did you have when you were pregnant?"

"I cried a lot, and over little things that were inconsequential."

Meridee grabbed her sister's shoulder. "Juliet, I've already cried at least three times today." She paused, her face growing pale. "I *never* cry."

"But you just told me there's no way you could be pregnant. You haven't missed a period, have you?"

"I didn't exactly skip it, but I didn't exactly have one, either." Meridee bit down on her lower lip.

"What are you talking about?"

Meridee explained about the mix-up in birth control pills and what the doctor had said would happen, including the fact that she might not have a normal period. When she was finished, she looked at her sister apprehensively.

"Now do you see why I'm worried?"

Juliet nodded sympathetically. "You're wondering if you mixed up the pills the weekend you spent with Zeb, aren't you?"

"Yes," she said shakily. "I...I just don't know what to do. The last thing I ever expected to have to worry about was getting pregnant."

"You don't know that you are pregnant," Juliet reminded her.

Meridee looked at her watch. "It's too late to call the clinic."

"You could get one of those in-home pregnancy kits. I've heard that they're something like ninety-nine percent accurate even if you're only a day late on your period."

Meridee snapped her fingers. "You're right. That's a good idea." She got up from the sofa, shoving the wedding album aside. "I'm going to get dressed and run down to the drugstore right now."

"Do you want me to come with you?" Juliet called after her as she headed toward the stairs.

Meridee shook her head. "I can do this. You go on home to Ross. I'll call you later."

A half hour later, Meridee stood in front of a drugstore shelf, staring blankly at products that suddenly had the power to change her entire life. Sandwiched between the contraceptives and feminine hygiene products were several brands of in-home pregnancy tests. She would have liked to open the packages to get an idea as to how they differed, but she was forced to rely on the labels to make her choice. As a result, she chose the brand that promised to be easy, fast and accurate.

Back home, in the privacy of her bedroom, she opened the box and examined the contents of the kit. Seeing the test vials and developer solution reminded her of the time she had received a junior chemistry set for her eleventh birthday. Despite her father's attempts to interest her in science, she had hated chemistry in school. It was the one course in college she probably wouldn't have done well in had it not been for the fact that she had drawn a great lab partner.

She sighed. There was no lab partner for this experiment, she thought grimly. "Damn!" she said softly as she stared at the kit. She wouldn't have had to perform the stupid test at all if Brenda hadn't left her pills where they didn't belong. Anger toward her absent sister festered inside her.

It was while she was reading the directions that she heard Brenda come home. At the sound of footsteps on the stairs, she stuffed the pregnancy test back into the box and hid it beneath her pillow. She was about to rush out into the hall and confront her sister when she stopped herself. She would only create more problems between the two of them if she were to try to talk to Brenda now.

Not wanting to say anything she'd be sorry for in the morning, Meridee waited until she heard Brenda's door slam shut, then went back over to her bed. She pulled the kit from under the pillow.

According to the instructions, she was supposed to wait until first thing in the morning to perform the test. Patience had never been one of Meridee's virtues. After only a couple of minutes of contemplation, she decided to do the test right away. If she were pregnant, she wanted to know—now.

Making sure Brenda's door was still shut, she walked down the hall to the bathroom. Following the directions carefully, she deposited a sample of urine in the vial, then waited a minute before adding the test strip. After five minutes, she rinsed the test strip and placed it in the developer solution.

"Oh, please, don't turn blue," Meridee whispered as she waited for the results. One minute passed. Then two. Then three. She pulled the test strip out of the solution and carefully examined the results. She grimaced. The pad wasn't white, but it wasn't as blue as the sample in the directions, either.

She decided to stick it back in for another two minutes. When she pulled it out again, it was still an ambiguous bluish-white. She reread the directions.

"If the result pad is white, the test is negative. You are not pregnant. If the result pad is blue, the test is positive. You are pregnant."

Meridee held the test strip up to the light. Although it wasn't as blue as she had expected it to be, it was definitely not white. She tossed the strip onto the vanity and sank down onto the toilet, dropping her head in her hands. "This can't be happening to me," she mumbled.

Only it was, she grimly acknowledged a few minutes later. Looking at the test strip, she saw that the error-control pad was white. She had done the test correctly. She, the woman who had vowed never to get married, was pregnant.

CHAPTER THIRTEEN

MUCH TO MERIDEE'S surprise, she didn't lie awake half the night pondering the subject of motherhood. However, the next day she found herself having difficulty thinking of anything but the possibility that her life was about to change drastically. She felt totally unprepared and ill equipped to deal with the situation. Nor would the problem stay quietly tucked away in the back of her mind.

When she got a message that Juliet had phoned while she was in a conference, Meridee debated whether she should call her back right away or wait until she was in the privacy of her home. Knowing her sister was probably going crazy waiting to hear from her, Meridee made the phone call from her office, making sure her door was shut before dialing her number.

"It's me," Meridee said when Juliet answered.

"Thank goodness!" Juliet said with a sigh of relief. "When you didn't call me back last night I was imagining the worst had happened."

"The worst did happen."

"Did you get a pregnancy-test kit?"

"Yes."

"And?" she probed.

Meridee swallowed—hard. "It was positive."

Juliet gasped. "You're kidding!"

"Of course I'm not kidding," Meridee snapped irritably. "Juliet, this is not something I would joke about."

"I'm sorry, Meridee, it's just that this is so unexpected. Are you sure you did it right?"

"The error-control pad indicated that I did," she said soberly.

"You should still see a doctor," Juliet advised.

"I know. I made an appointment for next week." She stared at the red circle she had drawn around the abbreviation "Dr." on the calendar.

"They'll run another lab test, and then you'll know for sure."

"Juliet, I think there's little chance I'm not. You said yourself these home kits are something like ninety-nine percent accurate."

"You could be in the one percent," she stated optimistically.

"I think it's a little more likely that I'm in the ninety-nine percent," she said grimly. "Don't forget—I screwed up taking my birth control pills."

"So how do you feel about all of this?"

"I feel numb. I never dreamed I'd be in this predicament."

"Have you thought about what you're going to do?"

"First I have to figure out how I'm going to get through the weekend." Meridee chuckled mirthlessly. "And I thought my biggest problem was going to be how to tell Zeb I had arranged for him to stay at Mom's."

"Maybe you should call and tell him not to come. You could always say you're not feeling well. I'm sure he'd understand if you told him you're having a relapse of the flu," Juliet reasoned.

Meridee had been thinking along the same lines all morning, and after talking with her sister decided that it would be better not to see Zeb this weekend. Her emotions were on a seesaw—a fact she attributed to her condition. As soon as she had hung up the phone, she called Zeb in New York.

However, she wasn't quick enough, for his secretary informed her he had left early and wouldn't be back in the office. When she tried his condominium, she got his answering service. Not knowing whether he would return to his apartment before leaving for the airport, she left the following message: "It's Meridee, just wanting to touch base with you. If you haven't left for the airport, call me. I'll be at the office until five."

It didn't surprise her when she didn't hear from him. At five-thirty, she left Krystalene and went home to change into a pair of white slacks and a sleeveless fuchsia tunic. After a light supper of melon and cottage cheese, she drove to the airport, her mind preoccupied with what she would say to him.

She had already decided that until she had her pregnancy confirmed by the doctor, there was no point in saying anything to Zeb. Having a baby would change the dynamics of their relationship dramatically and force them to make decisions she wasn't ready to make. They had decided only two days ago that they would continue seeing each other. How could they possibly discuss becoming parents when they were still trying to figure out how they felt about each other?

As she walked across the airport concourse in search of the gate where Zeb's plane would be landing, she saw a young couple pushing a baby in a stroller. When they stopped at a gate where passengers were boarding a jumbo jet, Meridee paused, too, her eyes drawn to the three of them. As the man set his briefcase down in order to give the woman a hug, Meridee's heartstrings were tugged as tears fell from the young mother's eyes.

She overheard the woman say, "Don't worry about us. We'll be fine." Then the woman lifted the baby into her arms and held it up so that the man could caress its cheeks with his finger before brushing a soft kiss across its forehead.

"Daddy will be back soon," he cooed. He waved goodbye and started toward the plane, looking back longingly over his shoulder as he disappeared down the walkway.

That could be me, Meridee thought to herself as she watched the young mother tuck her baby back into the stroller and head for the exit. The idea that she and Zeb could be in a similar situation next year filled Meridee with an unexpected sentimentality. In less than nine months, instead of getting up each morning and rushing off to the office, she could be staying home and caring for a baby. Balancing financial statements and auditing payrolls could be replaced with clipping coupons and changing diapers. Meridee smothered a laugh as she thought about changing a messy diaper. The picture of domestic bliss faded, and her expression became thoughtful.

She wasn't ready to become a mother. She wasn't even ready to become a wife, yet both possibilities loomed in the not-so-distant future. Panic threatened to weaken her legs as she hurried to meet Zeb's plane.

She had to remind herself that just because she was going to become a mother, it didn't necessarily mean she would become a wife. One was not a prerequisite for the other. She had always been untraditionally oriented. So why was she suddenly feeling so traditional? And why was marriage the first alternative that had come to mind when the test had been positive?

It must be my hormones, she thought morosely. They're out of whack and I'm not thinking clearly. She made a mental list of all the reasons she had avoided marriage in the past, a list that was immediately tossed aside the moment she saw Zeb walk through the Jetway into the airport.

He was wearing his usual attire—a Brooks Brothers suit with a crisp white shirt and a boldly patterned tie. Over his shoulder he carried a suit bag, and even though this was a pleasure trip, she'd venture to say his briefcase was in his other hand, hidden in the press of the crowd. The minute he saw Meridee, his eyes lit up and he gave her a smile that had a strange power over her heart.

As he finally worked his way through the gate, she saw that besides his briefcase, he carried a bouquet of cut flowers. He was the most handsome, the most romantic-looking man she had ever seen step off a plane, and she suddenly felt insecure about her relationship with him. Instead of throwing herself into his arms and kissing him, she simply smiled and said, "Welcome back."

Zeb had no such reservations and bent over to place a soft kiss on her lips before handing her the flowers. "These are for you."

She smiled warmly. "Thank you. They're lovely."

"Thank you for the houseplant. It's purifying the air in my living room," he said with a twinkle in his eye. Then he placed one more quick kiss on her lips and said, "I missed you."

She chuckled nervously. "It's only been thirty-six hours."

"The longest thirty-six hours I've ever spent," he confessed, gazing down at her with a warmth in his eyes that made her entire body feel overheated. He ushered her away from the other passengers and out onto the concourse. "How are you feeling?"

"I'm fine," she told him, ignoring the twinge of guilt that rippled through her.

"Thank goodness. All day long I had this terrible premonition that you were going to call me and tell me not to come."

The twinge became a pang. "I'm glad you're here. I would have been disappointed if you hadn't come." As she spoke the words aloud, she realized they were true, and the guilt disappeared.

"The only thing that could have kept me away would have been you being sick. You're sure you're okay?"

She couldn't stem the rush of pleasure that flowed through her as his eyes raked over her in a possessive manner. "Umm-hmm. Do you have any other luggage?'' she asked as they approached the escalator to the baggage-claim area.

"Unfortunately, I do. When I leave here Sunday I'm returning to Cincinnati, so I had to bring an extra suitcase,'' he explained as they rode the moving ramp down to the lower level.

"Maybe I should get the car and meet you out front?'' she suggested.

"If you'll take my briefcase, I can carry this and my other suitcase,'' he told her, gesturing to the suit bag slung over his shoulder.

In only a few minutes they were through the baggage claim and had his luggage stored in the trunk of her car. As soon as they had seated themselves in the Geo, Zeb pulled her into his arms and kissed her in a very thorough manner.

"There,'' he said when he finally ended the kiss. "I wanted to do that the minute I saw you, but I had my arms full.''

His lazy, intimate smile made her catch her breath. She kissed him a second time, then buried her face in his shoulder, hugging him tightly to her. All day she had been wishing he wouldn't show up, but now that he was here, she didn't want to let him out of her sight.

"It's going to be a great weekend,'' he promised, his lips close to her ear.

His body was firm and strong, giving her a sense of comfort as she clung to his shoulders. "It's going to be hot,'' she said, referring to the warm, humid air that had air conditioners throughout the city set at full power. "I hope you don't mind, but there's been a change in sleeping arrangements.''

"You want me to go to a hotel?"

She shook her head. "No, to my mother's. She has the pool, so you'll be able to swim whenever you like."

He lifted her chin with his finger. "I'm sure there's a good reason for the change of plans, but I'd rather be staying with you."

Meridee sighed. "I wish you were staying with me, too. When Mom suggested that you could be her houseguest instead of mine, it seemed like an easy answer to an awkward situation with Brenda. Now I'm sorry I agreed." Meridee straightened in her seat and stuck the key in the ignition.

Zeb reached over to run the back of his fingers across her cheek. "It'll all work out. I might not be able to wake up next to you in the morning, but we'll still be together."

Together. The word echoed in Meridee's mind often during the next forty-eight hours, for she and Zeb were seldom apart. Except for the fact that they didn't sleep together, Meridee got a taste of what it would be like to be living with Zeb. Although Kate fixed breakfast for him on Saturday morning, he spent the rest of the day at Meridee's.

Worried that she wasn't completely recovered from the flu, Zeb insisted they spend the day relaxing. After the two of them had taken a swim in her mother's pool, he hooked up her garden hose and washed her car while she rested in the shade of an oak tree, a glass of lemonade in her hand. They ate lunch on the picnic table in her backyard, then, clad in shorts and T-shirts, headed over to Como Park, where they strolled hand in hand through the zoo. Before returning home, Zeb

bought her an ice cream cone and rented a bicycle built
for two so he could pedal her around the lake.

On Saturday night, they helped to celebrate Kate's
and Donovan's birthdays at an elegant hotel that not
only had a first-class dining room, but a dance floor
featuring big band music. Throughout the evening,
Meridee had difficulty keeping her eyes off Zeb, the
subject of the baby never far from her thoughts. Because Donovan's son Rodney had a reputation for
playing pranks on his father's birthday, everyone was
surprised when the evening ended without any singing
telegrams or surprise guests.

To Meridee's relief, there were no family activities
planned for Sunday, not even the traditional family
dinner. Kate and Donovan had been invited to spend
the day in Wisconsin with friends who were celebrating their silver wedding anniversary, her grandparents
were attending a senior-citizens' picnic at Minnehaha
Falls and Brenda had decided to go with Ross and Juliet, who were taking Sara and Annie to Valleyfair
Amusement Park.

Meridee and Zeb found themselves truly alone for
the first time all weekend. As he sat stretched out on
her sofa reading the Sunday newspaper, she thought of
how natural he looked lounging in her living room.
What would it be like to live with him in the same
house twenty-four hours a day, three hundred and
sixty-five days a year?

She was lost in domestic daydreams when she heard
Zeb ask, "Have you ever thought about taking her to
dog obedience school?"

"What?"

"Vanna. Have you considered dog obedience training?" he repeated as the bichon bounced into the living room with one of Meridee's shoes in her mouth.

"She's been through dog obedience," Meridee said archly.

"Oh." Zeb's smile was sheepish.

As if to prove her point, Meridee said in a commanding tone of voice, "Vanna, release."

As she expected, Vanna didn't release the shoe, but continued to chew. Meridee repeated the command, then finally walked over to the dog and yanked the shoe from her mouth.

"Maybe you should try another school," Zeb suggested, hiding his grin.

She turned to face Zeb in a defensive stance. "Small dogs are much harder to train than large ones."

"I didn't know that," he said, getting up from the sofa and moving closer to Meridee. As he bent his head to hers, Vanna growled. "Is she going to do that every time I want to get closer to you?"

Meridee shrugged. "I don't know. I'll put her in the other room."

"No, wait." Zeb put his hand on her arm. "She's probably not going to get over her jealousy of me if you put her away every time I'm around. Why don't you just let her run around? If she barks, she barks."

"I suppose we could try it," she said hesitantly.

"It'll be fine. Pretty soon she won't care if I do this." He kissed her intimately. "Or this." He cupped a breast and kissed her again.

Vanna continued to bark, and Zeb finally said, "Maybe we should take her for a walk."

"Are you sure you don't mind?" She looked at him rather apprehensively. "Vanna's not very big."

"Do I look like the kind of guy who only walks with dogs that are over four feet tall and bring back dead animals?" he asked.

Meridee grinned and handed him the leash. But even after a leisurely walk around the lake, during which Zeb fiercely protected her from what Meridee labeled monster dogs, Vanna became no more fond of him, and the barking continued. Zeb and Meridee were able to ignore it until they were lying in her bed and Vanna sat on the other side of the bedroom door howling at being exiled from Meridee's room.

"Maybe you'd better lock her up," Zeb conceded in defeat, as he rolled his naked body away from Meridee's.

With a groan, Meridee climbed out of bed and slipped on her robe. She could hear Zeb mumbling something indistinguishable as she opened the door. Before she could scoop the tiny dog up in her arms, Vanna went streaking past, zipping around the room as though she were running on a racetrack. Zeb bent down to try to corral her, but she evaded his grasp, running down the hall and into the bathroom.

Meridee quickly shut the door on the dog. "Maybe I should just leave her in there," she said.

"She'll bark," Zeb growled.

"You're right." Meridee opened the door, and out came Vanna, her teeth clenching an empty box.

Up onto the bed she leaped, her prize held firmly between her jaws. It was Zeb who managed to get hold of her.

"Looks like she's been in your trash," he observed, prying the box from Vanna's teeth.

Meridee swallowed with difficulty, her heartbeat accelerating. The box that Vanna had dug out of the garbage was the one that had contained the in-home pregnancy test. She hurried over to the bed and tried to take the box from Zeb's hands before he had a chance to read what it said.

She wasn't fast enough. From the look on his face she knew immediately that he had seen enough of the mangled print to know what had been in the box.

"I'll be right back," Meridee said soberly, picking up the bichon and carrying her from the room.

When she returned, Zeb was getting dressed. As soon as he saw her, he asked, "Are you pregnant?"

It never even crossed Meridee's mind to tell him anything but the truth. "It appears that I am. The test was positive, but I haven't seen a doctor yet."

Zeb let his shoe drop to the floor. "You told me you were on the pill."

"I am. I was." She threw up her hands helplessly. "It's a long story."

"I think I'm entitled to hear it."

He was angry. Not happy. Not sympathetic. Not concerned. Just angry. She thought that it was a good thing she was numb, or else she might have reacted just as angrily and then they'd be fighting, resolving nothing.

She sank down beside him on the bed and quietly explained how she came to be in such a predicament, unaware that her eyes were silently pleading for support. Zeb didn't get the message. He couldn't, for the shock of discovering that he was going to be a father left his insides feelings like a pumpkin carved too many days before Halloween.

"You told me you didn't want any kids," he said in an accusing tone.

"I don't! You're acting as though this was something I planned." She swallowed the lump of emotion in her throat and said, "It was an accident."

He raked a hand across his forehead. "If only I'd known. I could have used something."

Meridee felt sick. This wasn't how it was supposed to be between two people who were having a baby. Remorse. Regret. Unhappiness. Tears fell onto her cheeks and she buried her face in her pillow.

Zeb tenderly lifted her into his arms, whispering belated words of comfort. Meridee wanted no part of it. "Why don't you just go back to New York and leave me alone?" she cried irrationally.

"Meri, please don't cry. I'm sorry," he said, refusing to allow her to pull away from him. "This is a real shock to me."

"How do you suppose I feel? I'm the one having the baby," she mumbled into his shirt.

"I know," he murmured, brushing his hand across the silky smoothness of her hair. "It's a shock for both of us."

After only a few moments, she lifted her head and straightened up. "Look at me. I'm a sniveling mess."

Actually Zeb thought she looked rather charming. Seeing her so red-eyed and vulnerable made his anger slowly dissolve.

"You're not a mess." He kissed her on the fore-head, as if she were a child. "You could never be a mess in my eyes."

"Don't say such things or I'm going to start crying again," she warned, reaching for a tissue on the night-stand.

Zeb stood and shoved his hands in his pockets. "All right. We have a problem here we need to solve. We're two intelligent adults—we can work this out."

All afternoon, Zeb kept repeating those words to Meridee, trying to convince himself as well as her that they would find an acceptable solution. The more he thought about her carrying his child, the closer he felt to her, yet ever since she had admitted she was preg-nant, she appeared to withdraw and become more dis-tant. Although they had discussed practically nothing else the remainder of the day, he still wasn't sure how she really felt about the baby, and it was with a strange sense of relief and sadness that he boarded the plane to Cincinnati on Sunday evening.

He wondered why he suddenly felt as though his life had become a riddle. The answer came to him while he was somewhere high above the clouds heading east on the jumbo jet. He was in love with Meridee. It was why he hadn't been able to get a decent night's sleep during the past three weeks. It was why he found himself thinking about her night and day. And it was why he wanted to be with her. Always.

The realization took his breath away. Until now, he had felt in control of his destiny, yet suddenly he felt unsure of himself. He looked at the pile of papers in his briefcase and thought about how meaningless they were compared to his feelings for Meridee.

He leaned back and closed his eyes, oddly at peace with himself. In his mind he conjured up a picture of domestic tranquility. The scene was his condo in New York. Meridee was there, a baby in her arms, welcoming him home after a hard day at the office. It was a scene he wanted to replay again and again. He smiled to himself as he thought of how unlikely it was that Meridee would want to become June Cleaver.

It didn't matter. He didn't want to become Ward Cleaver, either. But he did want Meridee in his life, and in a very traditional way. He wanted her for his wife. The challenge facing him was to convince her that she wanted him to be her husband.

Although Zeb would have liked to wait until he saw her again to declare his intentions, he couldn't resist calling her on Monday evening. She sounded surprised to hear his voice, which made him all the more insecure about her feelings for him.

Instead of asking him questions of a personal nature, she launched into the subject of his work in Cincinnati, as though their only connection was a professional one. He could have been talking to Griggs, so detached was her voice, and it didn't take long for Zeb to become impatient with her.

"Meridee, I didn't call to talk about business," he finally told her. "I called because I wanted to tell you I've been doing a lot of thinking."

"Oh?"

Again, her tone was cool, and his annoyance grew. "Yeah, and I figured that if I've been doing a lot of

thinking, you've probably been doing a lot of thinking, too. Am I right?''

''What are you trying to say, Zeb?'' she asked.

He took a deep breath, then blurted out, ''I want to
be a father to your baby, Meri, and not just in name
only and not from a thousand miles away. I want us to
get married.''

''Married?''

The way she repeated the word made it sound as
though he had suggested she grow a second head.

''I didn't want to do this over the telephone, but I'm
not sure when I'm going to be able to return to St. Paul
and I needed to tell you how I feel about you.'' He
paused, then said tenderly, ''I love you, Meridee.''

He thought he heard her gasp, and there was a pause
before she said, ''I love you, too, Zeb.''

''You do?'' His spirits lifted.

''Yes, I do. But that doesn't mean we should get
married.''

''Then what does it mean?''

Meridee sighed. ''We haven't known each other long
enough to be contemplating marriage.''

''What? Are there guidelines as to when it's proper
to discuss marriage?'' he asked, controlling his temper
with difficulty.

''No, but the only reason you're even suggesting it
is because of the baby.''

He regretted bringing up the subject during a phone
conversation. He should have waited until he could be
alone with her, when he'd be able to hold her in his
arms and convince her that what he said was true. ''I'm

suggesting it because I love you and I want to spend the rest of my life with you.''

''I don't see how that's going to be possible when you live and work in New York and I'm in St. Paul,'' she stated pragmatically.

Frustration welled up inside him. ''You wouldn't have any trouble getting a similar position with Denton in New York. Or if you wanted to stay home with the baby, I do make enough money that we could live comfortably on one income.''

''Zeb, I told you right from the start that I wasn't a traditional woman. I'm not into this housewife business. I couldn't stand being home every day grinding peas and carrots into baby mush. I have a career.''

''I wasn't suggesting you become a housewife if you don't want to. There are lots of marriages in which both parents work and the child goes to day-care.''

''Day-care? I don't want to leave my baby at a day-care center in New York.''

''They're no different from the day-care centers in St. Paul.''

''Maybe not, but I haven't even decided if day-care is what I want for my baby.''

''You just told me you're going to keep working after the baby is born. What alternative is there?''

''I don't know,'' she snapped. ''I've only known I was pregnant four days, I haven't got this figured out yet.''

Zeb was fast losing what little patience he still possessed. He found her attitude extremely annoying. She claimed she loved him, yet she was behaving as though she didn't want him taking part in the decisions that

272 SWINGING ON A STAR

would affect his child. "New York isn't all that much different from St. Paul."

"You're forgetting I have Vanna," she reminded him.

"Pets are allowed in my complex."

"But what would she do all day? You don't have a yard for her to run around in. She'd have to be shut in all the time."

Zeb heaved a sigh of frustration. "We could take her for walks. People do walk their pets in New York," he said tersely.

"She'd probably get attacked by some monstrous watchdog," she grumbled.

He sighed again. "Look, I can see that this was a mistake. We shouldn't be discussing this over the phone. I'm sorry I even mentioned getting married. Why don't we wait until we're together before we make any plans for the future?"

"When will that be?"

"Probably not for a couple of weeks."

"That long?"

Zeb couldn't figure her out. Just when he was expecting her to tell him she wanted some time away from him to think through their situation, she sounded as though she couldn't wait for him to return.

"You know where to reach me if you need me, but in the meantime will you think about what I said?" he asked.

"Yes, of course," she promised. "I'd better go. I'm giving a board presentation this afternoon."

Zeb told her he'd call her later in the week, then said goodbye. As he hung up the receiver, he sat staring at the phone, slowly shaking his head. Never had he imagined that when the day came and he proposed marriage to the woman he loved, he would do it over the phone—and be rejected in such a maddening way.

Meridee, too, was feeling stunned by their conversation. Even though the subject of marriage had crossed her mind, now that it had crossed Zeb's mind as well, it seemed too preposterous to consider. She knew that she had been short with him on the phone, but she knew that had she not told him she were pregnant, the subject of marriage wouldn't have come up. At least not now.

They needed more time. Time to really get to know each other. Time to work out a realistic solution to their job situations. Time to choose what they wanted their future to hold.

Everything was moving too fast—including her emotions. Besides having to accept the fact that she was going to be a mother, she had to deal with her feelings for Zeb. Never before had she loved anyone the way she loved him, and it left her feeling terribly vulnerable.

Ingrid's words echoed in her mind. *You can't love someone without taking a risk.* The question she had to answer was whether or not she was ready to risk not only her life, but her baby's as well.

The following morning Griggs called her into his office to inform her that Paul Morton, an executive from Denton Diversified, was visiting the Krystalene plant and wanted to speak to her privately in the boardroom. Thinking that she was going to be questioned about the quarterly financial reports, Meridee was taken aback when Morton offered her a position with Denton headquarters in New York.

Under any other circumstances she would have been flattered by the offer. But after her conversation with Zeb the day before, she couldn't help but wonder if he had set her up for a promotion with the home office. The more she thought about it, the more likely it seemed. She stormed back to her office, shut the door and called Zeb at his hotel in Cincinnati.

"I'm glad you called," Zeb said as soon as he heard her voice. "I miss you."

Meridee didn't hear the love and affection in his words. Instead, she leaped to the attack. "Paul Morton was here from the home office," she said accusingly.

"I know. Did the two of you get a chance to talk?"

"If you knew he was coming, you must know he offered me a position in the finance department at Denton's corporate offices."

"No, I didn't know, but that's great news!" he said. "Congratulations."

There was a brief silence, then she said, "I'm not taking the job, Zeb."

"You're not taking it?" He was completely bewildered. "Meridee, it isn't every day the senior vice-president in charge of finance at a firm the size of Denton offers you a promotion. I know you're close to your family and it would be difficult to move away from them, but this could be the opportunity of a lifetime."

"It's not because of my family that I'm turning it down," she said stiffly.

"Then what is it? We've talked about career goals. I thought this was what you wanted."

"What I wanted was to earn my promotion."

"What are you talking about?" he asked, puzzled.

"You arranged for me to get this job, didn't you?"

"If you mean did I write a glowing evaluation of your job performance at Krystalene, then the answer's yes. But if you're thinking I pulled strings with the New York office so you'd get the job, you're wrong."

"You had nothing to do with me being offered this job?" she asked skeptically.

"I told you, I recommended you as someone who possessed the right qualifications for advancement in the corporate structure. I didn't call the home office and tell them I wanted you to be transferred to New York if that's what you're thinking."

It was exactly what she had been thinking, but she didn't want to admit it. "I don't want to be given a promotion because of my connections."

He chuckled sardonically. "You're giving me too much credit. What happened to that self-confident, ambitious woman I worked with in St. Paul?"

Meridee had been asking herself that same question lately and hadn't been able to come up with an answer. Now that her relationship with Zeb was connected to her work, she found herself lacking confidence professionally as well as personally.

Maybe she needed a vacation, she thought wearily as she turned off her computer and locked her desk for the night. A few days away from her job might regenerate her sagging self-confidence and give her time to make some decisions about the future. On her way out of the building, she stopped by Griggs's office and did something totally out of character. She told him she was taking the rest of the week off.

CHAPTER FOURTEEN

TUESDAY NIGHT MERIDEE sat making a list of things she wanted to accomplish during the next three days. In no time at all she had filled a sheet of paper with all the things she hadn't had time to do: visit the library, go to a specialty shop that sold designer dog fashions, lunch with an old college friend who had been living in Chicago but had recently moved back to St. Paul . . .

"I'll be lucky if I get to do half of this," she told Vanna as she attached the list to the side of the refrigerator with a magnet. As she glanced out her kitchen window, she noticed that Juliet and Ross's van was parked in her mother's driveway. It served as a reminder that this was the last night Donovan and Kate were going to be home, for they were leaving for a long-overdue vacation. Donovan was speaking at an awards banquet for police officers in Duluth, Minnesota, after which he and Kate were planning to travel up the North Shore, where they would spend a few days at a resort on Lake Superior.

Wanting to say goodbye, Meridee slipped on a pair of sandals and walked over to their home. When she arrived, Brenda was outside with her nieces trying to fly a kite, while Ross, Juliet, Kate and Donovan sat around the kitchen table drinking coffee. From the looks on their faces Meridee wondered if Juliet had said something to them about her pregnancy.

However, she soon discovered the real reason for the grim expressions on their faces. As Donovan pulled up an extra chair, Kate rose to get her a cup of coffee, saying, "Ross and Juliet have had some bad news."

Meridee looked at her sister. "What is it?"

"Ross's mother's been in an accident," Juliet said quietly.

"How serious?"

"Serious enough that they suggested Ross fly out to be with her," Juliet answered.

Meridee reached across the table and covered her brother-in-law's hand. "Oh, Ross. I'm sorry."

Ross accepted her sympathy with a tired smile. "The doctors are hopeful, but I need to be there for her."

"Of course you do," Meridee agreed. "Both of you should go." She glanced at her sister. "You are going, aren't you?"

"I'd like to, but I can't. There's no one to stay with the girls," Juliet replied uneasily.

"What about Brenda?" Meridee asked.

"She has to drive Grandma and Grandpa down to Rochester on Friday," Juliet explained. "Grandpa needs to have his leg checked by the doctors at the Mayo Clinic and I don't want him to miss his appointment. You know how long he's been waiting to get in."

Meridee nodded in understanding, and Kate said, "I've offered to postpone our trip, but Juliet won't even listen to me."

"I can't let you do it. You and Donovan work too hard to cancel your vacation just to baby-sit my kids," Juliet insisted.

"I agree," Meridee said. "You shouldn't cancel your plans. Besides, it's not necessary. I can stay with the girls."

"You?" Kate and Juliet looked at her in astonishment.

"Yes, me. What's wrong? Don't you think I can handle two little girls?" she asked, her hands on her hips.

"What about your job?" Juliet said.

"It's not a problem. I'm on vacation for the rest of the week."

"Since when?" Juliet asked suspiciously.

"Since I decided it would be nice to take a few days off and get a little rest and relaxation," Meridee answered, ignoring the curious glances that were being sent her way.

"There won't be any of that with Sara and Annie," Juliet warned her, looking at her over the rim of her cup.

Meridee shrugged. "A change is as good as a rest, and taking care of two little girls can't be any more stressful than working for Griggs." She didn't miss the knowing glances her sister and her mother exchanged. "I can handle it."

Juliet remained apprehensive. "Are you sure you want to do this?"

"Of course I want to do this. You're my family, and if you can't count on family, who can you count on?"

Juliet and Ross appeared to be both relieved and grateful. After they had gone, Donovan excused himself to make a phone call, leaving Meridee alone with her mother.

"Why don't you want me taking care of Sara and Annie?" Meridee asked as Kate got up to refill their mugs.

"I never said I didn't want you to stay with them," Kate replied.

"You didn't have to. I could see it on your face. You don't think I can handle the job, do you? You think I lack the maternal instincts you and Juliet have," she said, hoping her tone didn't betray her insecurity.

"I think you have the same maternal instincts every other woman has. You just choose to ignore them," Kate answered, softening her words with a smile.

"You're wrong, Mother. I don't have any maternal instincts." She looked at her hands as she wrapped them around her coffee mug. "I wish I did, but I don't." Without any warning, tears spilled over onto her cheeks.

Kate slid over onto the chair next to hers and put an arm around her. "Meridee, what's wrong?"

"It's true, Mom. I don't have any maternal instincts," she cried, taking off her glasses to wipe at her eyes. "I want to have it. I should have it, but I don't. I'm de . . . defective," she hiccupped.

"You're not defective. Not one tiny bit," Kate said in a soothing voice. "You're bright and compassionate and so very special. What you've accomplished would make any mother proud." She handed her a tissue. "And contrary to what you may think, you do have maternal instincts. You just haven't had any reason for them to surface."

Meridee blew her nose. "Well, they'd better hurry up and make their presence known or I'm in big trouble."

Kate smiled gently and patted her hand. "You'll do just fine with Sara and Annie—with or without your maternal instincts. Just be yourself and everything will work out fine."

"It's not Sara and Annie I'm concerned about," Meridee said quietly.

Puzzled, Kate shook her head. "Then what is it? What's bothering you, dear?"

Meridee chewed on her lower lip as she sought the courage to tell her mother her news. "Mom, I'm pregnant."

Meridee had never seen her mother look so totally taken aback as she did at that moment. "Aren't you going to say something?" she asked.

"I don't know what to say," Kate answered, her face pale.

"It's all right," Meridee acknowledged with an understanding nod. "I felt that way at first, too. I was numb for days."

"I know this couldn't be something you planned."

Meridee's mouth twisted wryly. "No, it wasn't. This definitely isn't something I wanted to happen at this time in my life."

"Then how did it happen? I've always tried to respect your privacy, but I have to ask you—weren't you using any birth control?"

"Of course I was. Gosh, Mom, I'm not stupid," she snapped.

"I don't appreciate that tone of voice, Meridee," Kate said severely.

"I'm sorry. I didn't mean to bite your head off." Meridee sighed, rubbing two fingers across her forehead. "I was taking birth control pills, but I messed up on the sequence," she said, ignoring Brenda's part in the mix-up.

"Does Zeb know?"

Meridee nodded. "He found out last weekend."

"And what was his reaction?"

She frowned at the memory. "He wasn't very happy with the news. I thought that maybe after he left here I wouldn't hear from him again, but he called me the next day and told me he thinks we should get married."

"And how do you feel about that?"

"I don't want any man marrying me out of a sense of obligation," Meridee said, her back straightening with pride.

"You don't think he loves you?"

"Yes, but..." She didn't finish her sentence, unsure as to what her objections were to his proposal. "All I know is that this baby thing is complicating everything."

"Do you love *him?*" Kate asked, her eyes filled with compassion.

"I think I do, Mom, but..."

"Not enough to marry him? Is that what you're trying to say?" Kate looked at her inquisitively.

Meridee threw up her hands in frustration. "I don't know what I'm saying. I don't even know what I'm thinking anymore. I'm so confused, Mom."

"Of course you are. You're facing some pretty difficult decisions."

She turned her eyes to Kate in an appeal. "What would you do if you were me?"

"Meridee, I can't tell you what to do," Kate said gently. "And you don't really want me to, do you?"

She slowly shook her head. "I guess not. This is something I'm going to have to work through on my own."

"Don't forget about Zeb," Kate reminded her.

How could she tell her mother that Zeb was the biggest part of the problem? That her sudden inexplicable need to have a man in her life was frightening her just as much as the thought of having a baby?

"It'll probably be good for me to be with Sara and Annie. Maybe it'll help me take my mind off everything."

"It'll also give you a taste of what it's like to be a mom. I think you're going to discover you have something very special to give children," Kate said with a smile.

Meridee reached over to squeeze her mother's hand. "I can always count on a good healthy dose of optimism whenever I talk to you."

Kate returned her smile. "That's what moms are for. Remember that for future reference."

BY THE END OF HER FIRST day with Sara and Annie, Meridee was certain that her mother was wrong; she had definitely been shortchanged in the maternal instincts department. Despite the list of helpful hints Juliet had left for her, she managed to forget about Sara's swimming lesson and Annie's nap, which made both girls cranky and temperamental on the very first day of her visit.

She had always prided herself on being fairly competent in the kitchen, but then she had never catered to the demands of a seven-year-old and a three-year-old. Juliet hadn't told her that bread needed to be sliced diagonally instead of vertically, or that apples with the peel intact would cause little noses to wrinkle in distaste.

Nor had Juliet mentioned to her that in the game of Chutes and Ladders, Annie's marker could skip squares and Sara could have "overs" if she didn't like her spin. Or that Annie wouldn't go to sleep unless her covers were folded back so that the kittens on her sheet were visible. And Sara needed to put each of her dolls to bed before she could go to bed herself.

Before Juliet left, she had told Meridee that Sara had planned a pajama party for five of her friends. It was to be a camp-out in the backyard with all six sleeping in the big blue nylon tent Ross had erected before he left. When Juliet had suggested she postpone the party, Meridee had insisted she could handle six seven-year-olds telling ghost stories in a tent in the backyard. However, after her calamitous first day on the job, Meridee decided to play it safe and called Brenda to see if she would help out.

Meridee heaved a sigh of relief when shortly after dinner her sister showed up with a sleeping bag in hand.

"Where are they?" Brenda asked, grabbing a handful of the popcorn Meridee had just buttered.

"They're already outside in the tent staking out their territory," Meridee answered, filling the hot-air popper with more corn. "Boy, am I glad to see you."

"You look worn out. Do you feel okay?" Brenda eyed her curiously.

Meridee wiped her forehead on her shirtsleeve and said, "I'm tired. I can't believe how much work two little girls can be. And Juliet must spend half of her life in the car. It's take them to swimming, take them to dancing lessons, take them to 'tiny tots' in the park." She blew out a big gust of air. "I don't know how she does it."

"Maybe it's those vitamins she takes," Brenda suggested. "And she does eat a lot of health foods."

Meridee sat down for a minute, clutching her side. "It doesn't help that I have this pain in my side, either." She gently rubbed the area right below her waist.

"Aw, come on, Meridee. You're not going to pull a lame number on me, are you?" Brenda protested. "You said you needed help and I came. I wasn't expecting to have to take over."

"You won't have to take over, but one of us needs to sleep in the house with Annie and one of us needs to sleep in the tent with the girls." Meridee gave her sister the most pathetic look she could muster. "And I really do have a pain in my side...."

"And it might as well be me who sleeps outside, right?" Brenda finished for her.

"You did bring your sleeping bag," Meridee pointed out.

"All right, all right," Brenda conceded. "I'll sleep outside, but I do need to get *some* sleep tonight. Don't forget, I'm driving Grandma and Grandpa down to Rochester tomorrow morning."

"Do you honestly think that six seven-year-olds will last very long out there in the dark?" Meridee asked with a lift of one eyebrow.

Brenda shrugged. "We used to do it when we were kids."

"That's why I expect them to end up sleeping on the living room floor. We never made it through an entire night outside. Someone would hear a dog howl, and the next thing you knew it was a wolf's cry and we'd all scramble to get inside."

"Yeah, or else a cricket would find its way into the tent and frighten us out," Brenda mused. "All right. Give me the popcorn. I'll go join the little campers." She picked up the bowl of popcorn and started toward the door, then stopped. "Oh, I almost forgot to tell you. Zeb called today."

Meridee's heart began to hammer against her chest. "Did you tell him I was over here?"

"Umm-hmm. He told me to tell you he'd talk to you on Sunday."

"Didn't you give him Juliet's number?"

"Yes, I did, but for your information, he didn't call to talk to you, Meridee. He wanted to speak to me."

Immediately suspicious, Meridee asked, "What about?"

"He wanted to know if I had had any luck in finding another job." Brenda nonchalantly munched on the buttered popcorn.

"And what did you tell him?"

"I told him the truth." She popped another handful of popcorn in her mouth. "And it's a good thing I did."

"Why do you say that?"

"Because if he'd thought I'd found another job, he wouldn't have made his offer."

"What offer?"

"He said he'd try to arrange for me to get rehired at Krystalene."

"Leave it to Zeb to arrange jobs for people," Meridee said sarcastically.

"You don't think he'll do it?"

"Oh, he'll do it all right," she said.

"The thing is, it would only be on a part-time basis."

"Part time?"

"Mm-hm. That's part of the deal I had to make."

"What kind of deal?" Meridee asked.

"I agreed to return to the university to get a business degree. Zeb said he'll try to get me on some sort of work-study program. Apparently in New York, the employees who work for Denton are able to get their college tuition reimbursed if they're pursuing degrees that will help them in their work."

"And that's what he wants to happen at Krysta-lene?" Meridee asked, her attitude softening toward him.

"Yup. He said he's already recommended that the program be initiated at Krystalene. All that's needed is board approval from Denton."

Meridee could hardly believe he had done such a wonderful thing for her sister. And here she had practically accused him of causing her psychological damage! "I thought you didn't want to return to school," she remarked, still dumbfounded by Brenda's news.

"At first I didn't, but when Zeb was here last weekend he told me how important it was to have a college degree. I realized that I'm only fooling myself if I think I can get ahead without an education," she said, sounding more mature than she ever had in the past.

"When did he talk to you about the importance of a college education?"

"When we were dancing together at Mom and Donovan's party."

Meridee thought back to the night of the party and shook her head wistfully. She remembered watching Zeb dance with Brenda and thinking that Brenda was probably giving him a bad time. Seeing the serious looks on their faces, she had wanted to cut in, but decided to let the two of them work out their differences. Now she realized how wise that decision had been.

"He really is a smart man, Meridee," Brenda stated ardently, as if Meridee needed to be convinced. "If I were you, I'd keep my mouth shut about all those crazy ideas you have about not wanting to get married. The popper's empty," she reminded her, looking over her shoulder.

Meridee pulled the plug from the popper and was about to carry the second bowl of popcorn outside when the pain in her side became excruciating. "Ouch," she cried, doubling over.

"Are you sure you're all right?" Brenda asked, setting her bowl down on the table and coming to her sister's aid.

Meridee straightened with difficulty, then limped over to the refrigerator and pulled out six cans of soda. "Here. Take the pop outside. I'm going to stretch out on the sofa for a few minutes and see if I can't get rid of this." She left the room clutching her side.

Rest, however, did nothing to alleviate her discomfort. As the pain settled in the lower right-hand part of her abdomen, she knew that she needed a doctor.

"Brenda, quick! Get in here!" she called when she heard the back door open.

Brenda came rushing into the living room with Sara, Annie and a swarm of other little girls. They all gathered around Meridee's writhing figure, staring with open mouths.

"Meridee! What's wrong?" Brenda's eyes widened at the sight of her sister in such obvious agony.

"The pain is awful. I can't stand it. You're going to have to take me to the hospital," she replied, her voice thick with distress.

"To the hospital?" Brenda looked completely bewildered, standing statue-still.

"Yes, to the hospital. Get your keys." Suddenly Meridee realized the house was full of children. "Oh, forget it. Someone has to stay with the kids. I'll drive myself," she said, but the minute she tried to stand, she saw how impossible it would be. "I can't do it!" she cried. "It hurts too much."

Brenda snapped her fingers, and her face lit up. "I know. I'll call Gran. She'll send Grandpa George over," she said, pleased with her idea. Neither one of them noticed that Sara had walked over to the telephone and was already speaking into the receiver.

"Sara, who are you calling?" Brenda demanded as she went to use the phone.

"I dialed 911. My mom told me that if there's ever an emergency and she's sick I'm supposed to do that," she said in what had to be the calmest voice in the room. "Auntie Meridee's real sick."

AUNTIE MERIDEE *was* real sick, and all the way to the hospital she couldn't help but worry that her trouble had something to do with the baby. The minute the paramedics arrived she had told them she was pregnant. They immediately suspected that her acute abdominal pain was the result of an ectopic pregnancy. They explained to her on the way to the hospital that her fertilized egg, which should have been implanted in her womb, might have lodged itself in her fallopian tube. If that were the case, she would have to undergo surgery.

Meridee did end up having to sign a consent form for surgery, but not because of an ectopic pregnancy. Further tests and an examination at the hospital emergency room revealed that, contrary to what Meridee believed, there was no fetus growing inside her.

An inflamed appendix was causing the excruciating pain she was experiencing. Shortly before midnight she was wheeled into the operating room, where doctors removed her swollen appendix. The only relatives at the hospital were her grandmother and Grandpa George, who finally left after the doctor assured them Meridee had come through the surgery just fine and wouldn't awaken before morning.

Kate and Donovan stopped by the hospital first thing the next day, having cut short their trip as soon as Brenda telephoned them with the news of Meridee's operation. Still groggy from the anesthesia, Meridee didn't say much, but she squeezed her mother's hand and told her not to worry. Seeing her daughter's fatigue, Kate advised the other members of the family to let Meridee get some rest before they visited her.

While Meridee slept, Zeb sat wide awake on a plane, worrying about her. He kept hearing Sara's words on the telephone. "Auntie Meridee's not here. She went to the hospital because she had a real bad pain in her tummy and they had to do a operation."

Immediately, the thought of miscarriage had leaped to Zeb's mind. He had tried to get Sara to put Brenda on the phone, but the call had been disconnected, and every time he had tried to call back, he got a busy signal. He had dialed Meridee's mother's number, but there had been no answer. Nor could he reach her grandmother.

So he had done the only logical thing a man in love could do. He had packed his bags and got on the first available flight to Minneapolis-St. Paul. While waiting to board the plane, he had gone down the list of hospitals in the Twin Cities, calling each one of them in an effort to find out where she was. Just seconds before they announced the final call for his flight, he located her. Unfortunately, the only information they would give him over the phone was that she was out of surgery and resting comfortably.

Now he was wondering what he was going to say to her when he saw her. If only he had reacted differently when she had told him she was pregnant. Instead of blaming her, he should have been more supportive. He raked a hand through his hair, regretting the way he had handled so many things in their relationship.

The important thing was that she was all right. Until he had gotten the news that she was in the hospital, he hadn't realized the extent of her importance to him. Baby or no baby, he wanted her to be his wife.

EXCEPT FOR A BURNING sensation in her abdomen, Meridee awoke feeling surprisingly well. It was such a relief to be rid of the agonizing pain, she didn't mind the slight discomfort of the aftereffects of surgery.

There was a bouquet of flowers in her room, and she vaguely remembered her mother's comforting presence. When the nurse came in to check her vital signs, she confirmed that her parents had stopped in earlier and had left a message for Meridee to call when she felt up to having visitors.

Not long afterward, the door opened and in walked Zeb. He was pale and unshaven and looked as if he hadn't slept in a week. He stood in the doorway as though he wasn't quite sure whether he should be there. "Are you all right?" he asked.

"I'm a little sore, but I'm going to be fine," she told him, smiling weakly. "Come on in."

He came over to the bed then, studying her face as though he were trying to read something written there.

"You can sit on the bed if you want," she told him, and he carefully eased his body down beside her.

They sat staring at each other, until finally he took her into his arms with infinite tenderness. "Being so far away from you at a time like this was the worst thing I've ever been through," he murmured in her ear. It was the first time she had ever heard uncertainty in his voice, and she patted his back reassuringly.

"I know. But everything's fine now, and I'm going to be okay," she whispered.

He held her for several minutes, neither one speaking, until finally he set her back against the pillows.

"How did you get here so quickly?" she asked.

"I called Juliet's house and talked to Sara. When she said you were in the hospital, I took the first plane I could get on." There were stress lines on his face, and Meridee wished that she could erase them with her fingertips.

"It seems that Sara's quite a hero," she said with a smile. "She's the one who called 911 to get the ambulance. And it's a good thing she did. The doctor said the appendix was about to burst when they removed it."

"The appendix?" He gave her a puzzled look.

"I had an appendicitis attack. I thought you knew. Didn't you talk to Brenda?"

He shook his head. "Sara answered, and we were disconnected."

"So you came straight here not knowing what was wrong?" Suddenly she understood the reason for his anxiety.

He cupped her hand within his. "I thought you had had a miscarriage."

"Oh!"

"Does this mean the baby's okay?" His face lit up at the prospect, and Meridee felt a sudden sense of loss.

She looked down at their clasped hands. "There was no baby, Zeb," she said quietly. "I wasn't pregnant."

"But I don't understand."

She met his puzzled gaze. "I'm not sure I do, either. All I know is that when I got to the hospital last night they did a pregnancy test. It was negative." She looked down at her fingertips, thinking how ironic it was that when she was pregnant she didn't want to be, but now that she wasn't, she was disappointed.

Zeb didn't say anything, but simply rubbed a hand across the back of his neck. "We're not going to be parents."

She shook her head. "I spoke to one of the nurses about it this morning, and she told me that those in-home pregnancy tests are surprisingly accurate, but because I did mine at night instead of first thing in the morning, it might have given a false reading." Meridee found it embarrassing to explain how she had botched a simple five-minute test that held so much significance. She suddenly felt weepy, and a tear trickled down her cheek. "I'm sorry. I made a mess of everything."

"You don't need to apologize to me, Meri," Zeb said softly, wiping the tear away with his fingertip.

"I caused you some unnecessary anxiety," she said, sniffling.

"No worse than the anxiety I caused you over Brenda," he said penitently.

"It's not the same," she told him. "Besides, in my heart I know you did what was right."

"Well, it was an honest mistake on your part. I guess it'll just take me a while to adjust to the fact that you're *not* pregnant," he said.

"Are you sorry?" she asked, remembering how his face had lit up when he thought she hadn't lost the baby.

"I love you, Meri." He brought her hand to his lips and kissed it. "When you first told me you were going to have a baby, it was like a cold-water shock to my system. I felt like one of those guys who takes off all his clothes and jumps into the ocean in the middle of winter."

"You did look like you might turn blue," she teased lightly.

"After I started thinking about it, I discovered that I kind of liked the idea of becoming a father. I never thought I'd hear myself saying that out loud, but then I never met anyone like you before, Meri. I want to spend the rest of my life with you."

"Oh, Zeb." She wanted to tell him how she felt, but the words were stuck in her throat.

"I know you have your career and that you never planned on having a baby. I can live with that. I mean, I'd like children someday, but I'm not going to feel incomplete or anything if we don't have them. The im-

portant thing is that we have each other." He took both
of her hands and looked at her expectantly.

After swallowing several times, she finally found her
voice. "Does that mean you still want to get married?"

He grinned from ear to ear and reached inside his
pocket. "I brought something along just in case." He
handed her a jeweler's box.

Meridee opened the green velvet box and gasped.
Sitting inside was the most beautiful diamond solitaire
she had ever seen.

"Will you marry me, Meridee?" he asked as she
gazed in awe at the ring.

"What about our jobs?"

"I have it all figured out. If you don't want to work
for Denton, I'll apply for an assignment at Krystalene," he said, reaching into his pocket again. "And in
case you change your mind about living in New York,
I want you to look at this." He handed her a glossy
brochure.

She read the title out loud. "Doggie day-care?"

"It's just like children's day-care. The dogs get cared
for as if they were at home. There's social times, nap
time, training time . . . all sorts of wonderful animal
things," he assured her.

Meridee sat shaking her head. "I can't believe they
have doggie day-care."

"Why not? They have doggie toothpaste, doggie
designer fashions . . . even doggie braces," Zeb stated
dryly.

Meridee didn't know what to say. "Do you really
think it'll work?"

"The brochure says..."

"No, not the day-care," she interrupted him. "I was talking about us."

"It has to work, Meri. I love you too much for it not to work."

Her blue eyes were pensive, and she sat quietly for several seconds. "It's going to be risky," she said, breaking the silence.

A smile slowly spread across his face. "Is that a yes?"

Meridee smiled back and kissed him. They were interrupted by Brenda, who came bouncing into the room.

"All right, all right. None of that in here," she scolded. "There are sick people around."

"You're just in time to hear the good news," Zeb announced, getting up from Meridee's bed. He held her hand up so that the diamond was visible. "We're getting married."

"Just in time," Brenda said with a grin. "Meridee's going to need a new roommate when I go back to school."

EPILOGUE

"I THOUGHT YOU ONLY CRIED at weddings," Meridee said as she handed her mother a tissue.

"It's the christening of her first grandson. She should be a little misty-eyed," Brenda answered as Kate dabbed at the corner of her eye.

Kate smiled. "It is a joyous occasion," she said as she watched Donovan snap pictures of Juliet and Ross with their newborn son, Joshua Michael. They were in the church where all three of Kate's daughters had been christened, and were once more gathered to celebrate a new member joining the family.

"They do look happy, don't they?" Meridee remarked, looking on as Sara and Annie fussed over the tiny bundle in their mother's arms, grinning gleefully for the camera.

"That's because they *are* happy," Brenda pointed out. "Who wouldn't be, with a beautiful little baby like Joshua?"

Kate sighed blissfully. "A baby does bring something very special to a husband and wife," she said, giving Meridee a meaningful look.

Meridee eyed her mother suspiciously. "Is that a hint?"

Kate smiled and patted her daughter's hand affectionately. "I know better than to waste my breath," she teased.

Just then Zeb approached, smiling broadly. "I still can't believe how tiny those things are," he said in amazement, his eyes on eight-pound Joshua.

"Those things are called babies," Meridee pointed out lovingly, linking her arm through his. "Don't let Juliet hear you referring to her precious little one as a 'thing,' or you'll be stripped of your duties as godfather."

"How did rehearsal go?" Brenda asked her sister and brother-in-law.

"Every time Zeb picks him up he acts as though he has a carton of eggs in his hands," Meridee answered.

"That's because he's so small. I'm afraid I'll hurt him," Zeb admitted.

"It is a little scary being responsible for such a tiny person," she agreed on a note of wonder.

"You're not worried about that responsibility, are you?" Kate asked as Zeb and Meridee exchanged wary glances. "You two will make wonderful godparents."

"And it'll be good practice for when the two of you finally decide you want to start a family," Brenda added cheerfully.

Zeb cleared his throat. "We do need practice, don't we, Meridee?" he said with a grin.

Meridee nudged him with her elbow and gave him a reproachful look.

Kate and Brenda looked at each other, awareness dawning. "Zeb, why are you smiling like that?" Brenda demanded.

Zeb's cheeks reddened, and he looked at Meridee. "Maybe you should ask my wife."

Three pairs of eyes turned toward Meridee. She gave Zeb another censorious look and said, "We wanted to wait until Joshua's big day was over to tell you, but I can see by the look on Zeb's face that if I don't say something soon, he's going to burst."

Zeb grinned from ear to ear. "We're pregnant!"

Kate threw her arms around both of them, the tears falling once more as she offered her congratulations. "I can't believe this! You've only been married a year."

"A year and two months," Brenda corrected her. "Plenty of time to start a family. Congratulations, you two!" She gave them each a hug.

"But this is so unexpected!" Kate exclaimed.

Meridee could see that she had truly taken her mother by surprise. "You know what Dad always said..."

"Always expect the unexpected," Kate finished for her. She looked at Zeb and Meridee and gave them a warm, radiant smile. "Well, this truly does make this a special day. You must be on cloud nine."

Meridee gave Zeb's arm a squeeze. "Cloud nine? We're swinging on a star!"

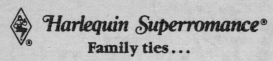

Harlequin Superromance®
Family ties...

SEVENTH HEAVEN
In the introduction to the Osborne family trilogy,
Kate Osborne finds her destiny with Police
Commissioner Donovan Cade.

Available in December

ON CLOUD NINE
Juliet Osborne's old-fashioned values are tested when
she meets jazz musician Ross Stafford, the object of
her younger sister's affections. Can Juliet only achieve
her heart's desire at the cost of her integrity?

Available in January

SWINGING ON A STAR
Meridee is Kate's oldest daughter, but very much her
own person. Determined to climb the corporate
ladder, she has never had time for love. But her life is
turned upside down when Zeb Farrell storms into
town determined to eliminate jobs in her company—
her sister's among them! Meridee is prepared to do
battle, but for once she's met her match.

Available in February

my VALENTINE 1992

Celebrate the most romantic day of the year with
MY VALENTINE 1992—a sexy new collection of four
romantic stories written by our famous Temptation
authors:

> GINA WILKINS
> KRISTINE ROLOFSON
> JOANN ROSS
> VICKI LEWIS THOMPSON

My Valentine 1992—an exquisite escape into a romantic
and sensuous world.

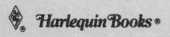
Harlequin Books ®

Take 4 bestselling love stories FREE

Plus get a FREE surprise gift!

Special Limited-time Offer

Mail to Harlequin Reader Service®

In the U.S.	In Canada
3010 Walden Avenue	P.O. Box 609
P.O. Box 1867	Fort Erie, Ontario
Buffalo, N.Y. 14269-1867	L2A 5X3

YES! Please send me 4 free Harlequin Superromance® novels and my free surprise gift. Then send me 4 brand-new novels every month, and bill me at the low price of $2.96* each—a savings of 33¢ apiece off cover prices. There are no shipping, handling or other hidden costs. I understand that accepting the books and gift places me under no obligation ever to buy any books. I can always return a shipment and cancel at any time. Even if I never buy another book from Harlequin, the 4 free books and the surprise gift are mine to keep forever.

*Offer slightly different in Canada—$2.96 per book plus 49¢ per shipment for delivery. Canadian residents add applicable federal and provincial sales tax. Sales tax applicable in N.Y.

134 BPA ADL3   334 BPA ADMH

Name _____ (PLEASE PRINT)

Address _____ Apt. No. _____

City _____ State/Prov. _____ Zip/Postal Code _____

This offer is limited to one order per household and not valid to present Harlequin Superromance® subscribers. Terms and prices are subject to change.

SUPER-91   © 1990 Harlequin Enterprises Limited

HARLEQUIN
PROUDLY PRESENTS
A DAZZLING NEW CONCEPT IN ROMANCE FICTION

One small town—twelve terrific love stories

Welcome to Tyler, Wisconsin—a town full of people
you'll enjoy getting to know, memorable friends and
unforgettable lovers, and a long-buried secret that
lurks beneath its serene surface....

JOIN US FOR A YEAR IN THE LIFE OF TYLER

Each book set in Tyler is a self-contained love story;
together, the twelve novels stitch the fabric of a
community.

LOSE YOUR HEART TO TYLER!

The excitement begins in March 1992, with
WHIRLWIND, by Nancy Martin. When lively, brash
Liza Baron arrives home unexpectedly, she moves
into the old family lodge, where the silent and
mysterious Cliff Forrester has been living in seclusion
for years....

WATCH FOR ALL TWELVE BOOKS
OF THE TYLER SERIES
Available wherever Harlequin books are sold

TYLER-G